Shadow Dancing

The Bedford County Series #2

Jennifer Sienes

CrossRoads Publishing

Chapter One

Rebekah

The memory was like a whisper that somehow found its way through the cacophony of the predawn morning. Instead of allowing it to take hold, I focused on the obnoxious thrum of the katydids, the sweet song of the awakening birds, and the tinkle of the wind chimes that hung outside my open window. The same breeze that put the chimes in motion rustled through the leaves of the old cottonwood tree that shaded my bedroom in the late afternoons. Rather than allow my mind to dwell on more recent events, I pictured myself swinging beneath that ol' tree as Daddy pushed me higher and higher.

If only I could hide away in a dream state long enough to get past this first anniversary. It was humiliating enough to be living at home again, but I couldn't cotton to having Mama and Daddy worrying I'd collapse from grief like a Victorian lady with the vapors.

I pushed the sheet aside and climbed from bed, my thin t-shirt sticky against my back. The room was bathed in darkness which brought some comfort. I'd always preferred dark to light. Best not to think too hard on what that meant for my spiritual health.

I raised the window higher to allow the breeze to cool my body and searched the shadows for the birds that were serenading the dawn. Although I'd been wrestling with God for nearly a year, the quote from Tagore came to mind—"Faith is the bird that feels the light and sings when dawn is still dark." Hollow and trite.

Dressed in a fresh t-shirt and jeans, hair pulled back in a ponytail, I eased down the stairs where a light shone from the kitchen. Daddy was sure to be sitting at the table tucked in the corner, with a cup of strong coffee and the Bible. It'd been that way for as long as I could remember. But when I entered the room, he was leaning against the counter sipping his coffee as if waiting on me. The florescent light above was too harsh for the early morning hour.

"Morning, Daddy. Everything okay?" I snagged a mug from the cabinet and filled it from the carafe cradled in the coffee maker.

"Just gettin' ready to go out and tend to the horses." He took a slurp of coffee and avoided eye contact. "Thought you might wanna have breakfast in town, maybe go by the cemetery."

Things'd be a whole lot easier if my family just went along with my fantasy that today was like any other day. "Taking care of the horses is my job, Daddy. Has been since I moved back home. Besides, I have to work at the vintage store this morning."

He scowled into his coffee. "Well, what about after? We could have lunch then go—"

"Can't, Daddy." The words came out in a rush over the quickening beat of my heart. "I'm waitressing over at the grill." I added a splash of milk to my coffee, although I wouldn't drink it now. It'd sit like acid in my belly. If I could just get through the day.

Daddy tilted his head with a sigh. "So, you gonna just pretend like nothin's different?"

"Trying to. It'd help if you play along." I hugged the mug to my chest and sent up a pointless prayer. Even if Daddy listened, I was pretty sure God wouldn't.

"If that's what you want. But you gotta know your sister and brothers are gonna be calling. Your mama had something planned, too, but since she's feeling poorly, you might could be saved from that."

"Poorly?" I set my mug in the sink. "What's wrong with Mama?" I could count on one hand the times she'd been sick and still have a digit or two left over.

"A little tired and weak, is all. Probably a touch of the flu." He rubbed a hand along the back of his neck, a sure sign it bothered him more than he let on.

"Is she awake?"

He nodded.

"I'm gonna check on her then. Don't worry about tending to the horses. I'll do that soon as I see Mama."

He held up a hand. "Look, Bekah."

I stopped at the doorway and turned to him. "It's fine, Daddy. Don't make a fuss, okay?"

He took in a deep breath and held my gaze. "You gonna at least see Mitch?"

Hearing his name only increased the knot in my stomach. "What for? It's not like he can change things." Bitterness was the product of a heart squeezed too long in a vice. I knew all the Scripture verses that warned against it—been raised on them since birth. Somehow, there was a wall between what ought and what was, and I couldn't seem to find my way over it.

The sun was just beginning to peek into Mama and Daddy's bedroom window as I poked my head in. Mama lay on her back, eyes closed. Although the bed was mussed with covers pushed to the footboard, the room was otherwise orderly as a nun's. Mama'd always kept a neat house and expected the same from her family. Even now at thirty-five, I couldn't leave my bed unmade or dishes in the sink.

"Mama?" I kept my voice low in case she'd drifted back to sleep. "You awake?"

She rustled a bit and attempted to sit up, but after a moment of floundering, gave up with a sigh. "You best not come in, Sweet Pea, in case I'm contagious."

"Nonsense." I pushed the door fully open and entered. It was disconcerting to find Mama not feeling well, like Dorothy discovering the Wizard of Oz was nothing more than a mere mortal hiding behind a curtain. I crossed the room and leaned over her, resting the back of my hand on her forehead. The familiar move snatched the breath from my lungs, and I schooled my features so Mama wouldn't notice.

"Me and Leah had a special day planned, but..." She took my hand as I settled on the edge of the bed. "Maybe tomorrow—"

"Don't you worry about it, Mama." There were dark circles under her eyes which heightened the pallor of her skin. "Like I told Daddy, I'm working at the vintage store this morning and took on an extra shift at the grill this afternoon. I don't wanna fuss. Can I get you some water or tea?"

"Working yourself into a stupor isn't gonna change things, Bekah. You can run all you want, but eventually, you gotta deal with it."

Tears bit at the back of my eyes. "Not today, Mama, okay? Now what can I get you before I head out to the stables?"

Once outside, the barn and horses offered a welcomed escape where I could breathe again. Cheyenne, Daddy's Australian shepherd, rustled from the corner while I drew in the scents of hay, straw, dust, and manure. Familiar and comforting. Horses and dogs weren't like people—they didn't ask questions when the tears fell or nag at you when you didn't feel like talking. I bent down to scratch Cheyenne's belly before moving on to the horses.

There were four stabled, and I let them out one at a time, lingering to bury my face in Siren's neck. She'd been mine since high school, and more loyal a companion I'd never found. Once they were fed and watered, I dug into mucking out the stables while Cheyenne followed in my path. It was a mindless task which gave me too much time to think.

Daddy and Mama weren't wrong—I was avoiding Mitch and running from something that would eventually catch up to me. But even a year later, I couldn't think straight enough to make a decision. It felt good to hang onto the anger and bitterness. It not only fueled me, it gave me a reason to get up in the morning.

I couldn't stay with my parents forever, and there was a deep need to start fresh. Living in a small town where everyone knew my business was not a tenable position to be in. I'd hidden away and licked my wounds long enough. Only two problems kept me here—lack of funds and motivation.

While I marched the possibilities for change through my mind, I was interrupted by Sister Sledge's "We Are Family," coming from my cell nestled in the back pocket of my jeans. *Leah.* I entertained the notion of ignoring the call but knew it would just be putting off the inevitable. Running from my life was one thing; running from my big sister was another.

I set the pitchfork against the barn wall while retrieving my phone. "Hey, Leah." I injected as much joy as I could into my tone, but it still came out sounding as if I'd just lost my last friend.

"Hey, Bekah. I just got off the phone with Daddy. He says Mama's sick?"

Relief drew a sigh from me. I'd much rather the focus be on Mama than on finding a way to take a tragic day and turn it into sunshine and roses. "Might be the flu," I confirmed. "Daddy's going to stick close to home today."

"So he said. Also said you've got yourself scheduled up."

"Yes," I said with gritted teeth. Seemed everyone had an opinion about my plans.

"Good. Gabe and I might come by the grill tonight. Of course, that's provided a miracle the size of Moses parting the Red Sea allows me to find a babysitter. I'll look in on Mama this afternoon, so you don't worry yourself about her."

I rested my forehead on the rough barn door frame and fought another bout of tears. Not because I was swimming in grief, but because Leah understood. I don't know what was more exhausting, wallowing in grief or pretending for family that everything was just fine. "Don't come over, Leah. If Mama's contagious, you'll be dealing with sick kids for two weeks. I'll come back by between jobs."

After we disconnected, I checked the time. 7:30. It was going to be a long day.

Mitch

Years ago, someone told me the key to a successful business was attitude. If I put out positive energy, things would be good. If not, it would tank. Sounded a little *woo-woo* to me. Might be he had a point. I clocked more deliveries over the last year than ever before but couldn't get a leg up. Previous ten years were more lucrative by far. How was a person supposed to be positive when life kept throwing butt-ugly punches at him?

I walked into the bar at six o'clock after two back-to-back hot shot deliveries—one to a power plant in downtown Nashville and another to a construction crew in Murfreesboro. The pay was good, but with my luck, I'd blow out the tranny in my truck or sit idle for the next week. I needed a distraction and figured a roomful of rowdy guys might just do the trick. Best way to forget my problems was to drink until I couldn't think straight.

Thursday night always seemed to draw a crowd, and tonight was no exception. Would've been smart to bring a friend, but the last thing I wanted was someone acting as my conscience. Enough of that went on when I was alone. God's honest truth, I was looking for trouble, and it didn't take long to find it.

Two rednecks sitting at the end of the bar making cracks at the waitress caught my attention. The girl couldn't have been more than a month over legal drinking age and looked about as natural to the setting as Rebekah would've been—which was not at all. She reminded me of a younger Bekah, actually. Brown hair, bangs, slender build. Only difference was she wore a pound of makeup. Probably figured it made her look older or get her bigger tips.

The guy to my left reached for his beer and jostled me. There wasn't enough elbow room to have a thought. "Sorry, pal. Place is packed tonight."

"No problem." I kept my gaze on the jokesters at the end of the bar as the waitress passed them with a tray of drinks. It looked to weigh more than her. One of the guys reached out and pinched her behind. She whirled around to avoid a repeat performance, and the tray wobbled precariously. She righted it in the nick of time, but not before alcohol sloshed onto the tray and floor. They cackled as if it was the funniest thing they'd ever seen.

"Pigs," I muttered. I wasn't the only one watching the scene, but no one looked like they'd step in.

The guy next to me leaned over. "You say something?"

I tilted my chin in their direction. "Those losers are harassing the waitress."

He chuckled. "She your girlfriend or something?"

I scowled. "Never saw her before. Doesn't make it right, though."

He peered around me to get a better view of the show. "She's just a kid. I got a daughter about that age."

"Yeah?" I took a swig of my beer. "How would you like it if a couple pigs like that grabbed her?"

He narrowed his eyes and shook his head. "S'not right," he slurred.

"No, it's not." Nothing riled me more than a bully. I slammed my beer onto the bar and stood. Perfect excuse to knock some heads together. "Someone needs to teach them a lesson."

He grabbed my arm. "They're kinda big, don'tcha think?"

"And so drunk, they couldn't hit the broadside of a barn." I maneuvered through the crowd, laser-focused on my target. The bartender leaned toward them and said something as he pointed toward the door. No doubt telling them to cool it or leave, but he didn't have the brawn to back it up. Either they were too stupid or too drunk to take heed, because when the waitress passed with another tray of drinks, one hooked an arm around her waist and reeled her in. The tray tumbled with a loud *crash* and a squeal from her as she jumped away.

"That's it," the bartender said. "I'm calling the sheriff, and y'all are gonna pay for those drinks."

"Hey, sweet thang," one of them called to the girl. "You wanna large tip, you gotta play the game." He slapped his thigh with a grin as if inviting her to take a seat.

I stepped between the terrified waitress and the drunks—close enough to smell their foul breath. A calmness washed over me like I was having an out-of-body experience. It'd feel good to bury a fist in their cocky faces. Break a few bones, even if they were mine. "I believe you were told to leave," I said through gritted teeth.

They turned to each other serious as a heart attack then burst out laughing again. "You gonna make us?" the bigger one said. Tree stumps in Louisiana had a higher IQ than him.

I grabbed a fistful of his t-shirt and drew him up off the stool. He was a head taller, but I'd built up enough mad over the last year to make up the difference. "Yeah, I think I will."

In a flash, fists and bodies were flying. Half the men jumped into the fray while the other half ducked out of the way. Before it was over, my knuckles were scraped and sore, one eye and cheek swollen, and my lip split. And it felt good.

Until I landed in a jail cell.

Drunk and disorderly were the charges. Only thing was, I hadn't been drunk. Didn't even finish half my beer. Disorderly? Well, I couldn't argue that one. Still, it didn't sit right being accused of something that wasn't true. Not the first time that'd happened, though. Mama used to tell me fare was the price you paid to ride a bus—she didn't have sympathy for whiners.

A deputy appeared at the cell I shared with three other guys all sleeping off the events of the night. "You made bail," he said, pointing to me.

"That was fast." I'd called Joe but didn't figure he'd show until morning. I pushed my sore body from the hard bench and shuffled to the door like an old man. Bad as I felt, it'd be worse once the stiffness settled in my muscles.

"It was a bum charge," the deputy said. "If things hadn't been so chaotic, you'd of just gotten a citation. The waitress and bartender showed up after closing to put in a good word for you. Just don't miss your court date."

"I won't." I trailed him down the hall and into reception. Joe stood propped up against the far wall, arms crossed.

"Thanks for coming so quickly." I patted him on the back.

"You might wanna consider sweet-talking Cassie after hauling me outta bed in the middle of the night. If it were any day but today, she'd of let you rot until morning."

While Joe's words washed over me, we stepped outside where the summer night was a good ten degrees warmer than the air-conditioned station. That reminder was all it took to drop kick me back where I'd started. Just proved what a fool I was. No amount of distraction was going to alter the truth of things.

"You wanna tell me what you were thinking?" Joe pushed a hand through his hair. "You look like the walking dead, by the way."

"At least I'm still walking," I muttered. "There are days I'd rather it be otherwise."

Joe turned to me, the muscles in his jaws clenching. "Sorry, man. I wasn't thinking." He moved down the quiet street toward his truck parked along the curb. This time of night there was no more than a few cars and the sound of katydids to break the silence. "You need to talk to Bekah, Mitch. Y'all can't keep goin' on like this."

"Your sister won't give me the time of day. Don't know if she ever will."

"Since when have you ever let someone stand in the way of what you wanted? Bekah included."

"It's not only about me. Can't force someone to do what they're not willing to," I said.

"So, you live separate lives as if nothing happened?" He shook his head. "It's crazy."

"I know it." I blew out a breath. "You mind driving me to the bar to pick up my truck?"

We drove in silence while the moist breeze that blew through the windows cleared the fog in my brain. I thought about the limbo Bekah and me had been stuck in for a year now. It didn't get easier—in fact, it just kept getting harder. Our marriage was non-existent, and the grief I'd sidestepped was every bit as deep as the day our lives came crashing down around us. I imagined it was the same for her. But what could I do if she wouldn't talk to me, or even look at me?

I suppose there were worse places to be than in limbo, but for the life of me, I couldn't think of any.

Chapter Two

Rebekah

It was now a year and a day. I lay in the dark, same as yesterday, but mixed in with katydids was the *pitter-patter* of rain drops and the low growl of thunder. A slight breeze skipped across my arms and face bringing with it the sweet perfume of hyacinth and magnolia. It was a small victory that I surpassed the anniversary without a complete meltdown, but a triumph, nonetheless.

Mama and Daddy were both asleep when I got in late the night before, so I was anxious to see how Mama was doing. After splashing water on my face and dressing, I slipped down the stairs relieved to see Daddy at his usual spot with his coffee and Bible. Seemed the world could always right itself as long as that remained true.

Not wanting to interrupt his studying, I got a cup of coffee without a word. Aside from the light fixture above the table, the rest of the room was in shadows. I glanced out the open window above the sink, but with the cloud cover, there wasn't even the slightest hint of a sunrise on the horizon.

"How'd you sleep, darlin'?" Daddy's low voice broke through the quiet.

"Good." I retrieved the cream from the fridge and poured a dollop in my cup before joining him at the table. "How's Mama doing?"

"Pert near the same." He scratched the gray stubble on his chin. "But you know how them flu bugs are. Could take a week or so to work its way through."

I worried my lower lip with my teeth as a thought occurred. "Seems an odd time to get the flu, don't you think?"

He frowned and shook his head. "Been known to happen." Reaching for his mug, he continued. "What d'you have planned for the day? Working both jobs again?"

I nodded. "Can't stay here forever, you know. Need to get a little nest egg together so I can find a place of my own."

"You already have a house, Bekah," he said with a scowl. "Don't you think it's time you and Mitch worked things out?"

"It's not as easy as all that." I ran a finger over the thick rim of my mug. I knew he and Mama thought I was doing things wrong, which was all the more reason to move out. It was hard enough to face my own disappointment without the added burden of theirs.

"No one said marriage is easy. And no one's gonna deny y'all have been through a rough time of it, but you don't just give up, Bekah. You think your mama and me haven't had our challenges?" He grunted. "Four kids, you're gonna have challenges."

Bitter tears bit at the back of my eyes as I sprang up. "I wouldn't know what it's like to have four kids, Daddy. Couldn't hold onto the only one I did have." I marched over to the sink with my full mug of coffee and dumped it down the drain. Clutching the edge of the sink, I fought to hold the tears back.

Daddy stepped up beside me, wrapped an arm around my shoulders, and pulled me close. He didn't say a word—didn't have to. We stood like that for a full minute while the calm finally took hold of me.

"We aren't gonna push you to do something you're not ready to do," Daddy finally said, planting a kiss on my head. "You take all the time you need, darlin'. We're always here for you."

I turned to wrap him in a hug before escaping to the barn. And although his words were meant to bring me comfort and relief, disappointment found its way in the mix as I ruminated on them throughout my day. It was true Joe,

Leah, Dan, and me might have given Mama and Daddy a few gray hairs over the years, but there'd never been anything catastrophic. It's not like they dealt with death or disease. None of us got into trouble—well, not much, anyway. Joe and Dan had a few tussles, but nothing earth shaking. Daddy just couldn't understand what I'd been through.

By the time I got to the grill late that afternoon, my brain felt as if it'd been boiled, mashed, and served on a platter. It would take all my concentration to keep from goofing up the customers' orders, especially on a busy Friday night.

The restaurant was set up like a sports bar with tables around the perimeter and three flatscreen TVs strategically positioned for viewing pleasure. I never was one to make idle chit chat and flirting confounded me, even though I'd been assured by Janice, a career waitress, that it'd garner larger tips. Even so, I did okay if I could just give good service. That meant no mistakes. Keep the refills coming, water glasses topped off, and the meal exactly as requested.

As far as careers went, this one wasn't exactly my dream job. Beggars couldn't be choosers, Mama was known to say, and I was in no position to turn my nose up at honest work. Without any experience, I was fortunate to have an in with the boss, although that didn't go over well with some of the other waitresses. Kimberley was one of them. We'd been to high school together, and she'd always seemed to look down her debutante-perfect nose at me. Joke was on her because we both ended up in the same place.

As I collected the dishes for table three, she leaned close to me in passing. "Got you a couple winners at table seven. Thought you might like to serve them, so I had Gil set them at your station." She gave me a wink and smirked, which didn't bode well. What was she up to now?

I balanced the full tray and moved from the kitchen to the dining room, averting my eyes from table seven. If Kimberley had something up her sleeve, I didn't want to lose my focus. Wouldn't do to upend a plate of food into a customer's lap.

I distributed plates of burgers and chicken fingers to the family at table three—a booth big enough for the six of them. "Can I get y'all anything else?" Although I sounded cool as a crisp cucumber, my heartbeat hitched up a notch in preparation for whatever awaited me next as I was assured all was good. I'd find out as soon as I deposited the tray back in the kitchen.

Table seven was an intimate booth tucked away in a dark corner, and I could only see one of the patrons from my vantage point. A young blond woman who wasn't at all familiar. Why did I let Kimberley work me into a dither? All it took was the hint of manipulation for me to react like one of Pavlov's dogs. As I drew nearer, I caught sight of a man sitting on the other side. The width of his shoulders, profile of his Roman nose, and strong jaw snatched the breath clear from my lungs.

Mitch.

My feet stuck to the floor like I'd stepped into a puddle of tar the moment recognition hit. Then I noticed his face. His left eye and cheek were black and blue, and his lip puffed up and split in the middle. Was he in a car accident?

When he spotted me, his mouth dropped open and his good eye widened. He was apparently as shocked as me. Was the flush that rose to his face from surprise or embarrassment for being caught with another woman? Not that it mattered to me one way or the other; it was just an observation.

"Bekah." He slid to the end of the booth and scrambled out. "When did you start working here?" His dark hair was longer than usual, thick with a slight curl.

"Never mind that." My gaze drifted to Mitch's girlfriend who watched our byplay with clear eyes. Either she didn't know Mitch was technically married or she didn't care. It was a miracle we hadn't crossed paths before, since Shelbyville didn't have a tenth of the population of Murfreesboro, which was, by Nashville standards, a small town. Made Shelbyville downright quaint.

Kimberley appeared with an empty tray tucked under one arm. "Need to keep the customers movin', Rebekah. Place is filling up. Table eight's waiting on you. Might want to get your husband and his girlfriend's order so we can get 'em outta here." She didn't wait for a response, and I doubt she took notice of the laser eyes I bore into her back as she retreated. There was no call for her to be ugly.

Mitch waved a hand toward his date. "This isn't what you think, Bekah."

"Doesn't make much difference either way." It was true. Mostly. "But I think it'd be best for both of us if you found somewhere else to take your date."

He latched onto my arm, and I stared down at it as if to make a point. His knuckles were scraped and swollen. So, it wasn't a car accident that got him banged up but a fight. Mitch could be a little hard-headed at times, but I'd never known him to be violent. Maybe he wasn't as immune to grief as I'd thought.

I tugged free of his hold and stared him down. The malaise that had been present for the last several months dissipated in that one moment of clarity. I couldn't stay in Shelbyville if I hoped to ever move forward. "I want a divorce."

Mitch

I'd never be accused of being a patient man, except in this particular situation. I'd given Bekah space to grieve, rant, and wallow. Enough. How dare she stand in the middle of a crowded restaurant and demand a divorce then turn and walk away like it was a done deal? She'd looked right through me as if I was invisible. A fire built up in my belly spurring me to finally take action.

I caught up with her as she approached the next table and nabbed her upper arm. "We need to talk." She twisted to get loose, but I was quicker this time and held tight. "You can't just demand a divorce and walk off like you're not throwing the last fifteen years of our lives down the gutter."

"We're not doing this here," she spat. "I'm working, and your girlfriend's waiting on you."

"She is *not* my girlfriend." My teeth were clenched so tight, it was a miracle I could speak at all. But the couple at the table were watching like we were the next best thing in reality TV. She was right—this wasn't the place. "What time do you get off work?"

"Eleven." She yanked free. "And I suggest y'all sit at the bar where I don't have to serve you or find another restaurant."

I let her go, but only because I knew we could hash things out later that night. When I glanced at my table, Tina was watching me, head tilted to one side. Probably trying to make sense of what she just witnessed. If she was smart, she would have hightailed it out as fast as she could.

I approached her but didn't slide back into the booth. "Let's go."

She shrugged and reached for her bag. "Where to?"

"If it's all the same to you, I'd rather sit at the bar. We can order dinner there." No way I was leaving the restaurant before Bekah got off work. Some might call it stalking, but I wasn't taking any chances.

"Don't matter to me one way or the other." She slipped the handle of her bag over her shoulder as she passed.

We found two empty stools at the end of the bar, and I had a flashback of the night before. I was getting my fair share of stares from people who didn't know me. Could only imagine what Bekah thought when she saw my battered face. This side of the restaurant, the noise level rose a notch or two, which would make conversation more challenging.

Tina leaned close. "It's none of my business, and y'all are welcome to tell me so, but who was that waitress?"

I snagged a pretzel from the bowl on the bar and popped it into my mouth. "My wife. Rebekah."

"Things aren't goin' so well, huh?"

I chewed a moment. "You could say we hit a rough patch, which is why you're here." I motioned to the bartender and pantomimed eating, so he'd get us a menu.

"She worked the backend of the business?"

"Yep. She was the brains of the operation."

The bartender approached with a couple menus. "Get you something to drink to start?"

"I'll have a gin and tonic," Tina said then looked at me as if for permission.

"A gin and tonic for the lady, and I'll have sweet tea." No way I was going to talk to Bekah with beer on my breath.

"You got it. I'll give you a couple minutes to look at the menu."

Once the bartender was gone, I turned to look at Tina. "To be fair, you should know there's a good chance this job is temporary."

Her mouth twisted. "From where I sat, it doesn't look all that promising."

Didn't look all that promising from where I sat, either, but I wasn't about to admit it aloud. "She'll come around." From my lips to God's ears. First time I ever took the saying to heart.

"Might as well get this job interview started," Tina said as our drinks were deposited in front of us.

It didn't take but a half hour to know Tina couldn't hack the job. She'd inflated her experience to the level of comical. What she called a bookkeeping background was balancing a checkbook. It was a wonder I hadn't figured that out over the phone when we scheduled the face-to-face. Bekah would often talk about how her God used unexpected circumstances to bring together His plan, and this kind of sounded the same. If I hadn't met with Tina, I wouldn't have known Bekah worked at the restaurant. All it cost me was dinner and a drink.

After Tina left, I hung around the bar nursing glass after glass of sweet tea, glancing at my watch every few minutes. Between the caffeine and sugar, I'd be up all night. Saw Bekah from a distance a time or two but didn't have a direct line to where she was working. Had too much time to think about the last several months and where I'd failed. Maybe it had been wrong to let Bekah leave, but I'd rather cut off my right arm than see her hurt any more than she already had been.

By 10:30, I was too restless to sit any longer, so I wandered around the dining room. The place was empty aside from a couple men in the bar. If there were no tables to serve, what was Bekah doing here? A well-dressed man came from the kitchen, rolling up the sleeves of his white dress shirt.

"Excuse me." My voice boomed in the quiet of the room. "I'm waiting for my wife to get off work. Rebekah Casey?"

He frowned. "Wait staff goes home at ten. Must have gotten your wires crossed."

Boy did we.

I sat in my truck for five minutes undecided. I had two choices—go home in defeat or fight. Never one to back down, as Joe had reminded me the night before, I made my decision. Bekah said we'd talk at eleven, and it was near that time now.

Rebekah's parents had a horse ranch just outside of town. Once I turned down their back country road, everything shifted. The katydids were louder, smell of hay and soil stronger, and the stars were brighter. I pulled onto their road and bounced along the potholes left by farm trucks and big rigs transporting hay rolls. Spent more hours than I could count on the Miller ranch riding the hay tedder and baler during harvest season. Not an unpleasant task.

The house was dark as pitch except for a light glowing from somewhere in the back. Bekah's bedroom, was my guess, given the late hour. John and Miss Anita kept farmers' hours—early to bed, early to rise.

I parked the truck at the edge of the drive and had to hope I didn't stumble in the dark. Worse thing this time of night was skunks. I made it to the porch and veered off the pathway to the left of the house. Brought to mind the time I'd snuck to her bedroom when we were dating, desperate to talk to her. We'd had an argument that evening about religion—or what she called relationship. She had it; I didn't. Her mama and daddy put a bug in her ear about something to do with ox and yokes. Made no sense to me. Thought it was pure nonsense to get her back to college. When she hadn't answered her phone, I showed up late to talk. I tossed pebbles at her window like I'd seen done on some movie, hoping she'd come out.

So fixated on that memory, the low growl in the here and now didn't register at first. I froze. "Cheyenne?" I peered through the dark looking for the shadow of the Australian shepherd that guarded the farm. "It's me. Mitch." What an idiot. Like she was going to understand.

Light flooded the area, and I squinted against it. Cheyenne was crouching low in front of me while the unmistakable *chh chh* of a shotgun being cocked registered. "Who's out there?"

My hands shot up in the air, and I slowly turned to face John Miller standing over me from the left side of the porch, rifle at the ready. "Just me, sir. Mitch."

He let the gun sag and scowled. "Son, what in Sam Hill are you doin' sneakin' around in the middle of the night? You about got yourself dead." He didn't look all that dangerous in his t-shirt and striped pajama bottoms, but the gun told a different story.

Cheyenne slipped up beside me as I lowered my hands. She nudged one, asking to be petted. *Traitor.* First, she turned me in; now she wanted to be friends. "Came to see Rebekah."

"You might could of picked a better time for a visit. Don't you think you're a little old for this nonsense?"

"Yes, sir."

"Go home, son. Things are sure to look better in the morning."

"Yes, sir." John Miller was the only person who had the power to make me feel like I didn't have but one oar in the water. Some things never changed.

Chapter Three

Summer 2008

Rebekah

Bekah wasn't home for summer break twenty-four hours before she slipped back into farm routine. Up early, turn out the horses, feed and water them and the chickens, gather eggs, muck the stables—all before breakfast. She used to think her life was about as exciting as watching hay grow and couldn't wait to go away to school. Now that she had, she discovered she was as comfortable with the college crowd as stilettos on cobblestones.

She couldn't wait to get home and wasn't too excited about returning to school in August. Life on the farm was predictable, yes, but comfortable too. She was even looking forward to baling hay this afternoon. Daddy and Ben had discussed it earlier. With the temps nearing ninety and low humidity, it'd be ready to go by four. Not a bad job since Daddy'd gotten a new, air-conditioned baler. In the meantime, she'd take a ride on Siren then spend an hour brushing her down.

Walking across the weedy grass pasture, she clicked her tongue to get Siren's attention. The Tennessee Walker's ears perked, and she meandered toward Bekah until they were nose to muzzle. "Wanna go for a ride, girl?" She ran her hand down the smooth mottled neck, scratched between her liquid eyes and forelock.

"Hey, Bekah. Welcome home."

Bekah turned to see Joe walking across the field with a guy she'd never seen before. Joe was always bringing home one friend or another. This one was taller than her brother by a head, dark haired, and lanky.

"Thanks." She took hold of Siren's halter and led her toward the guys. "You here to help with the hay?"

"Nah. I have a haul to make, and Dad says he's got enough help what with you riding the baler."

Bekah glanced at Joe's friend. Seriously cute. Dimple in his strong chin, regal nose, and lots of hair. Leah'd take one look at him and claim him for her own. Not that Bekah could blame her. She stuck out her hand. "Hi, I'm Bekah."

"Mitch Casey." His hand was strong and calloused in hers.

Joe slapped his forehead. "Sorry, guys. Somehow, I thought you'd met before."

"Nope," Mitch said. "Met your other sister."

"Leah," Bekah said. No one forgot Leah. Unlike the Biblical characters, Rebekah was the plain one, and her older sister the one that drew stares.

Mitch smiled, revealing matching dimples in his cheeks. "That's right. Forgot her name. Hear you're home from college."

He forgot Leah's name? Was this guy for real? "Yep." Siren nudged Bekah as if reminding her they had plans.

"Never been college material myself," Mitch said, his gaze steady and warm.

Bekah grimaced. "I'm not so sure I am, either."

Joe snorted. "What're you talkin' about? You're gonna be a vet. Can't hardly get a doctorate if college isn't your thing."

Bekah shook her head. For the brief time she'd been talking to Mitch, she forgot Joe was even there. What had gotten into her? She turned pleading eyes on her brother. "It just might be I'm not cut out for vet school. I'd appreciate it if you'd keep it to yourself for now. I'll talk to Mama and Daddy when the time's right."

"You're gonna leave them to pin all their college hopes on Dan?" He barked out a laugh. "Good luck with that." He gestured that Mitch should follow him. "Come on, Mitch. I need to hit the road. I'll drop you back at your place."

Mitch hesitated. "If it's okay with Bekah, I'd rather stay here."

Bekah's jaw dropped, and she shut it with a snap. He couldn't mean he wanted to hang out with her.

"You do," Joe said, "and you might get roped into baling hay. Not sure how you'll get home, either."

"I can give you a ride." The words were out of Bekah's mouth before she could stop them.

Mitch grinned, flashing those adorable dimples again. "That'd be great."

Joe frowned as a wrinkle formed between his brows. "Well, okay then. I'll see y'all later." He waved a hand and headed back toward the house.

Bekah chewed on the inside of her lower lip. Now what? "I was getting ready to take Siren for a ride."

Mitch gestured to the horse. "I take it this is Siren?"

She patted Siren's neck. "Yep. Do you ride?"

"Never have. Doesn't mean I can't." He squinted at the others in the pasture. "They appear harmless enough."

Bekah laughed. "Hard to believe you're from horse country and you've never ridden."

Mitch held out a hand toward Siren and let her sniff it as if she was a dog. "Not from here. Moved from Alabama with my mom a couple years ago." He rubbed Siren's muzzle with a gentle knuckle.

Bekah wanted to ask what brought them here, but she didn't want to pry. "Would you like to ride?"

He grinned. "You have one gentle enough for a beginner?"

"Sure." She turned to peer at the other three munching on grass in the pasture. "We got Little Foot, Daisy Mae, and Emperor. They're all pretty well behaved, but I think you'd like Emperor the best."

He slapped a hand to his heart and feigned relief. "Thank you. I don't know if my dignity could take riding a horse named Little Foot or Daisy Mae."

Bekah's shoulders relaxed, and it was only then she realized how tense she'd been. Her experience with boys, especially good-looking ones, could fit onto the end of a horseshoe. She'd always been relegated to the "friend" category. But when it came to horses, she was in her element.

"Let's get them saddled up then."

She collected a lead rope from the lean-to near the gate of the pasture and rounded up Emperor. As she led the horse out, she handed the lead rope to Mitch. "Follow me."

After she got Emperor and Siren saddled, she took Mitch through the basics—how to hold the reins, and how to use them to get Emperor to move left, right, and stop. "All our horses are neck-rein trained, which means they respond well to the reins. And they're very sensitive to them, so less is better."

Mitch nodded. "Sounds easy enough. What kind of breed is Emperor?"

"He's a Tennessee Walker. It's all we have. They're sure-footed and smooth." She raised her eyebrows at him. "You ready to give it a try?"

Although Bekah's family only owned eighty acres—a good portion of it for hay—the neighbors had an easy trail that meandered through their own hundred or so acres. There were plenty of trees for shade and a seasonal creek. When they reached the water, she crossed then turned to wait for Mitch to do the same.

Emperor knew he was carrying a tender foot and refused to cross just to be ornery.

"What do I do now?" Mitch held the reins high and spread wide, looking like the beginner he was.

"Take the reins like this." She showed him how to hold them in one hand low near the saddle horn. "Now, give him a little pressure with your heels and lean forward a bit."

Mitch did as he was told, and Emperor responded. "I did it!" He sounded as excited as a kid who just learned to ride a bike.

Bekah laughed. "You're a natural." A few more lessons, and he'd be cantering with the best of them. The thought pulled a frown from her. She was getting ahead of herself. Mitch was friend material. Or, more accurately, Bekah was friend material. Guys went for girls like Leah—fun, feminine, and a little fussy. The last time Bekah even wore mascara was…she couldn't remember. She got her hair trimmed every six months or so and would rather wear jeans and flannel than silk and satin.

When they arrived back at the farm, she led them to the stables. "We'll just get the saddles off them, and I'll give you a ride home. I can brush them later."

Bekah loosened the cinch on Siren and let the ends drop. She reached up to grab hold of the saddle, but Mitch stepped in.

"Let me at least put these away for you." He pulled the saddle off and straddled it on the rack like it weighed nothing while Bekah removed the blanket. "If it's all the same to you, I'd rather stay and help with the hay."

Bekah rested her hand on Siren's back and turned to Mitch. "Why?" She wasn't trying to be coy; she really wanted to know.

He shrugged. "I like hanging out with you. Thought maybe if I help with the hay, you'll let me take you out for a burger after."

Bekah's mouth went dry as a dusty trail. Did he just ask her out on a date?

Mitch

In his short twenty-two years, Mitch had his share of girlfriends. Never needed to work too hard to get a girl's attention. He'd inherited his daddy's looks. Drew the girls to him like honey, Mama said. But she'd been careful to remind him that being handsome was about as useful as gum on a boot heel.

Character was what's important. Considering his daddy had run out on them when he wasn't yet two, Mitch figured his daddy was sorely lacking in that department.

Mitch was committed to doing things different. He might resemble his old man, but that didn't mean he needed to act like him. Every time a girl flirted with him, it caused a fist to knot in his gut—like some kind of warning bell. He didn't trust flirty girls.

When Joe brought Mitch by the Miller ranch the week before, he'd said it was so he could meet his sister, Leah. "The two of you'll hit it off."

"You always try and fix your sisters up?"

"Just Leah." Joe snorted. "Don't know too many guys who'd take to Bekah. She's a tomboy that'd rather hang out with horses than people."

Mitch couldn't deny Leah was pretty, and she wasn't flirty like most girls. Still, when he looked into her eyes, there was no spark. Maybe he was fooling himself to think there should be. What did he know about love at first sight? He just knew she wouldn't be the one.

Bekah Miller was different.

Pretty? Not so you'd notice at first. But when she smiled, boy howdy, his heart about tripped out of his chest. It transformed her. Her dark bangs nearly caught in her eyelashes when she blinked, and those eyes were clear and true as could be. Couldn't quite figure if they were green or blue, but it didn't make much difference. They were beautiful.

He could tell Joe was confounded by Mitch's desire to hang out with Bekah after he'd dismissed Leah without a backward glance. Didn't matter. He wasn't going to miss out on the chance to get to know her better.

They finished their ride, which had him tense as a jack rabbit crossing a coyote's tracks at first. He was sure Emperor was going to upend him in the creek. Pretty soon, he relaxed enough to enjoy the easy motion and the feel of the saddle on his backside. By the time they got back to the farm, he understood Bekah's love of horses. They had a calming effect he could learn to love.

Bekah showed him how to brush Emperor, and they worked in companionable silence side by side. He'd never known a girl comfortable with quiet.

They usually wanted to fill it up with useless conversation designed to flatter and impress.

"Appreciate you taking me for a ride," he said after a bit. The soft brush made a *swooshing* sound as he groomed Emperor's dark brown coat.

"I'm just glad you enjoyed it. I love riding, but it's not for everyone." She patted Siren's rump. "You sure you wanna help with the baling? It'll be a good three hours before we're done."

"Maybe if I help, it'll get done sooner."

Bekah flashed him a grin over Emperor's back. "Afraid there's not much you can do. Daddy'll drive the rake, and I'll follow along with the baler. Course, Dan might be willing to take over baling if I ask him real nice."

Mitch frowned. "Don't think that would put me in the best light with your daddy or your brother." First impressions were important.

She laughed. "All right then. Let's go see if they're fixing to get started."

Bekah had been right—it was near seven before they were done, and there wasn't much for him to do but watch. It fascinated him how the baler drove over mounds of cut hay until it was full, wrapped them in twine, and dropped them like a chicken laying an egg. The field was dotted with the rolls by the time Bekah finished.

"You don't have to take me out for a burger," Bekah said as they walked toward the house. "Mama will have a late supper laid out, and you're welcome to stay."

"Would you rather do that?" Mitch tucked his hands into the front pockets of his jeans. He wasn't going to push her to do something she didn't want to, even if it was what he preferred.

She tucked a wayward strand of hair behind her ear and glanced at him. "I kinda had my taste buds ready for a burger."

He grinned. "Me too."

"Let me grab the keys to Daddy's truck, and we'll get going."

A few minutes later, Mitch jumped into the passenger side of the 2001 Chevy Silverado and sat back. Observing the hay baling process, he had a few questions. "Y'all use that hay you baled for the horses?"

Bekah shook her head. "We'll sell most of it. Kinda unwieldy to use bales that size with the horses, unless they're in the pasture all the time. We use the small rectangular bales that you probably see more often. That's a different process."

"You always lived on the farm?"

"Born and raised." She glanced at him. "What about you?"

"We moved around a lot." Mitch couldn't imagine staying in one place his entire life. Sounded good, actually. Once he got settled, he hoped to never move again. "It's been just my mama and me since I can remember."

Bekah stopped at a light and turned to him. "What about your daddy?"

He shrugged. "Took off. From what Mama's told me, we're better off without him." This was not what he wanted to talk about on their first date. "But your mama and daddy seem great."

"They are, actually. What d'you do for work, Mitch?"

"Been doin' this and that, but Joe's helping me get my own hot shot trucking business going. Seems like it's worked out good for him."

"Who knew my big brother could be someone's mentor?" The light changed, and she accelerated. "So, you're an only child?"

"Yep."

"I can't imagine what it'd be like to be an only child." She wrinkled her nose. "No one buttin' into my life or having to tussle with. I'd have my own room." She sighed. "Sounds downright boring." Her laughter filled the cab.

"You ever think of settling down and having kids?" Mitch blurted the question then tried to figure out how to get his size elevens out of his mouth.

Bekah's blue-green eyes widened. "Seriously? I'm only twenty years old. I can't figure out what I want to do with the next year let alone my entire life." She pulled into Krystal's parking lot, put the truck in park, and faced Mitch. "I heard somewhere that no one should make life decisions before they're twenty-five. That's when their brains stop changing."

His lips twitched. "I shoulda known better than to ask such a question on our first date."

Her cheeks turned a becoming shade of red as she opened and closed her mouth a couple times. "Date? This here's a date?"

"Maybe not a *typical* date," he said. "But we did get all gussied up, and I am buying you supper. I'd call that a date."

A smile bloomed as she gazed at his dirty t-shirt and jeans. Although she'd changed into clean clothes, he suspected he reeked a little of sweat, horses, and hay. "Well then, who am I to argue?"

It was in that moment he knew for sure he was hooked. No way was he going to wait five years to marry this girl. If he had his way, they'd have a passel of kids before they reached thirty.

Chapter Four

Rebekah

After giving Mitch the slip the night before, I had my nose so high I could drown in a rainstorm. There wasn't much I had control over, so this small slice of rebellion spurred me through my morning rituals. It almost had me convinced I was coming up on the other side of grief until my fingers crossed paths with the frame tucked into the back of my underwear drawer. A battle raged inside of me for a brief moment, knotting up my stomach. I could almost hear the Lord whisper, "Look at it, Rebekah. Hiding his picture away won't ease the pain from your heart."

I snatched my hand from the drawer and slammed it closed. I was halfway through my bedroom door when I felt a tug on my heart as clear as if someone had lassoed it with rope and cinched it around a saddle horn. How would I ever heal from this grief if I couldn't even look at him? Breath held, I eased the drawer open once again and reached into the recesses until I felt the simple wood frame.

I'd seen the five-by-seven photo a hundred times, yet not once in the last six months. When I moved from Mitch's house to Mama and Daddy's, I'd slipped it away for safe keeping. I still wasn't sure if it was the photo I was trying to keep safe or my broken heart.

Jonathon. Even at five, he was the spitting image of his daddy—at least when Mitch wasn't beat up and broken from some bar fight. The same green eyes, tousled brown curls, and strong chin. Tears welled in my chest as I thought about that little chin. Would it have grown a dimple to match his daddy's or stayed smooth like mine? My eyes soaked in the image of my sweet boy as if it would have to last me a lifetime. How could a God who claimed to be love do something so cruel as take my baby from me?

I slipped the picture back in the drawer and swiped the tears from my cheeks. There were days the world seemed too cruel to bear. The loss of Jonathon turned everything on its head, and for the life of me, I couldn't get it righted again. After schooling my emotions, I went downstairs with less confidence than I'd felt only moments before. God certainly had a way of humbling a body.

Daddy was in his usual place, but my gaze slipped down the hall to his and Mama's closed bedroom door. Was I the only one who worried it could be more than a flu bug? "Don't want to interrupt you, Daddy, but don't you think it's time you took Mama to the doctor?"

He looked up at me and nodded once. "Gone do that today, darlin'."

"Good." I crossed the kitchen and poured a cup of coffee.

He scratched his stubbled chin. "It's important to not let things go too long, don'tcha think?" Why did I have the feeling he wasn't talking just about Mama?

"Yes, sir," seemed the safest response. I took a sip of coffee and faced him. The overhead light wasn't flattering, but even taking it into consideration, it appeared Daddy'd aged a bit over the last few days. Most likely more worried about Mama than he'd let on.

"Caught that husband of yours sneakin' around the side of the house last night. Almost shot him."

I let out a gasp and the coffee went down my windpipe. I slammed the mug onto the counter, coughing so hard, my eyes watered. "What?" I finally managed to croak. Mitch wasn't one to take no for an answer, but the idea of him creeping around the house... and Daddy in wait with a shotgun?

"I done tol' you we weren't gonna push where you're not ready to go, and that's a fact. But if you promised to meet with him—"

"I didn't."

He stared at me with one eyebrow quirked in disbelief. Just like when I was little, and he'd caught me in a fib.

Clearing my throat, I dropped my gaze to my stockinged feet. "Not exactly, anyway."

"Only you and the good Lord know the truth, darlin'. I suggest you take it up with Him."

"Yes, sir." I was more concerned with how Daddy viewed me these days than God. We weren't exactly on speaking terms. Then I thought back to the nudge to take out Jonathon's picture. If that wasn't the Lord, then who was it? Might be He was talking to me even if I wasn't much into listening.

After finishing my chores and visiting with Mama for a bit, I went back out to the stables for some privacy and called Mitch.

"Bekah?"

"Daddy said you were sneaking around the house last night." Cheyenne sauntered up and sat on her haunches at my feet. I buried my fingers into the soft fur between her ears.

"About got myself killed." There was a definite edge to his voice. "If you weren't planning on meeting up with me, you coulda said so."

"Like you were going to take no for an answer." Still, shame had my face heating. Mama'd taught me better, but it was like bitterness and anger had taken ahold of me like a slow-growing cancer. What would it take to cut it out?

His voice broke into my thoughts. "Seems to me we could both grow up a bit."

I caught Cheyenne's ear between thumb and finger and rubbed it. "You're right, Mitch. I had no call to treat you that way."

"So, can we meet?"

"I gotta be at the shop at noon. If you have time before—"

"Meet you at The Coffee Break at ten?"

I nodded although he couldn't see me. "Yeah."

The Coffee Break was located in Shelbyville's town square anchored by the county courthouse which sat in the middle surrounded by quaint shops, restaurants, and several law offices. How one small town could keep so many lawyers in business confounded me. It reminded me of Mitch's battered face and the likelihood he'd be in need of one for himself.

I parked across from the Coffee Break at the back end of the courthouse. Maple and poplar trees were strategically placed around the perimeter shading the grass and gardens, making one forget that the business inside was often less than a pleasant undertaking. I waited for a car to pass before crossing the street and spotted Mitch standing on the sidewalk beside the door. A woman entering did a double take as if caught off guard by his black eye and split lip.

"You're causing a bit of a stir," I said, stepping onto the curb. He looked worse in the daylight than he had in the restaurant the night before.

He touched his lip and grimaced. "Not my finest moment." He opened the door and waited for me to precede him.

"Are you going to tell me what happened?" I threw over my shoulder. "Or should I wait for the local gossips?"

"One thing at a time. What can I get you?"

"Just a coffee." My stomach revolted at the thought of food. We hadn't had any real conversation since I walked out six months before in search of my sanity.

While we waited in line, I pretended to peruse the shelves of baked goods lined up in the glass counter to avoid Mitch's probing eyes. I wanted to be strong, and at the same time, my strength had always come from him. It was high time I found another source. Mama would say it should be the good Lord.

We filled our cups at the coffee station, and I searched for a place to sit. The room was long and narrow with tables along both walls—too close together for any semblance of privacy.

"Let's head upstairs." Mitch led the way up to the loft seating area, which was empty, and chose a corner table. He pulled out my chair and waited until I was seated before settling in across from me. "Now what's this nonsense about a divorce?" Mitch never was one to dance around a subject.

Heat stole up my neck and settled in my cheeks while a swarm of butterflies took off inside my stomach. He wasn't going to make this easy on me, and I was so tired. "We've been separated for six months, Mitch." Like he couldn't count.

The muscles along his jawline flexed, a sure sign he was angry. "That wasn't my choice, Bekah. You walked out."

I closed my eyes and sighed. "I was suffocating." I shifted in the hard chair and wrapped my hands around the paper cup. "Don't you understand? Every time I look at you…"

His eyes flashed as he leaned forward and placed his elbows on the table. "What? Every time you look at me, what?"

The accusation was too ugly and sinful to voice, even though it had plagued me more times than I could count. *Sticks and stones may break my bones, but words will never break me.* The childish chant tripped through my mind. But I knew words could cut more deeply than the sharpest knife.

"Every time I look at you, I have to stifle the urge to scream," I whispered. "You took my son from me, and I don't think I'll ever be able to forgive you."

Mitch

The accusation didn't come as a shock. Bekah had made it before. Maybe not in so many words, but in innuendo and double speak. In the way she'd cringed at my touch like a coon dog who'd been abused. But now that it was out there, what was I supposed to do? After Jonathon died, I'd given her all the space and time I thought she'd need to come to terms with the loss while I worked myself near to death to escape the pain. Instead of emerging from the cocoon of grief, she'd burrowed deeper into it as if it gave her some kind of sick comfort. I was no better off.

I wanted to throw accusations back, but where would that get me? The person I most wanted to protect was intent on splitting us up. Divorcing might be a temporary fix for her, but in the end, I knew without a doubt, it would destroy us both. Trapped, I had to at least try to get her to see reason.

"You think it's any easier on me?" The words pushed through the knot that sat in my throat. I understood that urge of hers to scream—had it myself more than once. It's what drove me to the bar two nights before. "You act as if you're the only one grieving here."

"Because you just went on with your life like nothing happened."

I rammed a hand through my hair. "What was I supposed to do, Bekah? Wallow in it like you? How would that pay the mortgage or put food on the table?" Or pay the funeral arrangements?

Tears pooled in her eyes and dampened her lashes. "You were supposed to protect him."

"There was nothing I could—"

"You told me to back off, Mitch." She swiped at the tears that trickled down her cheeks.

Not this again. "We've been over this so many times. Why do you keep bringing it up?"

"Because it's just sitting there, putting a wedge between us." The weak comeback was a contrast to her jutted chin and the flash of anger that shot from her eyes.

"It's there, alright. Because you won't let it go." I barked out a laugh that was anything but humorous. "You're beatin' an old dog to death. It's time we get past it, Bekah."

"I can't." Her voice broke, and she dug in her purse and brought out a tissue. "Don't you see?" she said, swiping at her eyes. "You were always on me about not trusting you with him. Being all the time overprotective. If I hadn't listened..." She blew her nose. "Jonathon might be alive today."

She was right about one thing—things might've been different—but not for the reason she believed. I could share that bit of truth with her, but in the end, it wouldn't make her feel any better. "I can't change what happened, Bekah. If I could trade my life for his, I swear with everything I have in me, I'd do it."

She took a deep breath and blew it out. "I don't doubt that for a minute, Mitch. But it doesn't change how I feel, and I don't see how to get past this."

My patience was wearing web thin. I took a deep breath. "Why don't we give it more time?"

With a shake of her head, she flicked her bangs into place and schooled her features. Gone was the emotion of only moments before. No tears, just determination. "I think it'd be best if we just go our separate ways. There isn't anything else to talk about." When she put her mind to it, the girl could freeze out a Tennessee August.

What happened to the faith she carried around like a shield for as long as I'd known her?

I muscled some control and sat back, matching her cool with some of my own. "You remember the first fight we ever had?"

A wrinkle formed between her brows. Either she was thinking on it or wondering what I was up to. "What about it?"

"Your mama and daddy got it into their heads that we shouldn't marry because I didn't believe like you did."

She chewed on her lower lip. "Yeah? So?"

"So, we've had more than one heated conversation over your belief in God or Jesus or whatever you wanna call it."

She huffed out a breath. "What're you getting at, Mitch?"

"You told me your mama and daddy would get over it eventually, 'cause that was the Christian way. It's all about what Jesus did and how y'all are to respond in like manner."

Her eyes narrowed as if she caught my train of thought and wasn't wanting to climb aboard.

"Where's the forgiveness you preach about, Bekah? For that matter, what about those vows we took? Better or worse? In fact, I believe you insisted on Scripture to that effect, didn't you?"

The grip on her purse was so tight, her knuckles turned white. "You think you're gonna bully me into staying married to you by throwing religion back in my face?"

"Thought you said it wasn't religion, but a relationship. Made all the difference, you said. Couldn't be all that great if you toss it out the minute things get tough." I was reaching but didn't have any other ammunition.

"We're not going there." She stood and worked the strap of her purse over her shoulder with shaky fingers. "Besides, if you're so evolved, how come you got into a bar fight?"

"Who said I did?"

"Please," she said with a smirk. "You don't think my brother and I talk? I believe he bailed you out."

So much for loyalty. "Some things are worth fighting over." It was a stretch. It's not like that waitress needed my protection as much as I needed the release.

She hovered over me. "You show off for some girl in a bar one night and are dating another the next. Doesn't sound like a guy devoted to his marriage. So, why are you holding on so tight?"

I shook my head and stood, my six-two frame now towering over her. A juvenile move to get the upper hand. "Never knew you to be one to jump to conclusions, Rebekah. Whatever helps you justify walking out on me, right?"

She put some distance between us and crossed her arms. "You're gonna tell me she was a cousin or a friend?"

"Nope. Neither of those things." The fact she was asking was a good sign. If she was really done with me, she wouldn't care. "If you must know, it was a job interview."

She snorted. "I'll bet. She has need of a private, hot-shot trucker?"

"I was the interviewer. Looking for your replacement."

Her eyes widened then narrowed. She was fixing to hit me with another zinger. "You think it's appropriate to hold interviews at a restaurant?"

"More appropriate than having her come into a married man's home, don't you think?" I snatched our coffee cups from the table, dropped them in the trash can, and sauntered out. Took every ounce of will power to walk away without glancing back. Sometimes, retreat was necessary in battle in order to win the war.

CHAPTER FIVE

Rebekah

I'd once heard there's a fine line between love and hate, and Mitch seemed determined to flirt with it. Some days, he could make a preacher cuss. Did he really think I'd have rather been immersed in grief like some kind of pig wallowing in slop? I'd tried every way I could think of to shake loose of the grip it had on me. Except one. But I wasn't about to ask the Lord to take away the pain He'd chosen in His infinite wisdom to inflict.

I pulled my truck into the paved parking lot at Vintage Decor & More and reached for the key with shaky fingers. I swear, hot oil was bubbling up my insides while smoke spewed from my ears. How in the world would I be able to work with customers in such an ugly mood? Closing my eyes, I let the cold air pour through the vents and work its magic. Deep breath in...*one, two, three*...deep breath out...*one, two, three*. A few minutes later, the scream that was doing its best to cut loose dissipated, and I was confident I could act like a mature human being. At least for one afternoon.

Heavy raindrops plopped onto the pavement as I opened the car door, and I inhaled the moisture that rose into the air. The only car in the lot was Darlene's, which was unusual. Although the shop was off the beaten path, it had developed quite a following since it'd opened the year before. Owner Charlotte Daniels had taken her love of repurposing vintage furnishings and infused her talent as an interior designer to create a unique shopping experience.

The old Victorian house, which Charlotte had inherited from her nana, had been renovated to accommodate the shop. The white wood siding was pristine against black shutters that bookended the tall windows. Its classic lines were softened by the curved flower beds that went around the perimeter of the building.

The wide front steps boasted pots of blooming geraniums, petunias, and cosmos. Cushioned rattan furniture was set to one side of the wrap-around porch with more potted plants—pink and blue hydrangeas, begonias, and impatiens. And several more I couldn't identify. Even my sour mood wasn't immune to the beauty of God's artwork.

As I opened the front door, the bell attached to the knob announced my arrival. An antique store counter was set up on the far side of the large foyer beneath a beaded chandelier. The light from it glimmered on the polished brass of the vintage cash register that sat atop—merely for aesthetics. We did our figures with the updated version tucked on a shelf beneath.

Each room was a creative setting that offered decor ideas for every budget. More often than not, shoppers would admit to purchasing more than expected in a desire to replicate Charlotte's creativity. And for those big spenders, they could hire Charlotte to design a room or their entire house.

It wasn't interior decorating or love of vintage furnishings that led me to this job. It was by chance that I ran into Darlene at the Piggly Wiggly a couple months before. I went to high school with her daughter Carla, who died of a drug overdose more than ten years ago. As soon as I mentioned I was looking for work, she offered the job. Although Charlotte was the heart of it all, her cousin Jenna and Darlene handled the day-to-day business. Fortunately for me, it didn't matter that I didn't know vintage from modern. I was capable of following orders. Not much different than waitressing, except tips weren't one of the perks.

"Hey there, Bekah." Darlene's stout figure emerged from the hall leading to the parlor. "Didn't hear you come in over the rain. Anything sweeter than a summer storm, I ain't never seen it." She drew me in for a quick hug. "You're a mite wet. Got caught in it, did you?" Her blue eyes latched onto mine and she frowned. "What's wrong?"

I had to chuckle. The woman had the instincts of a heat-seeking missile. "Goodness, Darlene. I just walked in the door."

"You put your pocketbook up, get yourself something to drink, and we'll have us a talk." She pointed a finger at me like she meant business.

"I don't get paid to talk." I passed by her and tucked my purse under the counter. Goose bumps skittered up my damp arms when a blast of air-conditioning whooshed from the brass vent behind the counter. "Jenna told me yesterday there's a load of old linens needing to be washed. Said they're in a box in the basement." One of the many conveniences of setting up shop in a real house was a laundry room. We also had access to a functioning kitchen and three bathrooms.

"Don't you worry yourself about those right now. I know when there's something up with you. You havin' another spell of depression?" Darlene was never one to tiptoe where she could trample.

"Not exactly." I combed out my wet bangs with my fingers and followed her to the hot pink velvet loveseat perched along the stairwell. Depression was a clinical term for a condition that seemed anything but clinical. I was plain sad. "Just had a spat with Mitch, is all."

"Oh?" Darlene settled onto the sofa with care. It had belonged to Charlotte's nana, and although most everything in the shop was for sale, this particular piece was held back for sentimental reasons. Couldn't see why anyone would keep it otherwise. Gaudy thing. But what did I know? She waved at me to join her. "You two workin' things out?"

I sat next to Darlene with a *humph*. "Hardly. Told him I want a divorce, and he acted like all I need is more time to get it together."

Darlene's eyebrow quirked much like Daddy's when he questioned my honesty.

I threw my hands in the air. "It's true. Said I should just get past it and move on, like Jonathon wasn't anything more than a pet dog or something."

She shook her head and clucked her tongue. "Sweet girl, you know I love ya, but either you're taking what he said and twisting it something ugly or you're puttin' words in his mouth. I don't know Mitch, but I know you. You'da never married a man that callous and uncaring."

"Maybe." Why did she have to be logical when what I wanted was someone on my side? "But the truth is, I don't think I can get past it, Darlene." I pinched the bridge of my nose against the threat of a headache. If anyone should be able to give me some hope, it'd be Darlene. "How'd you get past your grief after losing Carla?"

She shrugged. "It's not the same, child. Carla was a grown woman who made poor choices. I'm not sayin' I didn't grieve at the loss, but death came on the heel of poor choices, if you know what I mean."

I nodded.

"Your Jonathon?" She lifted her hands and shrugged. "He was a baby. Sometimes you just can't make sense of something so senseless."

That didn't help. In fact, it made me feel justified in my anger. "Which is why I no longer trust in the sovereignty of God," I admitted.

Darlene shook her head and sighed. "I understand your anger, sweet girl, but that's not a road you wanna travel for long. We don't get to know what God has planned, but that don't mean He isn't sovereign, and it don't mean He isn't good even when all we can see is the bad."

I swiveled on the loveseat and faced her. "How can you say He's good when He took my little boy from me?" I was strangling on emotional overload. "My marriage is destroyed, my relationship with God is tenuous at best, and most days I feel as if I'm suffocating." My voice hitched, and I dropped back onto the loveseat next to Darlene. With my elbows resting on my knees, I buried my face in my hands and practiced breathing. I was so tired of me.

Darlene's hand rested on my back for a moment before moving in slow, soothing circles. "I can't rightly say I know where you're coming from, Bekah. But I've been handed my own crosses to bear. Lost a husband to alcoholism, a daughter to drugs. My house burnt to the ground." She tapped me on the back like she wanted my attention.

I sat up and swiped at my bangs. Talk about a hot mess. Not only was I not working, I was keeping Darlene from working. I should be paying Charlotte rather than the other way around.

"But through all that, God has shown me mercy and grace. Whatever I needed, he provided. Maybe not in a way I'd of expected." She chuckled. "Who'd a thought the way to all this was me smokin' in bed and causing a fire?"

Her faith astounded me. After all she'd been through. "I feel like I'm just going through the motions. Jonathon's been gone a year now, and I'm no better now than I was then."

"That's not true," Darlene said. "From what you tol' me when we first met up, you couldn't even get outta bed the first month. Here you are, holding down two jobs and helping your mama and daddy out at the farm. That's progress."

"At a snail's pace." I shook my head. "I hate to say it, but the only way I'm going to get past this is to start over. I can't live with Mama and Daddy forever, and I can't go back to Mitch." It didn't help that every time I saw him, it nicked at the scar I'd developed over my heart.

"I know one thing for sure," Darlene said, pushing out of the loveseat. "You best not make big decisions when your emotions are running high. It'll lead you down the wrong path every time."

It felt as if my entire being was made up of emotions. Things were a whole lot easier when I loved nothing more than my horses.

Mitch

A last-minute haul to Nashville mid-afternoon put me smack in the middle of commute traffic going back to Shelbyville. Like a colony of ants lined up to return to their hill, except less productive. Nothing wasted more time than sitting in traffic. Didn't lighten my mood any. Fact was, it gave me too much time to think about Rebekah and her decision to split. If she got it into her head it's what she really wanted, there wasn't much I could do but stall her. Grief was a powerful motivator, but eventually, the fog would clear, and she'd see reason. I hoped.

She seemed to be of the mind that I hadn't been affected by Jonathon's death. Not true. Would it of made a difference if I told her it was all I could do most days to climb out of bed? That I could have sworn I saw Jonathon at least a dozen times, but it was just a figment of a grief-stricken daddy's imagination? That driving down the highway at that moment, just the thought of my little boy caused a knot the size of a softball to form in my throat?

Probably wouldn't make a bit of difference. She couldn't see past the haze of her own misery to care what it might be doing to me. Or maybe she felt it was justified, since she'd decided, without benefit of judge or jury, to condemn me for his death.

It was near seven before I turned down our road. Bekah's dream house sat in the middle of four acres. Nothing fancy, just a one-story ranch style. Space for a little boy to run with plenty of trees for climbing. Being mid-summer, the sun was still high, but my body was as worn out as if I'd been dragged behind a bronc. Two late nights in a row—one on a cot in a cell—had taken their toll. I'd microwave a frozen dinner and get to bed. Earlier I got going in the morning, better chance at contracting a couple hauls for the day.

The red Dodge truck parked alongside the house gave me pause. Why would Joe be here? If something had happened to Bekah, he'd of called. I parked and jumped out of the truck, my eyes searching him out. He sat in the shadow of the front porch on Bekah's white rocker. The one that needed a good scrubbing to clean it of the dirt and mildew collected over the last several months.

He stood as I walked up the path. "Wondered when you'd show. I was about to give up."

"Coulda called." I climbed the brick steps and tilted my head toward the door. "Wanna come in?"

"Sure. Won't stay long. Was passing your way and thought I'd stop by."

I unlocked the door and pushed it open for him to go ahead of me. "Got a bone to pick with you, anyway."

Joe stepped inside. "Yeah? What's that?"

I closed the door, headed to the thermostat just down the hall, and flicked on the air. "You told Bekah I'd been in a bar fight."

He spread his hands out and shrugged. "What was I supposed to do? She asked did I know how you come to have your face all beat up. Couldn't lie to her, could I?"

I waved a hand for him to follow me and headed to the kitchen where dirty dishes were piled in the sink. Meant to clean them up before I left the house this morning but had more important things on my mind. Like a wife who knew my business better than me. "She also knew you bailed me outta jail." I took two beer bottles from the fridge and handed him one.

He pulled a chair from the kitchen table and sat. "So, y'all are talking now?" He focused on picking at the label with a thumbnail, face set in a frown.

"One tense conversation this morning that stirred her into a hissy fit is not what I'd call talking." I sat across from him and noticed the slump of his shoulders. "Something going on with her I don't know about?"

He didn't respond.

"Hey?" I ducked to catch his eye and waved a hand in front of him. "What's wrong with Bekah?"

"It's not Bekah." He blew out a breath and looked at me. "Thought you should know Mama's been feeling poorly the last several days. Figured it was the flu or some kind of stomach virus. Daddy took her to the doctor today and they ordered all kinds of tests."

It took a moment to find my breath. I'd never known Miss Anita to be anything but the picture of health. "What'd they find out?"

Joe shrugged. "Don't know yet."

The incident with the shotgun the night before notwithstanding, John was the only father I'd ever known. Miss Anita treated me like her own, and there wasn't a finer woman alive, including my own wife and mama. What if it was serious? Just the idea of it made it hard to swallow.

Joe shoved his beer aside and rested his elbows on the table. "Reason I'm here, Mitch, is 'cause I'm a little concerned about Bekah. You know how she's been since Jonathon's death. What if this thing with Mama is bad? I mean, we'll all be broken up about it, but Bekah..."

I pushed a hand through my hair. "You don't have to tell me. She's a wreck, Joe. Told me this morning she wants a divorce. Can you believe it? Like walking away from me will somehow fix things."

Joe shook his head. "Not surprised, but what're you gonna do?"

"Stall her, I suppose." I took a pull from my beer. "Tried to reason with her, but it's like talking to a mule. I even went so far as to play the faith card this morning."

That pulled a grin from him. "How'd that work out for you?"

"Turned the tables on me. How'd you think I learned you ratted on me?"

"Sorry about that, bro. She's like a dog with a bone when she wants something." He sighed. "If Mama *is* sick, Bekah will nag her back to health."

The reminder wiped the grin clear off my face. "I'm sorry about your mama. I'll keep my fingers crossed."

His mouth twisted. "Appreciate the sentiment but crossed fingers are about as likely to make a difference as a witch doctor." He raised his beer. "We prefer to put our faith in Someone with a higher power."

Sounded like Bekah until a year ago. "Where was that higher power when Jonathon died?" I fiddled with my beer bottle. "Not to brush off your faith, but there's too much bad that happens in this world for me to trust in God." This wasn't the first time we'd had this conversation, and I was sure it wouldn't be the last. I slapped the table and stood. "I'm sure you wanna get home to Cassie unless you'd prefer a Swanson dinner. Roasted turkey with gravy and mashed potatoes."

He finished his beer and stood. "That's a hard pass. Cassie's the best cook this side of Nashville, so I'm sure she's got something better planned. You're always welcome to join us."

"Thanks, but I need to get an early start. See if I can get a couple hauls on the books for tomorrow." I followed him to the front door.

He turned. "You doing all right?" His gaze wandered into the darkened family room. The window shades were down, but the dark didn't hide the fact that it looked as if a tornado had struck.

"Nothing a few hours cleaning won't solve."

"How's business? You told me a couple weeks ago things was slow."

I crossed my arms and shrugged. "Don't have Bekah's magical powers of persuasion, I suppose. That girl could produce hauls from nothing." I snorted. "Been trying to find a replacement for her, but no luck so far."

He smirked. "Was that your date last night?"

I grunted. "Boy howdy, can't you and your sister find anything to talk about besides me?"

"Not so you'd notice." He grabbed hold of the door handle. "If I was you, I'd take that as a good sign, though. For someone planning to divorce you, she's plenty interested in your activities." He stepped through the door then turned. "Cassie might be willing to schedule your hauls along with mine. You want I should ask her?"

"All she can do is say no, right? Wouldn't be any worse off than I already am." I trailed him to the front porch. "You be sure and let me know when you find something out about your mama, okay?"

"You got it. I'll text you with Cassie's answer."

I stood on the porch and waved him off. The sun had slipped down behind the old oak that stood like a sentinel in the front yard. I'd planned on putting up a treehouse for Jonathon, but Bekah had nixed the idea. "He's too young," she'd said. "Wait a few years and then we'll talk." I'd accused her of being a helicopter mom more than once, all the fussing and worrying she did over him. And in the end, it turned out she wasn't fussing enough.

Chapter Six

Rebekah

Fingers of fog slipped through the trees cooling the morning air to a tolerable level. The earth was damp, and droplets of dew clung to the grass that bordered the horse path. I drew in the sweet scents of summer that were as familiar to me as orchard grass, horse manure, and leather while Siren and I rode the trail. Red oak and a variety of maple trees towered overhead enclosing us in a fantastical cocoon of protection where nothing evil could penetrate. No grief. No fear. No death. Was this what heaven would be like?

Siren's smooth canter, the rhythm of her shoes on the rocky path, and the sleepless night lulled me into a dream state where, for once, my heart didn't override my head as it was inclined to do. Since my set-to with Mitch the week before, he'd insinuated himself into my mind. If I didn't know better, I'd say he hired himself a voodoo priestess to cast a spell on me. More likely, it was the Holy Spirit trying to tell me something I wasn't quite ready to hear. It was easy enough to drown Him out with the worries I clung to like a morbid lifeline.

There were enough of them with Mama being called into the doctor's this morning. I wanted to go with her and Daddy, but she wouldn't have it. I'd spent the first thirty minutes they were gone changing Mama and Daddy's bed and tidying up their room. With Mama being down so long, things had gotten away from her. When it felt as if the walls were about to crush the life out of me, I saddled up Siren and escaped to the only place I seemed to find peace of late.

An hour later, we were breaking from the trees toward the stables when I spotted a figure leaning against the barn door. The closer we drew, the more the image took shape until I recognized it as Leah. Rather than urge Siren forward, I held her back as if by doing so I could postpone the inevitable. Only reason Leah would be here is if Daddy had called her. Of course, he might have called to give her good news, which she was itching to share with me.

Trying to decipher her mood, I studied her for the few minutes it took to get close enough to talk. The fact she didn't move toward me wasn't a good sign. It meant she wasn't in any more of a hurry to impart ugly news than I was to hear it. Even the *clip-clop* of Siren's shoes on the ground didn't draw her attention. My stomach twisted something fierce, and it was all I could do to hold down the coffee I'd had before leaving the house.

Once Siren was alongside Leah, I dismounted. My booted feet hit the ground, and my knees buckled so I had to grab hold of the saddle to stay upright. If I'd had the strength, I might have mounted up again and ridden so far nothing bad could ever catch up to me.

Leah finally lifted her head. There was a pallor beneath the tan of her face causing it to appear splotchy, and her eyes were swimming with unshed tears. "You need to go inside, Bekah. Mama and Daddy are back from the doctor, and Joe's here." She reached for Siren's reins. "I'll take care of Siren."

"Tell me." My lips were so stiff, it was a wonder words could find their way through them. "How bad?"

She glanced away for a moment and swiped at her eyes. "Please, Bekah." Her voice broke and she swallowed a few times before meeting my eyes. "Go inside and let them tell you. I can't." She tugged on Siren's reins and left me standing with no support.

My legs wobbled like a brand-new foal's as I made my way around the barn and to the house. I braced myself against the trunk of the maple Daddy had planted when he and Mama bought the farm some forty years before. Leah was just a baby then, and Mama was pregnant with Joe. Glancing up at the house, I drew in a deep breath and swallowed the knot of fear that sat at the back of my throat. Mama had been a rock when I lost Jonathon, and I wasn't about to be anything less for her and Daddy.

I pushed off from the tree and crossed the yard. My boots scuffed on the painted porch steps as I made my way to the kitchen door. Stepping inside the cool room, I hesitated a moment and listened to the murmurs coming from the family room. Daddy's low rumble in response to something Mama said.

"I'll check." Unlike Mama and Daddy's words, Joe's were clear. Determined steps preceded his entrance into the kitchen. "There you are. Mama was just asking about you."

My heart hammered in my throat as I eased my cramped fingers from the hold I had on the door knob. I searched Joe's features for some hint that things weren't as dire as Leah let on but found none. His mouth was set in a grim line, and his eyes reminded me of the day we buried Jonathon. I placed my hand over my heart and drew in a deep breath.

"Come on." Joe reached out. "I gotcha."

I stepped up to him and he wrapped his arm around my shoulders and walked me into the family room where Mama and Daddy sat side-by-side on the Naugahyde loveseat. Mama smiled up at me like she hadn't a care in the world while Daddy couldn't seem to raise his head enough to catch my eye. Joe walked me to the sofa, and we sat as if we were attached at the hip.

I tried to match Mama's smile, but I was sure it was a poor substitute. "Wha—" My voice came out sounding like a toad, and I swallowed a couple times before trying it out again. "What'd the doctor say, Mama?"

"Well, now." She grabbed hold of Daddy's hand with both of hers. "It's like this, Sweet Pea, doc says I have cancer."

Cancer. Joe's arm tightened around me as if he was holding me upright, and it gave me the strength to match Mama's calm demeanor. "I'm so sorry, Mama." Despite my determination to be courageous, tears bit at the back of my eyes and near choked me to death. "What's the plan? You gonna do chemo or radiation?"

Daddy's head seemed to sink even lower. "She don't want to do chemo," he mumbled.

"What are the other choices?" Wait. I was getting things backwards. Maybe there were other ways to approach the treatment. "What kind of cancer is it?" I glanced from Mama to Daddy and back again.

Joe kissed the top of my head. "Listen, Bekah. Mama's got stage four pancreatic cancer." His voice hitched, and he squeezed my hand. "There's nothing they can do for her."

As the words sunk in, I pushed away from him. "That makes no sense, Joe. She's only been sick a week." I looked at Mama. "You've only been sick a week, right, Mama?"

Daddy dug his thumb and forefinger into his eyes like he was trying to stop the flow of tears while Mama patted his leg and addressed me. "I've been feeling off for a while, Sweet Pea. I thought it was nothing, but, well…" She shrugged. "Guess I was wrong." Her smile wavered.

I crossed the room and knelt at her feet, pulling her in for a hug. "It's okay, Mama. Everything's gonna be okay." We sat like that for a while, me patting Mama's back and she patting mine as if she hadn't just shared a heartbreaking bit of news.

When I finally sat back, I took Mama's hands and looked into her clear eyes. How could she be so calm? "There's gotta be something we can do."

Daddy sat up straight, blew out a long breath, and pinned me with a look. "Your mama, the doctor, and me have talked, darlin'. We gotta do things your mama's way. She don't want to be hopped up on that poison."

Even knowing it might be the only way to keep Mama with us longer, I nodded. "I understand." There had to be other options, though. "Maybe a special diet." The idea took hold, and I squeezed Mama's hand. "I've heard all sorts of things have been cured with the right foods."

"Sure, Sweet Pea," Mama said, patting my hand with her free one. "We can try that."

"Bekah." I turned at the sound of Leah's voice and found her standing in the doorway motioning me to come with her. "We gotta call Danny."

After giving Mama and Daddy a hug, I pushed off the floor with a sigh and followed Leah into the kitchen. "I'm guessing Dan'll wanna fly out as soon as possible," I told her when we were alone. "Sarah will have to get her mama to watch the kids or get some time off of work."

"He'll be here end of the week," she said, hooking her hair behind her ears.

It took a moment for my brain to connect the dots. "You already called him?"

She nodded.

"Then why—"

"Because we need to talk." She took my hand in hers. "Let's step out." What could be so important she'd interrupt my conversation with Mama? Once outside, she leaned against the porch railing. "I know you want Mama to be better, but she needs you to be okay if she's not."

I shook my head. "This isn't about me. It's about Mama. I'm just thinking there ought to be something we can do to fight this."

Raising her hands, she waved them as if erasing my words. "You're makin' it about you, Bekah. You can't fix this. Mama has already decided on palliative care, and you pushing to try other things is only gonna put more pressure on her."

Palliative care? "Are you saying Mama's just decided to give up and die?"

Mitch

By the time I stepped out of the courthouse, the morning fog had given way to pure heat and humidity. Should have been thanking whatever power saw fit to give me a hundred hours of community service and a fifty dollar fine in lieu of jail time. Instead, I was frustrated over losing a day's work and grumbling about life in general. Not the least of which I didn't know where I'd find the time to donate the required hours and keep the business going.

Todd slapped me on the back as we moved down the courthouse steps. "Could have been worse," he said. "We got a break with Ellie Woods and Judd Lassiter's affidavits. Made you sound like a bona fide hero. Didn't hurt, of course, that it was your first offense."

The bartender and waitress weren't obligated to step in and save my hide, so they did me a definite solid. "Yeah, you gotta point. Should stop by the bar and thank them."

"No, you shouldn't. Send 'em a note instead, would you?" Todd stopped on the sidewalk and cut me a look. "And stay outta the bars, Mitch. You do this again, and there won't be any leniency."

"Appreciate your help, Todd. Don't know where I'd be without it."

"That's what friends are for. It's good for me too."

I snorted. "How do you figure?"

"Pro-bono work never looks bad on a resume. Shows how charitable I can be." He tugged at his tie with a grin and nodded across the street at The Coffee Break. "How 'bout I buy us some lunch since the day's gotten so late."

"Sounds good, except I'm buying. It's the least I can do." My plan had been to search out a haul for the afternoon, but after everything Todd had done for me, it'd be downright rude to rush off.

The Coffee Break was the go-to place to eat on the square if you wanted it quick and good. Problem was, they were usually packed until closing mid-afternoon. Todd grabbed the only table available downstairs while I stepped into line to order. Glancing around the room, I recognized a couple sitting at a table tucked in an alcove at the front. Keith and Mindy Taylor. My gut clenched at the reminder of the ugliest day of my life. For a full five seconds, it was all I could do to take a decent breath. They'd been part of the group at the pool party the day Jonathon died. Hadn't seen them since. I turned away hoping they wouldn't notice me, although in a restaurant the size of a postage stamp, it was like hiding a horse in an outhouse.

"What can I get for you today?" Evelyn flashed her customer-service smile, which shifted when she recognized me. "Hey, Mitch. I haven't seen you for a while."

"How ya doin', Evie? Was here last week, but you must've been off."

"Had to take my Benji to the doc's. The kid went and broke his arm. Can you believe that?" If she was expecting an answer, she didn't wait for it. Her smile disappeared as quick as a lick. "How's Bekah doin'?"

I wasn't about to air my marital issues with a line of customers listening to every word. "Fair to middling." I shot a glance at the specials written on a large board on the wall. "I see you have a few new specials." She took the cue to cut the chit-chat.

After I finished ordering and paying, I accepted the metal clip with my number on it and made my way through the line to our table. I sat across from Todd, which conveniently put my back to Keith and Mindy, and blew out a breath. "Hope you're not in a hurry, 'cause it might could take a while."

"Think that couple behind you is trying to get your attention." Todd nodded toward the front window.

I closed my eyes for a sec, wishing I was anywhere else. There was nothing to do but turn and offer a wave.

"I take it you're not best buds or anything." Worst part of having a lawyer for a friend was they tended toward the nosey side. Occupational hazard.

"Used to be. Now it's just awkward." I started to say more when a hand landed on my shoulder. Forced smile in place, I turned to greet Keith. Instead, I came face-to-face with Brother Paul. May be the lesser of two evils but not by much. He had a few more lines in his face, and the fringe of hair that surrounded a bald pate was whiter, but other than that, he didn't look much different than the day of Jonathon's funeral.

Paul removed his hand from my shoulder and held it out. "Mitch, my boy. Good to see you."

"Brother Paul." I made quick work of the handshake hoping he'd move on.

He then offered it to Todd. "Paul Marshall. Pastor at Mount Hermon First Baptist."

Todd hesitated a moment while his gaze flicked to mine before he took Paul's hand. "Todd Murray. Pleased to meet you."

"The same." He shifted to let someone pass. "Would you mind if I sit a moment?" He indicated the empty chair at our table.

"Not at all." Todd leaned over and pulled it out. "Can we order you something to drink?"

"That's kind of you, son, but I won't be long." His attention turned to me. "Just thought I'd inquire about Miss Anita. Have you heard anything?"

"Uh, no." The question threw me off my game. Of course, Paul would be part of the inner circle of Bekah's family, which meant he should have known about our separation. And if he knew about our separation, why would he assume I was in the loop? "Have you?"

Mouth pulled into a frown, he shook his head. "Nope. Been prayin' it's nothing more than a nuisance, but I have a feeling it's more serious than that."

Todd leaned in. "Who's Anita?"

"Bekah's mom," I said, my attention still on Paul. "Why do you think that?"

He shrugged. "Stopped coming to Wednesday night church meeting a few months ago, which tells me she's not feeling herself. And since I only see her once a week or so, changes tend to stick out."

A knot formed in my belly. I'd been of the mind it wasn't much, either, knowing Miss Anita the way I did. "What kinda changes?"

"A yellow cast to her skin, weight loss, more of a shuffle to her steps each time. Asked her about it a time or two, but you know Miss Anita. She would like to pass before she'd complain." He pinned me with a keen eye. "When's the last time you saw her for yourself?" So, he did know about the separation.

"Been a while," I mumbled. Shouldn't have let my problems with Bekah cause a wedge between the in-laws and myself. If Joe hadn't been more friend than kin, we'd of drifted too.

Paul fiddled with the clip that held our number. "Was at the courthouse just a bit ago and couldn't help but notice y'all there."

I glanced at Todd who merely raised his eyebrows at me. "I swear this town's so small you couldn't have a thought without your neighbor hearing it."

Paul held his hands up. "None of my concern. Just wanted you to know I'm here if you need me."

I crossed my arms and grinned. "Now why would you make an offer like that to a sinner like me?" He knew I didn't follow his religion.

"Truth is, Mitch, we're all sinners. Just so happens mine is covered by the blood of Jesus. Not here to convert you, just here to give a hand where I can."

"Here we are boys." Evie appeared with a tray of food and drinks. "Who has the strawberry salad?"

I pointed to Todd. "Goes to the California-born health nut."

When the food and drinks were dispersed, Todd looked at Brother Paul. "Sure we can't get you anything?"

He scooted his chair back. "Nah. I'll get outta your hair. You just let me know if I can help. You know where to find me."

As Paul turned, Todd glared at me and tilted his head at him. He mouthed something, but since lip-reading wasn't in my wheelhouse, I had no idea what it was. He leaned closer, his tie now dipping into his salad. "Community service," he whispered.

He made about as much sense as spending a dime to save a nickel. "What about it?"

"Brother Paul." He threw a hand toward Paul's retreating back. "The church counts as community service hours."

I shook my head and picked up my BLT. "Not gonna happen, bro. You think I want Bekah's family pastor to know I was arrested? Fact he's aware we're separated is bad enough. No need to give him more ammunition."

"And you're delusional if you think he doesn't have the inside scoop on the happenings around here." He reached for his napkin and swiped at a glob of dressing on his tie. "And if he doesn't have enough work to get you your hours, he knows someone who does."

"Forget it—" The buzz of my cell cut me off, and I had to cough up the bite of sandwich that caught in my throat. Joe. It had to be about Miss Anita. I picked up the phone and glanced at Todd. "Gotta get this."

CHAPTER SEVEN

Rebekah

Raised in the church, I started memorizing Bible verses before I could even read. To this day, I could quote Psalm 23:6 about goodness and love following me. Or James 1:17 telling me every good and perfect gift is from above, or a passel of others that assured me of God's great goodness and mercy. Mitch accused me of forgetting everything I'd believed in when things got tough. Although I pushed back some, he was right. Where was the promise of Romans 8:28? For those who love God, all things were supposed to work for good. How was losing Jonathon, and now Mama dying, working for my good, or anyone else's for that matter?

How would Daddy get along when Mama was gone? They'd been together forty-two years, and I just couldn't imagine one without the other. It was their marriage that showed me people could love unconditionally, even if I failed at it myself. Mama was only in her mid-sixties—too young to die. But then hadn't God already proven there was no such thing?

I pondered these things while tidying up the house and preparing food for the family meeting. Or, more precisely, a partial family meeting. Mama and Daddy had taken a drive and planned to stop somewhere along the way for a picnic.

It was our best chance to discuss how we'd handle things from here on out. Leah and Joe would be at the house at noon, and Dan was still sleeping off his late-night arrival, having driven from Atlanta the night before.

Why was food the focus for every occasion whether it was grieving over a loss or celebrating a beginning? Would we even be able to eat the sandwiches and potato salad I made and stored in the fridge along with sweet tea and lemonade? The fixing of it was more to keep busy than anything else. Once that chore was done, I scrambled to find something else to occupy my hands, even as my mind was bursting with thoughts too troublesome to contain.

I took a basket from the pantry and slipped outside to Mama's garden where her tomatoes were big as softballs. The sun baked my back as I rubbed one of the deep green leaves. The pungent scent flooded me with memories of planting and sowing in this exact spot with Mama. From the time I could remember, this was her happy place. I plucked some of the ripened tomatoes off the vine and moved to the next row.

The squash was bursting with more than we could eat in five summers, so I snapped off some of the buttery-yellow blossoms. Mama wasn't eating much, but she'd never been able to turn down my stuffed blossoms. The ricotta and parmesan would give her some needed calories and a little protein to boot.

"For a split second, I thought you were Mama tending the garden that way."

Standing, I craned my neck to see Dan leaning his elbows on the fence appearing as relaxed as you please. But the circles beneath his eyes and strain around his mouth told a different tale. None of us would walk through this season unscathed—least of all the baby of the family.

"You get some decent rest?" I lifted the basketful of produce—must've been ten pounds worth—and carried it to the gate.

Dan unlatched it and took the vegetables from me. "Much as I could. Got in around three. Hope I didn't wake y'all."

"I heard you come in, but I wasn't asleep. No one's doing much of that these days." I led the way across the patchy grass. "How's Sarah and the girls?"

"Good. Sarah just got word yesterday of a promotion, so it means longer hours for her."

I stopped at the steps and turned. "Are you doing okay with her gone so much?"

He shrugged. "I knew what I was gettin' into marrying an architect." He shifted the basket onto a hip. "Just makes it a little more challenging for me to get my classes done. Didn't think I'd be a house daddy forever. At this rate, I won't have my business degree until Molly's in college."

"Can't you work when they're in school?"

"Oh, didn't I tell you?" He grimaced. "We decided to homeschool them. For the most part, I'll be with 'em all day, every day." He marched past me and climbed the stairs to the back porch, his shoulders slumped as if weighed down. Was it from the load he carried in his arms or the one at home?

A thought occurred to me in that moment. If I were going to justify it, I'd have claimed it was another nudge from the Lord. But even in my sad state, I knew He'd never condone running from my problems. Tagging behind Dan, I said. "What if I came out there to live?"

"What d'you mean?" He pushed through the screen door into the kitchen and set the basket on the counter.

I followed, letting the door slap shut. "After Mama..." I couldn't abide the thought, let alone say it out loud. "Once Mama doesn't need me, I can move out there and help y'all."

He leaned his backside against the counter, crossed his arms, and looked at me like I was as pitiful as a three-legged dog. "I don't know, Bekah. The house is hardly big enough for the four of us. We only have but two bedrooms, and—"

"No, no, no." I waved my hands in the air. "I didn't mean I'd move in with you." Perish the thought. "I love you and your family to pieces, Baby Brother, but I wouldn't do that to either of us. I'd find a place of my own, but I'd be close enough to be available when you needed me."

Eyes down, he shifted his stance and crossed one ankle over the other. "You offering to do this for me or for you?"

I shrugged. "A little of both, I suppose."

Before he could say more, the sound of tires crunching on the gravel drive drifted through the screen door. Dan looked out the window above the kitchen sink. "Looks like both Leah and Joe are here." He turned to me. "Let's talk about this later, okay?"

Either Dan was relieved by the interruption or anxious to see Leah and Joe. I liked to think it was the latter but suspected otherwise. I understood the need to escape. Hadn't I been perfecting that move myself for a year?

I set up the table with the food I'd prepared and set out place settings while my stomach revolted at the thought of eating. My hands shook like a drunk coming off a bender as I took ice cube trays from the freezer, cracked them loose, and filled four glasses. It was a wonder I survived the loss of Jonathon. If it'd been possible to die from grief, that would have done me in. But now with Mama's diagnosis and my marriage turned into a heap of cold ashes...how close was I to the breaking point?

"There you are." Leah stepped inside and let the screen door slam as she studied the food-laden table. "You have quite a spread here, Bekah. Shouldn't have gone to so much work, I don't think anyone's going to feel much like eating." She crossed the kitchen and pulled me in for a hug, ice cube tray and all.

"It gave me something to do. You know what they say about idle hands and the work of the devil." I stepped out of her arms and tried to smile but failed. "What are we gonna do?" My voice wobbled like a spanking new bike rider.

Leah fingered a strand of hair from my face. "That's what we're here to figure out. We're all of us in this together, Bek. It'll be okay. I promise." Her own smile was a little shaky.

Ever since I could remember, I'd admired Leah. Four years older, she'd always been my champion whether it was to pave the way with Mama and Daddy, protect me from a schoolyard bully, or teach me how to be a girl, which didn't come natural for me. I'd have rather hung out with horses than people, so it was a pure miracle Mitch had ever glanced my way in the first place. But more than anything, I'd trusted that when Leah said things would be okay, she was speaking truth. This was the first time I wondered if she might be as lost as me.

After everyone had a plate of food, we got down to business. Leah, being the eldest, slipped into the lead.

She took a sip of her lemonade and wiped her mouth with a napkin as proper as the Queen of England. "We need to figure out if we should try and care for Mama ourselves or bring someone in."

"What d'you mean bring someone in?" Joe leaned his elbows on the table. "Like hire a stranger?"

"Mama wouldn't like that," Dan said. "And I don't think Daddy would be none too happy about it, either."

I swiped a finger on the condensation from my glass of tea. "He wouldn't complain if it was best for Mama. And Mama wouldn't complain because she doesn't like to make a fuss." I looked at Leah. "But like you said the other day, it's important to keep things as stress-free as possible for Mama."

"So, what do we do?" Joe asked. "Take turns watchin' over things?"

Dan cleared his throat. "I can't hardly do that from Atlanta. Doesn't seem fair that things fall on y'all because I don't live closer."

"Nothing you can do about that, Danny," I said. "Besides, how are any of you gonna be able to pitch in much? Y'all got kids and marriages." Unlike me. There was nothing dividing my time, and I had lived off the generosity of Mama and Daddy for far too long. "I'm already here, so it makes sense that I take care of Mama."

Leah shook her head. "You can't do that alone, Bekah. You have two jobs and the farm." She glanced at Joe and Dan. "And I'm afraid the worse Mama gets, the harder it'll be on Daddy to keep up. When Gabe's nana got sick, it took as much a toll on his mama as it did on his nana. It's draining physically and emotionally."

A glance around the table, and it was clear they were all avoiding direct eye contact with me. It didn't take a kick in the head for me to realize they weren't too keen on depending on me for Mama's care. They probably thought I'd crack under the pressure. Might be they were right.

Mitch

Mount Hermon First Baptist was located off the square a couple of blocks. As churches went, it appeared average. There must've been near twenty of them in Shelbyville alone, each a paragon of brick and stone with a steeple stuck high in the sky as if reaching for the heavens. I couldn't tell one from another—Baptist, Methodist, Church of Christ, or some odd name that didn't reveal its denomination. I just knew Bekah's family had been attending Brother Paul's particular institution since John and Miss Anita were married.

And though Bekah and I were married there, too, it didn't mean anything to me other than it was her wish. Tradition, or some such, was her reasoning. She probably hoped I'd be so overcome with the power from above, I'd convert the minute we got hitched. The fact I hadn't succumbed to them didn't mean I wasn't aware they existed. That kind of power, whether I bought into it or not, deserved respect.

So it was, I stood outside the church on Saturday night. I'd wrestled with Miss Anita's diagnosis since Joe called and laid it on me. Stage four pancreatic cancer. If Jonathon's death hadn't convinced me that God wasn't as merciful as He'd have people believe, this would have.

"Can I help you?" A man about my age stood in the cavernous doors at the top of the concrete steps. He had an official air about him, though he was dressed much like me. Maybe an associate pastor? Why else would someone hang out at church on a Saturday night unless obligated?

"I'm looking for Brother Paul." Thought using the pastor's proper title might ease any suspicions the man might have. My bruises had healed for the most part, but there was still a tinge of yellow around my eye, like a patch of jaundice.

"He's next door at the parsonage. I could ring him if you'd like."

"That'd be appreciated. Tell him Mitch Casey's here to see him, would you?"

"Sure thing." He pulled a cell phone from his back pocket and made the call. A moment later, he descended the steps. "Said to come right over. I'll show you where it is."

"Thanks." I followed him to the east side of the church where a cottage-like structure stood under the canopy of an old oak tree. The brick house was small but charming, with flowerbeds surrounding the exterior.

As we came near the front door, it swung open, and Brother Paul stepped out. "Could of knocked me over with a feather when Aaron told me you were here." He had a napkin tucked into the neck of his shirt, and it struck me I'd interrupted his supper.

"If this isn't a good time, I can come back."

He waved me in. "Nonsense. You're welcome to join me. Barbecued a rack of ribs, and I'm happy to share." He glanced at Aaron. "You, too, son, if you'd like."

Aaron waved him off. "Nice of you to offer, Paul, but I have supper waiting on me at home." He stepped out of my way so I could enter. "Good to meet you, Mitch. Hope to see you again."

"Thanks, Aaron."

Brother Paul's home was neat and tidy, unlike my own. A bookcase, filled to capacity, took up one full wall in the family room. I pointed to it. "You like to read?" Brilliant repartee, but I was out of my element. Felt as if I was infringing on holy ground.

"Best way to learn." He indicated I should follow him. "You like ribs?"

"Who doesn't?" The kitchen was as orderly as the family room. Maybe it was high time I did some cleaning. If Bekah saw the mess, she'd pitch a hissy fit for sure. She may not be residing there at the present, but that wouldn't lower her expectations one bit.

"Have a seat." He pulled a chair from the kitchen table then crossed to get another plate from the cabinet. A pile of ribs, doused in sauce, sat like some kind of offering. There was corn on the cob and coleslaw as well.

"If I didn't know better, I'd say you were expecting me." My stomach grumbled. Might as well take him up on his generous offer.

He slid a plate in front of me. "Sweet tea? Water?"

"Whatever you're havin' is fine."

Once he was settled across from me, he nudged the plate closer. "Dig in. I've already prayed over it but feel free if you'd like to offer up some thanks."

Way to make me feel ungrateful. "I'm sure you got it covered."

"So, what can I do for you, besides offer sustenance?"

I reached for a rib. "I didn't know if you'd heard about Miss Anita's diagnosis."

He shook his head. "Not a word. Left a message the other day, but they haven't called back. You?"

I took a bite from the rib and licked my lips. Seemed downright sacrilegious to be eating while discussing Miss Anita's bad fortune. "Joe called the other day just after you left the coffee shop. She's got stage four pancreatic cancer." Even though I'd repeated it in my mind a dozen times, it still seemed unreal.

Brother Paul dropped his rib and gathered the napkin from his neck. Wiping his mouth, he stared ahead as if trying to decipher the information. "That's about the worst news you coulda brought."

I snatched a napkin from the holder in the middle of the table. "Yeah."

"Have you talked to Rebekah yet?" He pushed his plate aside as if his appetite was now gone.

"No. I wanted to, but..." I wiped my hands and mouth. "Joe said the family was getting together earlier today to figure out a plan. Miss Anita doesn't want to undergo treatment."

"Can't say I blame her." He twisted his mouth then sighed. "If they don't come to church in the morning, I'll give 'em a call." He pinned me with a look. "Wanna share what's goin' on with you and Rebekah? I'm real good at keeping secrets, seein' as it's part of the job description."

His offer pulled a smile from me. The man had a way about him, I'd give him that. They say confession's good for the soul. "Bekah's got it in her mind we should split up. Somehow, she believes gettin' away from me will make it easier on her."

He frowned. "What d'you think?"

"I think she's running away from something she can't rightly escape. And losing Miss Anita might just be her undoing."

Brother Paul sat back and stared at me like he could see clear to my soul. It made me feel like a colony of ants was crawling around inside of me. "I'm grateful you saw fit to come by with this news, but I'd of found out sooner or later."

"I suppose." I kept my eyes glued to the wadded napkin on my plate and tried not to squirm like a kid waiting on a scolding from the principal.

"You wanna tell me the real reason you come by?"

It wouldn't surprise me none if he already knew. "Thought maybe you might have some volunteer work around here you could throw my way."

He chuckled. "Now why would you wanna hang out here when you can't hardly abide the place?"

I reasoned a few answers in my head to see what might put me in the best light, but nothing clicked.

"Could it have something to do with the bruises on your face? They appear to be healing up nicely, by the way," Brother Paul said.

I blew out a breath. "Got myself jammed up a week or so ago."

"Looks more like a fight to me," he drawled.

I straightened my spine and faced him like an adult. "Yes, sir. Would it make a difference if I told you I was protecting a young woman's honor?"

He laughed. "If you say so. What's the charge?"

"Drunk and disorderly." I looked him straight in the eye and raised my right hand. "But I swear to God, I wasn't drunk. Didn't even finish a beer."

He quirked an eyebrow. "Surprised you'd swear to a God you claim to not follow. How many community hours you need?"

The man was downright spooky. "A hundred."

He nodded. "I think we can work something out."

Chapter Eight

Rebekah

When I lost Jonathon, it took all the strength a body had just to breathe. It was weeks before I was able to push past my despondency enough to even drag my broken self from bed. As hard as I'd been on Mitch, he was the only anchor I had at the time. Now with Mama, I didn't have that luxury. And I didn't have the freedom to just give up and hide away from the pain. As long as she was with us, I had to be strong for her and Daddy.

Work was my salvation. The busier I stayed, the less time I had to wallow. Friday and Saturdays, Leah agreed to sit with Mama while I worked at the store. It cut my hours some, but I had to prioritize. Daddy was available for evenings while I waitressed, and Joe promised to look in on them the nights I was gone. Serving customers kept my mind occupied since it took every cell in my brain to get the orders right. So, it was no surprise when I stood in front of the customer at table four that I didn't recognize him as Brother Paul until he spoke. Gone was the suit-and-tie pastor. Instead, dressed in a red t-shirt, he looked like any other old man.

"It appears they've got you running around like a chicken with its head cut off." He smiled and set his menu aside.

I'd never seen him in the restaurant before. Of course, that didn't mean much, since I'd only been waitressing a couple months. "I don't suppose it's our beer selection that brings you here."

"Heard about your mama." There it was. He was a man on a mission. Even in the shadows of the booth, the droop of his eyes communicated the same sadness that plagued my own heart.

I glanced around to be sure no one was listening. Mama's illness wasn't a secret, but it would be easier for me if I could keep work and family separate. "This isn't the place, Brother Paul."

He held up both hands. "Not here to ruffle feathers, I assure you. I'm just here to offer whatever help I can."

"I'm sure Mama and Daddy would take some comfort if you stopped by and visited."

"But not you?"

"No, sir." I held the order pad aloft. "So, what can I get you?"

Lips pursed, he picked up the menu. "What d'you recommend?"

"Depends on your preference. We got a nice New York steak or beef ribs if you're wanting red meat. There's a fish special, but I'd give it a pass if I were you. The roasted chicken is popular with a side of mashed taters and green beans."

"I'll take that then. And a glass of sweet tea."

"You got it. I'll put that order in right away, and—"

"Do you get a break, Rebekah?"

The question didn't make sense to my befuddled mind. "Sir?"

"I asked if you get a break. A little time so we maybe could talk where you'd be more comfortable." He sat back and clasped his hands on his belly, relaxed as you please.

"I'm early shift tonight, so I get off in about an hour." The moment the words were out, I wanted to shove them right back in. What in the Sam Hill prompted me to be so accommodating? I wasn't in need of his spiritual guidance, and to pretend otherwise would be a flat out lie.

"Perfect." He beamed up at me. "I'd appreciate it if you could give me a few minutes before heading on home."

Without being rude, there was nothing to do but agree.

An hour and ten minutes later, I stepped outside to catch the sun setting behind a bank of fluffy white clouds. It brought to mind the times I'd lie with Mama on a blanket in the yard, and we'd spot animals in the cloud formations. No matter how they were splayed against the cerulean backdrop, I found horses every time. Even when it was pure strain on my part, Mama always claimed to see them too. Whatever I wanted in life, Mama wanted it for me. It'd always been that way. Unconditional love.

The thought of it formed a knot in my throat, and I sent up a prayer that Brother Paul had changed his mind about meeting and headed on home.

"There you are." He stood at the edge of the parking lot and lifted a hand. Of course. Why would God see fit to answer a prayer now, when He'd been so miserly with them in the past?

The air hadn't cooled much, and the humidity boosted it by a good ten degrees. Perspiration popped up on my forehead and upper lip as I crossed the lot to meet him. The urge to rush home to see how Mama was doing thrummed through every nerve fiber. I didn't know how much time I had left with her, so I treasured each minute like a precious jewel.

"Do you mind if we walk?" He indicated Main Street south which would eventually drop into River Bottom Park.

"Ten minutes," I said, making a point to look at my watch. "I really wanna get home to Mama."

He nodded. "I promise to be quick about it."

We moved across the lot, and when we reached the sidewalk, Brother Paul stepped around me so he would be on the street side. Daddy always did the same walking with Mama, Leah, or me. He told me once that it was the chivalrous thing to do, which didn't make sense to my ten-year-old self. It was later I discovered the practice came from the Middle Ages when a knight kept his right hand free to retrieve his sword and defend his lady. My respect for Brother Paul rose by a degree or two when he acted in kind.

"If I didn't say it in the restaurant, I want you to know how sorry I am about your mama," Brother Paul began. The rumble of his low voice cut through the traffic that whizzed by on the street.

"Thank you. It doesn't feel real, you know?" A horn blared, and I winced at the intrusiveness of it.

"Yes." He cleared his throat. "You often hear people say, 'I know just how you feel,' but the truth is we can't unless we've actually lived it. I'm not going to tell you I know how you feel, Rebekah. But I am going to tell you that God does. He holds every tear you've ever shed in the palm of his hand."

I swept a strand of sweat-damp hair from my face as a surge of anger heated my cheeks. "A fat lot of good that does me," I spat.

He tucked his hands into the pockets of his slacks. "You have every right to be angry."

That was unexpected. "Yes, I do, even if it doesn't change anything."

"It changes your relationship with your Heavenly Father. Instead of moving toward Him, you're moving away. The same goes for your relationship with Mitch."

I rubbed my forehead and fought the tears that threatened at the back of my eyes. "With Mitch, it's more complicated than you know."

"Maybe you can explain it to me."

We had reached the end of busy traffic on Main Street, and the sudden quiet was deafening. There were no car engines or horns or other pedestrians to drown out the clamor in my mind. "I'd rather not, if you don't mind." Just what I needed—one more person on Team Mitch, someone else to point out that I was called to forgive as Jesus forgave my sins. Leah, Mama, Daddy, and even Darlene made it sound like it was easy as pie. Just forgive. Two little words that were near impossible to do.

Brother Paul placed a light hand on my arm. "We need to head back to your car if I'm going to keep my promise of ten minutes."

We walked in silence for a time while I ran all the arguments I could think of through my mind. I wanted to stay angry with God; I needed to stay angry with God. It was all I had left to hold me up.

"You think it might be good for you to come back to church?" Brother Paul finally said. "I'm sure it'll do your mama a world of good to have you there with her." That was a low blow.

I glanced at him as we crossed the street into busier traffic once again. "Ever since I can recall, I've attended church on Sundays and Wednesday nights. I learned my Bible verses, got myself baptized, and did everything that was expected of me. I come to realize it doesn't matter if I'm there or not; God's gonna do whatever He wants regardless."

"That could be your issue right there, Rebekah."

"What's that?"

"You somehow think you've earned God's favor by doing what's right. Attending service isn't for God; it's for you. I take the blame for that missed theology. Should have taught y'all better. You're in a bad spot right now, and God gets that. He's strong enough to take your anger and merciful enough to use it."

Mitch

Mount Hermon Baptist Church looked to be a simple building from the outside. From inside? It was two floors of convoluted hallways going every which way. I was trapped in a full-size maze designed to test my navigational skills. I'd spend half my community service hours just finding my way from one place to the other.

Sunday school classrooms and a fellowship hall covered the first floor while more classrooms, the church sanctuary, and Brother Paul's office were on the second. And every one of them needed a good coat of paint. Boy howdy, did I ever walk into that one, but I was too grateful to grumble. I could work whatever hours fit my schedule, as long as it wasn't on Sunday. "It's the Lord's Day,"

Brother Paul had said. That left Saturdays and nights after I completed my hauls for the day.

My second evening, I was finishing up the first classroom. The work was easy, the room air-conditioned, and I had the place to myself. Only problem with doing mindless work was it allowed me more time to think than was healthy. I'd left Bekah at least five messages, none of which she'd responded to. I knew she was hurting, but the girl could surely make a preacher cuss. I was of a mind to show up unannounced but didn't figure that would play out in my favor.

Wet roller in hand, I stepped back and admired my work. It was amazing what a fresh coat of paint could do to a room. This one was a light blue. Kind of reminded me of the sky.

"Nicely done."

I spun around to find Paul standing in the doorway. I had music blasting through my phone, so I hadn't heard his approach. "It's passable," I said as I turned the music off.

"You're just bein' humble." Paul's gaze wandered around the room as if inspecting the work. "Thought you said you didn't have any painting experience."

"I don't, but it's not rocket science. All it takes is good tools and a steady hand. You supplied the first, and I supplied the second." I reached to dislodge a plastic grocery bag from the wad on the floor with my free hand and slid the wet roller inside.

He tapped the low table in the center of the room. "Seems like it was only yesterday Rebekah was in this classroom. I can still see her with her pigtails and cowboy boots," he said with a chuckle. "She was a quick learner, that one."

Even though I didn't cotton to the idea of church, there was something sad in knowing she was now rejecting what she'd once loved. "Can't believe I'm saying this, but I'd feel some better if I knew she still had her faith to cling to. I never realized before how much a part of her was tied to this." I flung an arm out to encompass the church. "I'm watching her fade away, and there isn't a darn thing I can do about it."

"She's goin' through a rough patch," Paul said. "There comes a time every person's faith is tested in some way. We either move toward God or step away from Him."

I pondered his words while I retrieved the trim brush from the edge of the paint can. Was Paul speaking from personal experience or in generalities? A mason jar filled with paintbrush cleaner sat in the corner, and I plunked the brush inside to soak then turned my attention to him. "That include you?" It was an offhanded question that didn't expect an answer.

He nodded. "Afraid so. Had myself a crisis of faith right before I came to pastor this church. This was my fresh start."

Bekah said she wanted a fresh start too. Was she intending to run off somewhere else to get it? Squatting down to place the lid back on the can of paint, the questions tugged at my mind like an impatient two-year-old. "That must've been over forty years ago," I said. "Didn't you marry Bekah's parents?"

"I did indeed." He frowned. "I was twenty-five when I lost my wife and baby daughter in a car accident."

His confession hit me square in the gut like a sucker punch. It was near impossible to survive the loss of Jonathon. What if I'd lost both him and Bekah? "I'm sorry. I can't even imagine."

"Most people who'd say that, I'd tend to agree with. But reading the expression on your face right now, I'd say you *can* imagine. You know what it's like to lose a child, and I get the feeling you're worried about losing Rebekah too."

I averted my eyes and reached for the hammer to secure the paint lid. "Yeah. But it's not the same. She's not dead." I pounded on the edges of the lid until it was sealed tight.

"If you don't mind me asking, how long have y'all been separated?" He sat on the small table and crossed his arms.

"More than six months now." I grabbed a rag from the pile I'd left in the corner, took the paintbrush from the cleaner, and wiped it down. "If I could just reach past all that pain and anger..." I shook my head. "I'm at a loss. I think it's all the harder because Jonathon was our miracle baby. Took us eight years to get pregnant. Not that the answer would be to have another child. It's not like replacing a puppy."

"No, it's not." Paul's response was slow as if he had something else on his mind.

"Did you ever think about getting married again? You were practically a kid when you lost your family."

"What's that?"

Yep, he was somewhere else. "I asked if you ever thought about remarrying. Starting over, you know?"

"Never found anyone who could hold a candle to my Caroline." He smiled and clapped his hands together once. "We're gonna have to put our heads together and see if we can't move Rebekah along a little."

I barked out a laugh. "Isn't manipulation against your rules of conduct or something?"

"We'll just set things in the right direction and let the Holy Spirit do the heavy lifting." His eyes perused the room again as he stood. "You're doing a good job here, Mitch. You'll have this place looking spanking new in no time." He walked out the door and lifted his hand in a wave.

The abrupt departure left me scratching my head. What had just happened? Something smelled off, and it wasn't paint fumes. I gathered up my supplies and carried them into the next classroom. I tried to picture Bekah as a little girl running down these halls, pigtails flying behind her. It was an image that tugged a smile from me.

All the years Bekah pushed and prodded to get me into this church. Never could I have imagined a bar brawl would accomplish what she couldn't. Not that I bought into the whole religion thing, but there was something peaceful about the place. Could be it was just the quiet. Then again, maybe there was more to it than I'd been willing to see before.

No matter. I had another ninety-four hours to figure it out.

Chapter Nine

Rebekah

When life was good, taking things for granted was easy as slipping into a comfortable pair of old jeans. There was no question about where our next meal might come from, or how Mitch and I would pay the mortgage, or even where we'd spend the holidays.

If I'd learned nothing else over the last year or so, it was that I should take nothing for granted. Almost everything I'd held dear had slipped through my fingers or was working its way to that end. And so it was with Mama. Still, I was honored to be able to care for her in this season of her life—and death, apparently. And it made me wonder at God's timing. There was a truth that poked its way into my head then retreated again like a fearful turtle ducking inside its shell for protection.

I wouldn't have been able to help Mama like I was if I'd had Jonathon to tend to. It wasn't as if I was the only person who could care for Mama. I was merely the most convenient.

Early Saturday morning when I spotted the dirty dishes piled in the sink and on the counter, I growled through gritted teeth. Joe struck again. I was not only the most convenient but the most malleable to boot. Every night he stayed with

Mama and Daddy, he played the good son and cooked up a mess of food. Only problem was, he wasn't good enough to clean up after himself and left it for me.

A headache throbbed at the base of my skull like Ritchie Albright was playing a drum solo. I turned on the hot water and reached for the dish soap. It'd been past midnight when I got in after working at the grill, and I'd purposely avoided the kitchen. It would have been a pure miracle if I could get five hours of sleep, and knowing what awaited me would have had me fuming mad all night. Me and Joe were about to have a come-to-Jesus meeting.

"Morning, darlin'."

I craned my neck to see Daddy shuffling in, Bible tucked beneath one arm. He was still in his robe and slippers, which had become his habit since Mama's diagnosis. Before then, he was up, dressed, and halfway through his Bible reading before I made an appearance. Now, he lingered in bed with Mama like he was soaking up what time he had left with her.

"Morning, Daddy. Did you sleep well?" I wiped my hands on a dishtowel, poured him a cup of coffee, and took it to the kitchen table.

"Better 'n you, I'm sure. Heard you come in past midnight." He pulled out his chair and eased into it like he'd aged ten years in the last couple of weeks. "Sorry about the mess in the sink. Thought Joe was gonna take care of it before he left last night. Must've gotten too late. Said he had somethin' cooking with Brother Paul and had to get home by eight."

Brother Paul? What was the pastor up to now? "Don't you give it another thought." I returned to the dishes and flipped the water faucet handle harder than necessary. It surely wasn't Daddy's fault his son was a slob. Well, maybe a little. The nut didn't fall far from the tree—that was for darn sure. "How's Mama doing this morning?"

"Afraid she didn't sleep much. Need to talk to the doc about increasing her pain meds." He took a slurp of his coffee, set the cup down, and opened his Bible. "Dad blast it," he muttered.

I whipped around from the sink. "What is it, Daddy? You okay?"

"I'm fine," he mumbled. "Left my glasses on the nightstand." He planted his hands on the table for leverage and started to rise.

"I'll get them. You just stay there." I waved him back down and wiped my wet hands on my jeans as I crossed the kitchen.

The bedroom was dark except for a nightlight that shone from the master bath. I could just make out Mama's form under a pile of blankets. The house was near eighty degrees, and Mama always wore a nightgown. She should have been roasting, but instead, she was huddled like it was dead of winter and the heat was on the fritz.

I felt my way around the bed, careful not to bump it. By the time I'd reached Daddy's side, my eyes had adjusted enough to the dark to spot his glasses set atop his latest book.

"John, are you gettin' up now?" Mama's sudden voice startled me, and I fumbled the glasses.

Quick reflexes and a little luck had me clutching them to my chest. "It's me, Mama. Bekah. I'm just getting Daddy's glasses. Didn't mean to wake you. Go on back to sleep."

"Come sit with me a spell, would you, Sweet Pea? Seems you're always rushin' around." Her voice was groggy and slightly slurred.

"Let me give these to Daddy, and I'll be right back." I slipped out of the bedroom and eased the door near closed. She'd be asleep by the time I got back, just like she was every morning. *The mind is willing, but the body is weak*. Mama had been living out that adage even before she'd been diagnosed. Why had she hidden her illness for so long? If she'd been open about it, they might have been able to treat the cancer before it spread.

After delivering Daddy's glasses to him, I checked on Mama again. Sure enough, she was softly snoring. I returned to the kitchen and the casserole pan with baked-on gunk. Looked like some kind of cheese and noodle concoction. "What did Joe make for y'all last night?"

"Hmm?" He looked up from his reading, eyes like an owl behind the glasses. "Oh, he made lasagna."

Not likely. "He *made* lasagna, or he heated up a lasagna Cassie made?"

He shrugged. "Makes no difference. Tasted good just the same. And your Mama ate for once."

Sibling rivalry reared its ugly head and turned my blue eyes green in a flash. Just as quick, shame tamped it back down again. So, what if Joe was the one who got Mama to eat? Still, it was just like him to take the credit when Cassie did the work and then leave the mess for me to clean up after waitressing all night. Pettiness was not a pretty color on me.

I blew out a breath. *Get ahold of yourself, girl.* It sure didn't take long for that ol' sin nature to take over. What did I expect when I turned my back on the One who made me better? I finished the last pan and put it in the dish drainer atop the already precarious pile. Better to focus on the work I had to get done before leaving for the shop. I promised I'd work an eight-hour shift, then it was back to the restaurant from six to midnight again.

Daddy slid his Bible aside. "What's your schedule look like today?" The man had a way of reading minds. Always had.

I poured myself some coffee and sat with him. "Same as last weekend. Leah'll be here before lunch and stay until Joe arrives." I still had to muck out the stables, feed and water the horses, and gather the eggs. If I was quick about it and settled for a power bar for breakfast, I might find an hour to take Siren for a ride. Poor girl was going to feel neglected if I wasn't careful.

"We got the hay to cut and bale sometime this week," Daddy said. "A course, I could hire the work out if it's too much." He didn't have to remind me that hiring out would cut the profits to near nothing.

"Maybe you could talk to Joe tonight and see if he can spare some time. Might have to do it Sunday, though." Daddy had been a stickler about keeping Sunday sacred, but I didn't know where else we'd carve the time.

Unless I quit waitressing. Thirty hours a week that could be put to better use.

"Now's not the time to put the good Lord on the back burner," Daddy said. "He'll find us the time."

A few minutes later, I was out at the stables. My body was working while my mind was pondering. Waitressing brought in more money than I could earn at the shop because of tips. I'd been squirreling away every dollar I made in anticipation of a fresh start, but that wouldn't be possible as long as Mama and Daddy needed a hand. When my life came to an end one day, I would most likely have more than a few regrets. The time I spent caring for Mama wouldn't be one of them.

Once the choice was made, breathing got a little easier. If only all my decisions were so quick to come by.

Mitch

There used to be a routine to Saturday mornings, but it fizzled like a Fourth of July sparkler after Jonathon died. I'd awaken slowly with Bekah spooned against my chest, her warm body pressed up against mine. Even now on some mornings before full consciousness, I could swear the sweet floral scent of her shampoo still clung to the pillowcases. Wasn't possible since I'd changed them several times. Not as much as Bekah would have, but enough that her scent was long gone.

Since Bekah left, Saturdays were just another workday. I'd get ahold of dispatch by six and contract whatever hauls I could. That changed when I got slapped with community service hours. It'd take near a year if I stuck to the occasional evening, so I'd promised Brother Paul every Saturday until it was done. Didn't help my bank balance, but I figured there were more important things than money—and one of them was clearing my accounts.

The upside to the situation was that Paul didn't want me showing my face before eight. Left me time to sleep in some. The sun was clear up by six, weaseling its way between the blinds. *Just another thirty minutes.* I squeezed my eyes tight and wished for sweet oblivion. Almost worked, too, until my cell phone pinged. *Who in the world would text so early in the morning?*

I rolled to my side and dragged the pillow over my head in one swift move. Didn't do no good. My cell phone pinged again, and I sat bolt upright. Rubbing at my eyes to clear them, I reached for my phone on the nightstand. Joe.

Come 4 breakfast

Can't

Why not?

The heck with this. I thumbed in his number and scratched my bare chest waiting for him to answer.

"You coming?" he answered.

"Are you nuts? It's only six. What're y'all up so early for?"

"Cassie's makin' pancakes and eggs. Get yourself dressed and head on over." He *was* nuts.

"You're crazy." My voice rose a couple octaves. "Even if I didn't think you lost your last marble, I couldn't drop everything. I gotta work at the church today."

His voice was muffled like he was talking to someone else. "Says he can't."

There was a scuffling sound and then Cassie's voice came over the line. "Mitch Casey, I'm cooking up a stack of flapjacks for you with a side of eggs easy-over and crispy bacon. You'll have plenty of time to clock some hours once we're done with breakfast. I'm not about to take no for an answer, so get your sorry butt outta bed, get dressed, and get over here." Then the phone went dead.

I stared at my cell. Was this what an out-of-body experience was like? Was someone punking me? No, it was definitely Joe and Cassie. *I* called them, not the other way around. What was a body to do? Cassie said get over there. I wasn't going to argue. Besides, flapjacks and bacon were powerful motivators.

Half an hour later, I pulled my truck up their long, asphalt driveway. Unlike me, Joe made real good money with his hot-shot trucking business, so he was living in what I teasingly called the upper crust of Shelbyville society. Of course, the real uppity-ups were those with the million-dollar horse ranches.

"Uncle Mitch!" The squeals reached my ears as soon as I hit the ground. Jane and Gracie came bounding down the porch steps, and I planted my feet so I could take the impact when they threw their little bodies at me.

"Well, aren't y'all a sight for sore eyes." I gathered them in my arms and basked in the unconditional love. Nieces were the best.

"Mama said you was comin' for breakfast." Gracie swept the flyaway strands of blond hair from her face. She was the exact age Jonathon was when he'd died, and the pain of it pierced my heart for a beat or two.

"She was right, 'cause here I am."

Jane, an older version of Gracie, wrapped an arm around her little sister—a move that seemed to come as natural as breathing to the nine-year-old. "She made pancakes and even squeezed the orange juice herself." Her eyes were wide as dinner plates as if she'd never experienced such a thing. Might be I wasn't the only one who thought things were a little hinky.

"You don't say." I ruffled her hair. "So, what's the deal, huh? I don't believe I've ever been ordered"— I grinned—"I mean *invited* to breakfast before."

"You'll see," Jane sing-songed.

Joe ambled down the stairs. "Okay girls, go inside and set the table for your mama."

I watched them scamper back into the house, shot Joe a withering look, and threw my hands in the air. "What's the deal here? You dragged me out of bed and ordered me over here to have breakfast? Since when?"

"What're you griping about. I didn't get to sleep in either." He gave a come-along wave and followed the girls.

I trailed Joe into the house where the smell of flapjacks and bacon had my mouth watering. At least they hadn't lied about the food. I wouldn't leave hungry—that was for sure.

Cassie stepped from the kitchen, a warm smile lighting up her brown eyes. "I'm so glad you could make it, Mitch." She moved in for a hug, and all I could do was stand there with my mouth hanging open.

"It's not like you gave me a choice now, did you? I told Paul I'd be at the church by eight, so if that's not gonna work out, I'd appreciate y'all letting me know so I can give him a call. And while you're at it, could someone please tell me what is goin' on here?"

"Don't you worry yourself over Brother Paul." Cassie latched onto my arm and pulled me into the kitchen. "'Cause he's right here."

There at the large oval oak table sat Paul and a little boy I'd never seen before. Frowning, I held onto the back of a chair and looked from one to the other. "Someone want to tell me what's going on?"

"Why don't we all sit?" Paul waved a hand to include the group. "Once I pray over our food, we can clear everything up."

There was scraping of chairs on the tile floor as everyone took a seat. Paul held out a hand to Cassie on one side of him and the little boy on the other. Gracie slipped her tiny hand in mine, and when I glanced on my other side, Joe's was waiting. Felt a little silly taking his hand, but I'd feel even sillier if I made an issue of it, even in jest.

"Heavenly Father, we thank you for the opportunity to come together and share this meal. We are grateful for the provision You've blessed us with and for the provision to come. We thank you in advance for the work that You will do in the future. We pray this in our Lord and Savior's name, Jesus Christ."

"Amen," the crowd mumbled.

I took the platter of flapjacks, forked a couple onto my plate, and passed it on. All the while, I kept one eye on the quiet boy sitting beside Paul. He hadn't said a word or even offered a smile, but his amber eyes seemed to take in everything around him. He had thick brown hair cut like a bowl around his head which added a doe-like quality to his soft features. If I had to hazard a guess, I would have put him at four or five.

"Now that we're all settled, would someone like to introduce me to this young man and tell me what's going on?"

Joe pointed his fork at the boy. "Meet Caleb. Caleb? This is the girls' Uncle Mitch."

Caleb watched Joe without saying a word.

"Pleased to meet you, Caleb." I offered him a smile, but he responded with a blank stare. Was he not able to talk?

Cassie cleared her throat. "Caleb's going to be staying with us for a while." She turned to the boy. "Isn't that right, sweetheart?"

He nodded once then picked up a piece of bacon and bit into it.

Paul cleared his throat and caught my eye. "Caleb lost his parents last week in an auto accident."

I stopped chewing and choked down the bite I had in my mouth as Paul's words took root. If there was anything sadder than losing a child, it was a child who lost both his parents. My brain froze, and I couldn't come up with anything to say.

Paul continued. "As you can see, he's a little tongue-tied." He patted Caleb's hand and smiled at him. "But we're going to do something about that, aren't we, son? And Mr. Mitch is going to help us."

Chapter Ten

Winter 2015

Rebekah

In the middle of Rebekah's junior year in high school, Cora Leigh Reynolds mysteriously disappeared over Christmas break. One of the teachers claimed her family moved to Florida, but that wasn't true, because her mama was still seen in the Piggly Wiggly, and her daddy frequented the Farm Supply on a weekly basis. Rumor ran rampant throughout the school—Cora Leigh got pregnant, and her parents shipped her off to some maiden aunt. Everyone expected her back senior year, but she didn't turn up.

This alone would have been enough to keep Bekah from the boys had any been interested in the first place—which they weren't. They didn't go for girls in ponytails and the faint whiff of eau de equine. It was fine with Bekah. It made things real simple while she was single. But things were different now. She'd been married going on five years and still no baby.

Anovulation. Before Bekah was trying to get pregnant, she thought this was a blessing. While other women she knew, including Leah, griped about their monthly visitor, Bekah was only too happy that she didn't have that problem. "Guess I've just not been given the gift of hospitality," she'd joke with Leah. She only had to deal with hers every couple of months or so.

"It's most likely the cause of your infertility," Doctor Lenora, her OB-GYN had told her. "If you aren't ovulating regularly, the chances of getting pregnant are diminished."

And to think the one thing Bekah once feared might be a near-impossibility now that she desperately desired it. She and Mitch did the research, and she checked off one recommendation after another. She cut back her caffeine intake which didn't do more than make her tetchy. Increased exercise gave her more energy and a toned body, but not the belly bump she desired. She took prenatal vitamins with folic acid, which improved her hair and skin. Big whoop. She wanted a baby, not thicker hair.

She was being particularly ugly one morning, whining to Mitch like she didn't have everything else a body could want—a sweet, supportive husband with a successful business, healthy enough that she could do anything she put her mind to (except get pregnant), and a family straight out of a Norman Rockwell painting. Maybe God had already given her as much as she deserved. Only so many blessings per person, and she'd reached her capacity. Would she have traded any of those things for a child? No, but it didn't console her.

"I don't know God like you do," Mitch told her as she snuggled up to him on the couch with her head tucked just so beneath his chin. "But I have a hard time believin' that's how He operates."

"It's not fair." Bekah had her five-year-old niece's whine perfected to the precise pitch. "Leah's got three kids already, and she and Gabe are fixin' to have another one. Joe's got one with another in the oven, and even Dan has one, and he's three years younger than me. Why can't I get pregnant? I'm not asking for a passel of kids. Don't even want a passel. Just one."

Mitch kissed the top of her head. "You know, babe, there's more than one way to have a family."

She pushed away from him as if he suddenly reeked to high heaven. "Don't start that again, Mitch." Curled up in her corner of the couch, she tossed an ugly scowl his way. "I told you already that I don't want to adopt."

He reached out and drew a finger down her cheek, followed her jawline, and stopped at her chin which he raised until their eyes met. "Yes, you've made it clear as can be that you don't want to adopt. Only thing is, the why of it is a bit muddy."

She shrugged out of his reach, pulled her legs to her chest and wrapped her arms around them. Head resting on her knees, she stared at nothing as her eyes blurred with unshed tears. "You don't get it."

Mitch blew out a breath and hopped up only to plunk himself onto the coffee table in front of her. He filled her line of vision with a face that warred between impatience and confusion. His brows were drawn together over eyes filled with compassion. "Babe, I can't get it unless you tell me. Unlike the heroes in those ridiculous romance novels you read, I'm not a mind reader. And I hate to break it to you, but real men aren't. We're just doing the best we can with the limited brain power we've been given. That might could be something you should talk to your God about."

Despite her sour disposition, Bekah's lips twitched. If Mitch wasn't a mind reader, how did he always manage to find the right thing to bring her out of a mood? "I don't want you to think any less of me," she finally admitted.

His eyes twinkled. "How could I possibly think less of you?"

It took his words a moment to sink in, then Bekah freed her legs to nudge him with a foot. "Ha ha."

His smile vanished and his eyes homed in. "Tell me, babe. I want to understand."

She sighed. Even after five years of marriage, being vulnerable with Mitch was like wading in a river full of copperheads. Each step in was with the fear of getting bit. Maybe if he'd struggle now and again, it would even things out some. But as it was, sure as she was sitting here, she'd share too much one of these days, and a huge spotlight would shine on her failure.

Mitch rubbed her leg. "I can see the wheels turning in that pretty head of yours. You wanna let me in?"

"It's just..."

His eyebrows arched.

"What if we get a child I can't love?"

His eyes widened. "I don't see how that can happen. You're—"

"Scared, Mitch." She pulled her legs up again and took comfort in the confinement of space like stabling Siren during a storm. "You make it all sound so easy. Adopt a child and everything will be perfect. But I've done almost as much research on adoption since you first brought it up as I have fertility. It's not like taking possession of a puppy you can train. It's a living, breathing child with issues. Anything from Reactive Attachment Disorder to PTSD."

Mitch spread his arms out. "It doesn't have to be that way, Bekah. We can adopt a baby, if that's what you want."

Chin jutted, she shook her head. "You're not hearing me, Mitch. You get it into your head something is going to be a certain way, and you believe it. But I'm terrified we might bring a child"—she threw her hands in the air—"or a *baby* into this house that I'm not capable of loving. Then what? I suck it up and raise it without the complete and total love it deserves? I can't do that." That level of failure would be her undoing.

He slapped his thighs and stood. "Then what d'you wanna do, Bek? I can assure you until I'm blue in the face that you're incapable of *not* loving. I see it whenever you work with your horses or play with your nieces and nephews. But you don't want to hear it."

Her nieces and nephews got on her nerves a lot more than she let on, and horses were easy. They were, well, horses. They didn't talk back or get an attitude for no reason. They didn't have hormonal issues or get their noses out of joint if one of the other horses got a touch more grain or a few extra brush strokes. But Mitch wouldn't get that. Why couldn't she be as sure of herself as he seemed to be?

"Look, babe. Whatever you want to do, I'm open." He planted himself on the couch next to her and pulled her resistant body in for a hug. "Heck, I'll even sacrifice myself and make love to you every day if that'll increase our chances."

"Dr. Lenora said our chances increase if we abstain until—"

"Never mind," he said on the tail end of a sigh. "I can see you're of no mind to be swayed by my attempt at humor."

The thought that had been niggling at her for weeks filled her mind to bursting. "What about revisiting fertility treatments?"

"Anything but that, Bek. We already tried Clomid, and you had some mighty serious side effects."

"*We* didn't try Clomid. I did," She snarled.

He patted her back. "Glad to see those mood swings aren't an issue anymore."

She stuck out her tongue, although the impact was lost on him since her head was buried in his shoulder. "There are other drugs I can try. And if those don't work, we can try IVF."

"Yeah, 'cause those drugs would be super easy where Clomid was near torture. And if you survive those, then you might just get the passel of kids you said you don't want. Quints are all the rage these days."

She closed her eyes with a sigh. "I used to think your sense of humor was endearing. Now it's just downright annoying."

"Better than the alternative, babe. Believe me."

Shoulders back, Bekah lifted her chin. "It'll work out just fine. You'll see."

Mitch

There was no denying Mitch wanted kids. All things being equal, which he knew they weren't, he'd have been willing to subject his body to undergo a massive overload of hormones to get the job done. Had he even hinted to Bekah that it might be harder on his end of things than hers, she'd have taken his head off—even without being loaded up on Clomid. She was a real peach to live with. Even her mama said, "Bless her heart," on a regular basis when she talked about Bekah during that trying season.

Didn't matter that the doc assured them the side effects were only seen in a small percentage of patients—if it was a side effect, Bekah had it. Nausea and vomiting, mood swings, insomnia, hot flashes, and headaches so fierce she couldn't get out of bed some days. It took all the romance clear out of the equation. Two months into it, they had to give them up. Or rather, *she* had to give them up. He wouldn't make the mistake of using the collective "we" again. He might have been born at night, but not *last* night.

Now that her body was clear of the drugs, why couldn't she see reason? Did she really think she'd get jammed up trying to love a child? There were days Leah's oldest could curdle the skin clear off an armadillo, but Bekah never lost her patience. Even when that vein in her neck throbbed something fierce, she kept it together.

If Mitch could give her the moon and stars, he'd do it. The problem was they came with a hefty price tag. Where did she think they'd get that kind of money? And then, if they were fortunate enough to be successful with a first try after going into debt by $25,000 what would they do if there were multiple babies? It was enough to make his head spin clear off his shoulders. Given all the options, it didn't take an Ivy League education to know that adoption made sense.

But how could he get Bekah to understand without losing any of his coveted body parts?

"Bek?" He rubbed the top of her head with his chin while the scent of her shampoo tickled his nose. Lazy winter Saturday mornings were the best. Bekah cuddled against him on the couch while fake logs burned in the gas fireplace.

"Hmm?" Her response was slow and sleepy. Maybe it'd be better to let the conversation die a natural death. Then again, walking away from a problem never fixed it. Didn't his dad's abandonment teach him that?

He kissed her head. "I don't want you goin' through anymore treatments."

"I know, babe. But it'll be okay." She twisted until she was tucked more firmly under his arm.

He chewed on the inside of his cheek and stared into the fireplace as if the answer would miraculously appear. *You do that, Lord, and I'll be the first in line to sign up for Team God.* He continued to wait, but no answer was forthcoming. *You had Your chance.* Why was it Bekah pushed so hard to have her own baby like anything else wasn't good enough? A baby was a baby, wasn't it?

"You know how much it costs for a round of IVF?" He kept his voice low like talking down a skittish horse.

"Mmm. Not cheap."

"More 'an I make in four months. Where would we get that kinda money, Bek?" He drew slow circles on her arm with his thumb. "And what if it didn't take the first time?"

"I'm young and healthy," she mumbled. "It'll be fine."

Images of her flickered in his mind—hanging over the toilet, crying uncontrollably, hiding away under the covers. Weeks of her snapping at him for every misstep. How could she forget? Or maybe she didn't care. "Bein' healthy didn't make a difference when you were on Clomid. You still got sick."

She pushed out of his arm. "I don't care, Mitch. It's worth it to have a baby."

"For who?" He winced at the sharpness of his voice. So much for not stirring up a hornet's nest. Rubbing his forehead, he drew in a deep breath. "Sorry I snapped."

"Is it the money?"

Needing some space, he jumped up and began pacing the small family room. Where it was cozy only moments before, now perspiration popped up on his forehead and sweat pooled in his armpits. This was one of those stages in their marriage where he could make it or break it. Not that Bekah would leave him over this, but it could cause a fracture that might never properly heal. A tender spot that they'd prod over and over again like a tongue returning to a sore tooth until the infection might be irreparable.

"It's a lot of things, Bek," he said after weighing his response. "Since you asked about the money, let's tackle that one first."

Sitting up straight, she folded her arms as if preparing for battle. "Fine. I know it's expensive, but it's not like I'm asking for an extravagant gift. I want to be able to have a baby. *Our* baby." Score one for Bekah.

How could he argue that? She never asked for anything—other than feed for Siren. "Okay, I suppose we could take out a second mortgage." And hope like heck the trucking business didn't bottom out. "But a bigger concern is the hormones, Bek." He sat on the coffee table and took her hands in his. "You might've blocked it, but it about killed me to see you so sick." He gave her a lopsided grin. "And you about killed me every time I looked at you sideways. I can't be much use to you if I'm sleeping in the doghouse all the time."

Eyes softening, she chewed on her bottom lip. Bekah never was one for high maintenance, so he imagined it didn't sit well with her that she had an attitude that could rival a Kardashian when she was hopped up on hormones. "I'll give you that one." Score one for Mitch. "But we don't know for sure that it'll be a problem."

Were they willing to take that chance? It was clear she was. "Okay. Let's assume for the sake of argument that you handle the drugs fine and in vitro takes first time out."

She nodded, a soft smile communicating that she was ready to tackle the next point.

"What if there are multiple births?"

The smile melted. "Well..." She cleared her throat. A stall tactic, he was sure. "I guess twins wouldn't be the worst thing that could happen. We'd be like one and done."

What was she talking about? "One and done?"

Her head bobbed. "Yeah. Two kids in one fell swoop. Our family would be complete."

Mitch rubbed his brow. "And if there are three, or God forbid, *four*? How are we going to afford that being mortgaged to the hilt?"

She rolled her eyes. "I have faith that God will provide, Mitch. You're worrying before you have a reason to."

There were days he wondered if Bekah left her brain back in the barn. "If we have four babies, it'll be too late to do anything about it. We'll be living like Ma and Pa Kettle right down to the rickety flatbed, because that'll be all we can afford."

She scrunched up her nose. "I had no idea you were such a worry wart. If you had faith, you'd save yourself a lot of stress."

"If *I* had faith?" He said, poking his own chest with a finger. "If you had faith, you wouldn't be rushing ahead to get pregnant when God clearly has you waiting for a reason."

She slumped back, mouth open. "How can you say that?"

He reached out to take her hands, but she recoiled. "Babe, I'm not the one who said it. You did. How many times have you told me I needed to trust in your sovereign God? I'm just parroting back your own words." They'd flown from his mouth without thought. It wasn't like he'd planned to throw her faith back in her face.

Her fingers covered her mouth while her eyes widened. "Oh my word, Mitch."

"What?" She merely looked at him with tears swimming in her eyes. "'Oh my word what Bek? What'd I say that has you looking at me like I kicked your puppy?"

"I've been like Abraham running ahead of God's plan."

"Abraham? Abraham who?" He searched his memory bank for someone they knew by that name. "Are you talking about Abe Meadows?"

She shook her head, releasing the tears. "In the Bible. His disobedience eventually caused the birth of Islam."

A thrumming started in Mitch's temple. "Okay, I don't have any idea what you're talking about, but if it's important to you that we try in vitro, we can—"

"No." She squeezed Mitch's hands. "No. You're right. If God wants us to have a baby, it'll happen."

The thrumming was now a full-blown drum solo. "So, no in vitro?"

She shook her head.

"And adoption is out too?"

"If God wants us to have a baby, it'll happen." She drew in a deep breath and let it out slowly. But he couldn't hardly miss the sadness that lurked in her eyes or the way her chin wobbled.

Chapter Eleven

Rebekah

The days blended together like a child's painting where layer upon layer of color saturates the paper resulting in a blob without any defining characteristics. It was a blessing to be able to take care of Mama and Daddy, but it also made me yearn for my own life—and Mitch. It was bad enough that I'd awake from dreams where he was so real, I'd reach out to the other side of the bed to feel his warm body and find nothing more than a rumpled sheet. But he'd started to show up in brief moments throughout the day, as well. The whiff of his scent, the intense blue of his eyes, the rasp of his beard on my cheek.

"It's downright obnoxious," I told Siren as I brushed her coat. "He's wearing me down, and he's not even here."

"Who's not here?"

Joe's booming voice in the quiet of the stables had me jump clear out of my skin. Siren bolted in response, and it took some soothing to settle her. "You oughta know better than to startle a horse." The snarl was part reaction mixed with a lingering annoyance for the mess he'd left in the kitchen a couple nights before. I still hadn't called him to task for it.

"Well, aren't you delightful this morning?" Joe scratched between Siren's ears and grinned down at me. "Get up on the wrong side of the bed, did ya?"

"Not enough sleep is all." Between late hours at the restaurant and Mitch haunting my dreams, there wasn't a whole lot of rest happening. In fact, it took me a full ten seconds to remember what day it was. "What're you doing here so early? Shouldn't you be on your way to church?"

"Shouldn't *you*?" he said with a smirk. Always good with a quick-witted comeback, Joe was. Right up there with *na-na, na-na, boo-boo; stick your head in doo-doo.*

"Once Mama and Daddy leave, I've got some cleaning to do. Only time Mama gets outta bed these days is to use the toilet or go to church." I ran the brush down Siren's neck. I wasn't sure who needed it more—her or me. "Might be the last time she gets out."

Joe was quiet while he retrieved a second brush and worked Siren's other side. "She didn't look too good when I was here last night. I'm surprised she's going today."

I wrangled with the idea of scolding Joe for leaving the sink filled with dishes, but it would be petty and immature. I ran a hand down Siren's smooth neck. "You know Mama," I said on a sigh. Our eyes met over Siren's back. "So, what are you doing here, really?"

"As soon as the coast is clear, I'm gonna bale the hay. Can't put it off much longer."

"Daddy wouldn't want you doing that on a Sunday, Joe. I asked him about it, and he was pretty clear."

He smiled. "Why do you think I need to wait 'til the coast is clear?"

There wasn't much Daddy could do about it once Joe got started. "Is it your plan to coax me into helping?" I could always put off the housework until another time. The sheets really needed doing, though, and—

"Nope. Mitch is on his way."

"Mitch?" His name squeaked out of my mouth like one of Cheyenne's chew toys.

"Sure. Hope you don't mind."

"Why should I mind?" But the sudden increase of my heart rate told a different tale. "Just so you know, I would of been willing to help out."

"You got enough to do what with work, taking care of Mama, and cleaning up my dirty dishes," he said with a smile. So, he wasn't a complete bonehead. He rested his hands on Siren's back. "The reason I came early is 'cause there's something I wanna tell you."

My hands stilled. Was it Mitch? Could be that bar fight put him in a bind. "What?"

"You're gonna tell me the timing of this stinks, and you'd be right." He shrugged. "But we don't get to be in charge of things."

So, it wasn't about Mitch. My shoulders relaxed, and I could breathe again. Then what was he yammering about? "Are you gonna get to the point or beat it to death?"

He scowled. "You know, Bek, you could learn a thing or two about the art of conversation."

I tilted my head and raised my brows.

"Fine." He blew out a breath. "Cassie and me took in an orphan."

"You're fostering a dog?" What was so all fired important about that?

"When have you ever heard of a dog bein' referred to as an orphan? No, not a dog. A child. A little five-year-old boy."

It took a moment for my head to put context to his words. "What? Why? Life isn't challenging enough as it is you have to complicate it some more?"

He tossed the brush into the bin and raised his hands in surrender. "I know. I said the same thing, but God doesn't always work according to our timeline. It's not Caleb's fault his parents died last week."

The shock of his words had my mouth hanging open for a moment. "Both of them?"

"Killed in a car wreck on I-65."

I pressed both hands to my chest. "Well, if that isn't the saddest thing I ever did hear. Bless his heart."

"Right?" He hung his head. "You know the Youngs from church?"

"Older couple that always sat in the back pew?"

"That's them—Frank and Sylvie." He scratched his brow. "It was their son and his wife. They lived in Lewisburg and were heading down from Nashville when it happened."

"So, they didn't attend our church?"

"Didn't attend any church that I know of. The Youngs are older than Mama and Daddy, and in no condition to take in a child. Not sure what's gonna happen to him long term, but for now, he'll stay with us." He checked his watch. "I'm gonna get things started. Daddy should be pullin' out any minute."

I walked Siren out to the pasture where she had plenty of grass to munch on, the shade of a red oak, and the other horses to keep her company. What I wanted to do was saddle up and ride, but it would have to wait for another time. The sun was already high with only a cloud or two in the sky. It would be a hot one today, topped off by another shift at the restaurant. My intention had been to give notice the night before, but the boss wasn't in, and I didn't feel right not doing it in person. Not after he'd given me a break.

I secured the stable gate, turned, and smacked into a very wide, t-shirt-clad chest. Mitch's hands clamped down on my upper arms as he steadied me.

"You okay?" The same Mitch-scent that had been teasing me lately assaulted my senses, and I shook my head to clear it.

"Sorry, I didn't see you there."

"Your head was in the clouds," he said, dropping his hands. "Sure you weren't hurt?"

"I'm fine." I glanced away not wanting to have both his scent *and* his blue eyes haunting me for the rest of the day. "Joe's getting the baler ready. He was waiting until Mama and Daddy were gone."

He planted his hands on his hips. "Went past them coming down your road. Stopped to say hi, and I told 'em I was coming to see you." I could feel his gaze searching my face, but I didn't bite. "Didn't want to be a liar so thought I better make it true."

"Well, you saw me, so you're good." I stepped around him, and his hand on my upper arm stopped me. "Look Mitch, I don't want to be rude, but I gotta lot of work to do before they get back."

"The fact you don't wanna be rude is progress, right?"

I gave a noncommittal shrug. One minute I was dreaming about him and the next I couldn't get away fast enough.

"I need to ask a favor, Bek." His gaze was on the pasture rather than me, which made it easier to stay put.

"Okay. Can't promise you I'll do it, but you can ask."

He waved a hand toward Siren who stood in the shadow of the shade tree. "You got good horses here."

That was random. "The best."

"You remember the first time you took me riding?"

"On Emperor." The memory tugged a grin from me. "Thought you were gonna be sick for sure."

"You have a way about you, Bek." He turned his eyes on me before I could avoid them. A tingle of awareness moved up my spine. "A gift with horses."

"I suppose." My brain must've been befuddled, because he wasn't making sense. "Didn't you say you had a favor to ask?" *We're burning daylight here.*

"Do you think horses can act as a connection for someone who's shut down?"

"Are you feeling okay?" I itched to touch his forehead for evidence of a fever, so I tucked my hand into my back pocket.

"I have a proposition for you."

Mitch

I would never have claimed to be an expert on women. Fact was, they remained as much a mystery to me as they ever did. You'd think after being raised by a single mother and married fourteen years, I'd have an inkling or two. You'd be wrong. Bekah was forever doing the opposite of what I expected. Thought

I'd have to hogtie her to the pasture fence before she'd give me a listen, but she looked up all attentive-like pretty as you please. What was that all about?

"A proposition?" Her eyebrows disappeared behind her bangs, and if that wasn't curiosity in her eyes, I'd eat a cow pie.

I snapped a quick nod. "Joe tell you about Caleb?"

Her mouth turned down, and she leaned her backside against the pasture fence. Sunlight glinted off her dark hair like streaks of red fire. "The little boy who's staying with them a spell? Just that he lost his parents. I didn't ask, but I assume he's an only child."

"And his daddy was an only child, so he's most likely looking at foster care down the road." I had a distinct connection with the boy since I'd been one lick of luck away from the same fate.

"What a sad situation."

This was where having a little understanding about women's logic would have come in handy. If I said the right thing the wrong way or the wrong thing the right way, I would be dead in the water. Seemed I was always sticking my size elevens into my mouth around Bekah. Did she have any idea the power she had over me?

I tucked my hands into the front pockets of my jeans and cleared my throat. Each second I stalled gave me a little more time to decipher the best approach. Of course, I tried every which way in my head on the drive over, but nothing clicked. "The thing is, Bek, Caleb hasn't spoken a word since the accident."

A wrinkle formed between her brows and her eyes kind of melted like she was near tears. My own throat constricted to see it. That tender heart of hers got me every time.

"He—he wasn't in the car with them, was he?"

"Thankfully, no. He was staying with Bobby's parents."

"Bobby? Was that his daddy's name?" She smoothed a strand of flyaway hair off her face.

Nodding, I took note of the changes in her since last time we were together. There were dark circles under her eyes, and her cheeks had a hollowed-out look about them. Surely, Miss Anita's illness was taking its toll. "And Stacey was his mama. But from the minute Frank told Caleb about the accident, he hasn't breathed a word."

Bekah rubbed a hand over her heart as if massaging an ache. "That poor little boy. He must be terrified, and I'm as sorry as I can be, but what does that all have to do with me?"

"Brother Paul was of the mind that you could work some of your horse magic with Caleb. Might help him to open up enough to talk."

"Horse magic?"

"Yeah. You know, put him on Siren or Emperor, or whoever you think best, and work with him. Teach him to ride. You've said yourself that riding is therapeutic."

She huffed out a breath. "Well, yes, horses can be very therapeutic, Mitch. That's why there's a therapy horse ranch right here in Shelbyville. Clearview Ranch, I think it's called. Why don't y'all contact them and see if they can help?" She shuffled around like she was getting ready to stomp off. Couldn't say I blamed her. I thought it was a stretch myself, and I wasn't the one already worn thin caring for my mama.

"They have very limited hours and lots of rules, Bek. I know it's an imposition, but—"

"Even if I had the time, which I don't, I'm not qualified." She bit at her bottom lip and paced, hands flying in the air. Was she nervous? "What if I made things worse? Have you thought of that?" It wasn't an outright no, which was a good sign. If Bekah didn't want to do something, she dug in her heels.

"Can't see how you can make things worse. And I know you're already workin' two jobs and caring for Miss Anita, but it might be good for you too." Get her focus on something besides herself for a change.

She stopped mid-pace and pinned me with an accusation. Might be I went a little too far. Would I ever learn to stop talking long enough to think first? "What d'you mean 'good for you too'?"

I backpedaled so quick it was a wonder I didn't topple over on my rear. "You're all the time stuck inside, is what I meant." Yeah, that was a good argument. Should have started with it. "You're tied up at the shop or the restaurant.

And when you're here with your mama, I'm guessing it's a lot of time inside cooking and cleaning up after her."

The heat left her eyes, and she shrugged. "That's true, but as you just pointed out, there's enough already on my plate. It doesn't leave me time for one more chore, Mitch. I haven't had a chance to ride myself in the last week. Where am I supposed to find extra hours to tend to a little boy I don't even know?"

"I'll help, Bekah. You need me to run a load of laundry or do some vacuuming while you work with Caleb, say the word, and I'll do it." Of course, why would she want me hanging around when she'd been working so hard to get away from me?

She snorted. "Since when have you done any of those things?"

I folded my arms. "Since you walked out more 'n six months ago. Might not do as good a job as you, but I'm not living in a pig sty, either." That wasn't completely true. I still hadn't tidied up the house like I'd planned, but she didn't need to know that.

Gazing past me, she gnawed on her lower lip again. She was thinking on it which was a parting of the Red Sea miracle right there. Then she rounded on me, and I tensed in preparation for whatever she'd throw my way. "Joe told me you were doing some community hours for Brother Paul."

Joe talked more than a group of gossipy women. "Yeah. So?"

"Where would you find time between that and work to help out around here?"

"Don't you worry about that. When I make a promise, I keep it." The moment the words were out, I heard the accusation in them and winced.

It might be Caleb had the right idea not speaking his mind. Maybe if I took a page from his book, my marriage wouldn't be in shambles.

CHAPTER TWELVE

Rebekah

Lust. It was one of the seven deadly sins for good reason. It made a person do things they knew would lead to trouble. It was the only excuse I could come up with for allowing myself to be talked into something I had no business doing. Horse magic? It was lust for my husband that had me falling for that line. I blamed it on my dream of him the night before last. There was nothing magical about my way with horses. I just loved them—sometimes more than people. And definitely more than Mitch once I realized he'd manipulated me into taking on the broken heart of a child.

Caleb.

Jonathon was the same age as him when he died, which was one reason right there I shouldn't have agreed to spend time with the little boy. How could I not be overcome with the loss of my own baby when I looked into Caleb's eyes?

Cleaning up after supper that evening, I berated myself for being so gullible. Should have left the mess for Mitch since he was bringing Caleb by after he finished his hauls for the day. He'd promised to help out, and I'd already come up with a laundry list of unpleasant tasks for him while he waited. We'd just see how well he could keep his word. There was never a shortage of chores around here. Seemed I was always cooking, cleaning, changing beds, or harvesting the garden. I was plumb tired, but in a good way. I actually slept a full seven hours the night before, which was a first since losing Jonathon. And no dreams that I could recount.

"You're gonna wear a hole in the Formica if you keep that up, Bekah." Daddy came through the kitchen door, wiping the sweat from his brow with his sleeve. He'd been grumbling since last night about Joe baling the hay on a Sunday and went out to inspect the work for himself. "Somethin' eating you?"

"No, sir. Just cleaning up. Got a casserole in the fridge for supper." I'd been doing my level best to cook foods that would entice Mama to eat. Tonight would be chicken enchilada with sour cream. It wasn't Cassie's lasagna, but it might be a close second.

Daddy got himself a glass of water and downed it at the sink. "You waitressin' tonight?"

"No, sir. The restaurant's closed on Sunday and Monday. Remember?"

He nodded. "The weather's coolin' down some. Might want to take yourself on a ride. Would surely ease my guilt at you having to slave away 'round here."

I patted his arm and collected his empty glass. "No need for you to feel guilty, Daddy. I don't mind a bit. Besides, Mitch talked me into working with the little boy staying with Joe and Cassie." Daddy must've known the family since they went to the same church. "He said Caleb's the Youngs' grandson."

He sighed. "Sad business that was." He shook his head and rubbed the back of his neck. "From what Keith told me, his boy and wife spent a lot of time whoopin' it up in Nashville. Liked the bar scene, I guess. Turns out they were drunk when they got into that accident. Not the first time, neither."

That put an ugly spin on things. My fingers clenched so tightly around Daddy's glass, it was a wonder it didn't crack. The child needed nurturing, not some grief-stricken woman teaching him to ride a horse. "I don't know what good I can do, but there it is." That poor child.

Daddy put an arm around my shoulders and gave me a little shake. "You never know how the Lord will spin things, darlin'. You have a good heart, though, and I'm sure as can be that it'll benefit the boy."

"Just don't know why Mitch is the one bringing him. Why not Joe or Cassie? It's their place he's staying at."

"Like I said, you don't know how the Lord's workin'." Daddy chuckled. "I'm fixin' to head into town to pick up a few supplies. You need anything?"

"Nothing you can buy at the store." What I wouldn't give to have a Fruit of the Spirit shop. Need a little patience? We got you covered. How about some joy? It'll cost a bit, but it's available too. But God didn't work that way. Mama told me more than once, anything worth having had to be earned the hard way. Wasn't that the truth?

Ten minutes later, Mitch texted that he was on his way. Before heading out to saddle Siren, I went into Mama's room to check on her. After church yesterday, she'd slept until supper and went right back to bed after. The pain meds made it tolerable, but she was weakening more and more every day. It would be a pure miracle if she lived until Thanksgiving. Four months.

Her bed was empty, and I heard her rummaging around in the bathroom.

I tapped a knuckle on the door. "Mama? You okay?"

She muttered something I couldn't make out. When I eased the door open, she was stooped over the sink, hands gripping the counter. "Sweet Pea, I'm afraid I made a mess in the bed." Her voice cracked, and her face crumpled.

I took a quick survey of her nightgown and saw the damp stain. My chest went heavy as my heart broke clear in two to see my stoic childhood hero embarrassed by what she couldn't control. I had to swallow the fist-sized lump in my throat before I could speak. "It's okay, Mama. We'll get you cleaned in a jiffy. Think you have enough energy to sit up for a while? We can stream an old movie on TV for you." How else could I change the sheets?

She gave me a watery smile. "That'd be nice. Feels like I've been livin' in this bed since we got the diagnosis."

I gave her a quick sponge bath, changed her gown, and was getting her settled on the couch when I heard scuffling sounds coming from the kitchen. A quick check of my watch told me it was most likely Mitch. "I'll go get you some juice, Mama." I handed her the remote.

Mitch was filling a glass of water at the sink, a small boy by his side, when I walked in. Two pairs of eyes turned to me. I ignored the older for the younger, and with my emotions already taxed, it was nearly my undoing. How could anyone deny this little one anything he wanted?

Caleb was small for five—not much taller than Jonathon had been at four. His thick, brown hair was cut in a bowl style that brushed his brows above clear, hazel eyes. He was thin with high cheekbones and a dimple in his strong chin.

"Hey, Caleb." I bent down so we were at the same level and held out my hand. "My name's Bekah. It's so good to meet you."

His small fingers closed around mine. Would it scare him if I pulled him in for a hug? Best to not take the chance. Instead, I smoothed a hand over his hair and glanced at Mitch as I rose. "Can we talk outside for a minute?"

He frowned. "Everything okay?"

I held up a finger then rummaged in the pantry until I found a package of Daddy's coveted Moon Pies. With a light hand on Caleb's shoulder, I walked him to the table. "Here you go, sweetheart. Would you like a glass of milk?"

He turned solemn eyes on me and nodded.

Once he was settled with his snack, I grabbed Mitch's arm and pulled him onto the porch. Despite feeling duped into spending time with Caleb, my stomach clenched at the thought of disappointing him. "This isn't going to work out today."

He sighed and rubbed his brow. "I know this is hard, Bekah, believe me. He's so much like—"

I waved away his words. "That's not it. I mean, yes, it brings back painful memories, but that isn't why it won't work. It's Mama."

His brow crinkled. "What's wrong? Does she need to go to the hospital?"

"Not quite that dire." Would it betray Mama to share her humiliation? But this was Mitch. He loved her almost as much as I did. "She had an accident in bed. I have her set up on the couch, but I need to get the sheets changed before she gets too tired to stay up. I'd have Daddy do it, but he's not here."

He shrugged. "So? I'll do it."

"Wh—what?" There must've been something wrong with my hearing.

"I already told you I'd help out so you could work with Caleb. I meant it. Tell me where the clean sheets are, and I'll get to it."

Who was this man, and what did he do with my husband? Mitch couldn't rightly be called a chauvinist, but I'd never known him to make the bed, much less change it. "Why make the bed?" he'd say. "You're just gonna mess it up again later."

Now here he was offering to do something that'd give most men the willies. "Well, if you're sure."

After getting Mitch what he needed, I set a glass of juice on the coffee table in front of Mama who was focused on the television. She was snuggled up on the couch with a pillow supporting her back and a light blanket over her lap, even though the air-conditioner was set to eighty. I'd sweated away more calories since she'd gotten sick than I ever would dieting. Mitch didn't know what he'd gotten himself into.

"What're you watching, Mama?" I fussed with her blanket.

"*Dirty Dancing.*" She glanced up at me. "Did you know Patrick Swayze died of pancreatic cancer too?"

Even though I fought it something fierce, Mama was resigned to her fate. That one-stop fantasy shop for Fruit of the Spirit should have included a side of courage. I'd pay a premium price for it just to see me through the next few months.

Mitch

It was hard to face Miss Anita. I hadn't seen her since Bekah left me. Hadn't even tried. I wasn't proud of it—fact was, the longer I stayed away, the more the shame took hold. It didn't strike me when I told Bekah I'd help that I'd be put in the awkward position of facing the in-laws. Last time I saw John, he greeted me with a shotgun. Fortunately for me, Miss Anita was a genteel lady who wouldn't harm a fly let alone a wayward son-in-law.

Figured it was best to tend to the chores before I sat with her. Uneasiness trailed up my spine when I entered Miss Anita and John's bedroom. I'd seen it only in passing on my way to use the bathroom over the years, where a quick glance showed it to be like every other room in the house—spotless and organized. Now, it was a sickroom with a tray of prescription bottles, a box of tissues, and a tube of lotion on what I assumed was Miss Anita's side. John's nightstand had a stack of books, the top one the Holy Bible, reading glasses, and a notebook.

The bed was a rumpled mess of sheets and blankets. I reached for the pillow to strip it of the case and caught a whiff of urine that had my stomach rolling. I made quick work of gathering the soiled sheets, mattress pad, and blankets, the heaviness of my limbs and sudden tightness in my chest hampering my movements. How could Miss Anita's life come to this? If anyone deserved a sweet death, it was her.

I carried the linens to the washer and got the first load started before going back in to remake the bed. I was no expert. Had more experience short-sheeting beds than making them, but I took meticulous care as if Miss Anita were standing over me.

I expected to find Bekah's mama asleep when I slipped into the family room. But she was not only awake, she offered me a soft smile. "Come sit a spell with me, Mitch." She swept a hand toward John's recliner.

My brain shut down as I eased into the chair. There was a movie playing on the television, but the volume was down so low, it was doubtful Bekah's mama could hear it. She wasn't watching, that was for sure. Instead, her eyes followed my every movement. Had she been waiting for me? A well-deserved dressing down, maybe?

Anything I might say would sound trite in light of the situation, but I cleared my throat and blurted, "I'm so sorry, Miss Anita." My voice hitched, and I dropped my head. *Don't go making a fool of yourself by crying.*

"About what, sweet boy?" She smoothed a hand over the blanket covering her legs. The house was like a sauna, but she seemed cool as peach ice cream. "That you haven't come by in a month of Sundays or that I'm dying?"

I ran a hand through my hair. "Both. I stayed away so long, it made it near impossible to find my way back."

"This hasn't been an easy year for anyone, Mitch, but most especially for you and Rebekah. What do you plan to do about it?"

"About what, ma'am?" There were so many choices.

"My daughter, of course. I can't imagine you're happy with the situation as it is, are you?"

"No, ma'am." Elbows on my knees, I braved a first glance at her, and my heart sank. Could've talked myself into believing she wasn't really dying if I didn't see it for myself. Her once rosy face was now yellowed and sagging, and her eyes appeared as bruised as mine had after the bar fight. She'd lost weight too. A lot of weight.

"So, what do you intend to do about it?"

I rubbed my eyes with a finger and thumb to stop the tears that burned at the back of them. "Bekah's a strong-willed woman," I finally managed.

She folded her hands in her lap. "She comes by that naturally, you know."

In spite of the ache in my throat, my lips twitched. "Yes, ma'am."

Miss Anita's eyebrows arched. "You don't believe me."

I shrugged. "No disrespect, Miss Anita, but I've never seen you anything other than soft-spoken and gentle. Bekah"—I barked out a laugh —"can be very vocal."

She smiled, and her eyes lit up the same way Bekah's did. "Believe me, you aren't telling me anything I don't already know. A strong woman needs a strong man. Otherwise, she reacts out of insecurity and fear. I'll have you know, John had his hands full when we first married."

That was hard to believe. "So, what changed?"

She fingered the blanket covering her. "He grew in his faith and learned how to lead me as a godly husband should." She wriggled a finger at me. "I know what you're thinking. You don't believe in God, so how could you possibly be a godly husband?"

I opened my mouth to deny it, but there was more truth than not in her accusation. "If nothing else has proven to me there is no God, Jonathon's death and your cancer would be enough." Heat rose up my neck and sweat broke out on my forehead. "How can you believe in a God who makes this stuff happen?"

She clucked her tongue. "Oh, Mitch. God doesn't make it happen. He may allow it, but He certainly doesn't cause it. You'd have to understand we're all sinners saved by the grace of Jesus Christ."

I scraped a hand through my hair. "Well, I can't deny I've done some sinful things in my life, but I have a hard time believing you have. And I know Jonathon didn't."

"You'd be wrong on both accounts, son. But this isn't something I can convince you of in one short conversation. Besides, I'm too tired to try right now. Just promise me something, will you?"

Would she ask the impossible of me? Course, it was Miss Anita, and I trusted her more than my own mama. "What?"

"You at least seek it out for yourself. If you truly love my daughter and want your marriage restored, you need to at least look into it before you discount it out of hand."

It sounded like a hefty promise. "How do I do that?"

"It starts with prayer. Ask the Lord to open your eyes and then dig into His word to see what He reveals. Can you do that?"

I stood and bent over her to plant a kiss on her paper-thin cheek. "Anything for you, Miss Anita."

"Not for me, Mitch. For you. And for Bekah. Now, be a sweetheart and help me to bed, will you?"

After I made sure Miss Anita had everything she needed, I wandered outside to see how Bekah and Caleb were getting along. I tucked the odd request away to think on another time. There was nothing I could do about it at the moment anyway.

Not wanting to intrude, I watched from the shadow of an old oak that stood halfway between the house and the stables. Bekah had Siren haltered and saddled. She crouched down next to Caleb as the boy reached up and touched Siren's velvet-soft nose. The horse stomped her back foot, and Caleb jumped like he'd been stuck with a hot poker. I'd expected to see him on Siren's back, but it appeared he wasn't ready for that step, as tentative as he was.

"It's okay, sweetheart." Bekah's voice was low and soothing. "She's not going to hurt you. I know it's kind of scary because she's so big, but she's a very gentle girl."

Caleb hesitantly reached up again, and Siren nudged his hand. Was that a giggle I heard coming from the boy? After a few more attempts, Caleb was running his small hand along Siren's muzzle as if it was the most natural thing.

A memory of Bekah working with Jonathon played through my mind. By the time he turned five, he was riding like a pro. She made sure he was safe—always with a helmet—but she didn't hover. Was it because she felt confident in Siren's gentleness and her own ability as a teacher? It was the only explanation. Which meant she didn't have the same confidence in me, because when I tried to teach him anything, she hovered. Swimming lessons, fishing, sledding. She stood over me as if I couldn't keep him safe. Miss Anita had said a woman who isn't led well reacts out of insecurity and fear. Was I to blame for this whole sordid mess?

If you'd not gotten on me about being an overprotective mom, maybe things would have turned out different. Jonathon might be alive today.

"Would you like to ride her?" Bekah's voice broke me out of the trance.

Caleb stuck his hands behind his back and shook his head.

"Okay, that's fine. What about just sitting on her while she stands still? I'll even hitch her to the fence, so you don't have to worry about her going anywhere?"

After a moment, he nodded once.

She'd have the child riding inside of a week. Horse magic. I'd say she hadn't lost her mama magic, either.

Chapter Thirteen

For a full twenty-four hours after working with Caleb I was grinning like a dead pig in sunshine. I never was partial to that saying, but it was appropriate. Every time I pictured the delight in that boy's eyes, I couldn't help but smile. He'd giggled when Siren's velvety nose pressed against his neck, and his little mouth had formed an "o" when he combed his small fingers through the horse's mane. Perched atop Siren's back, the child's eyes grew big as saucers. Siren may have been therapeutic for Caleb, but Caleb was therapeutic for me. The fear I had that it would somehow make the ache over Jonathon's loss unbearable blew away like dandelion dust.

My steps were lighter throughout the next day as I did my morning chores and prepared a meal for that night's supper before heading to the restaurant. They faltered slightly a time or two when I caught Kimberley's sneer as I crossed the dining room to attend to customers. But it didn't matter—after my shift, I was meeting with Dale, the manager, to give my two weeks' notice.

Apron in hand, I stood at the threshold of Dale's office where he sat behind his desk, eyes glued to the computer screen. This would be easier if he was an unpleasant sort. Instead, though I'd had no experience, he'd given me a chance and had been both encouraging and supportive. Now I was going to pay back his kindness by quitting after only a few months.

He glanced up and smiled a welcome. "Come in, Bekah." He waved me forward.

"I don't want to interrupt your work."

"Please, interrupt. Been looking at the computer so long, my eyes are starting to cross. Have a seat and tell me what I can do for you."

Prepared for a quick escape, I perched on the edge of the chair. "I'm afraid I need to give my notice."

His smile melted. "I'm sorry to hear that. Seems like you were just getting the hang of things."

Poor man was either blind or too good for this world. Every night was a comedy of errors. I had trouble getting the orders straight, couldn't carry near the load the other waitresses managed, and just last week, I dropped a full tray of food. It was only by the grace of God it didn't land on anyone. I was doing Dale a favor by quitting before I caused a real catastrophe. "I appreciate you saying that, even though we both know it's not true."

He was too kind to agree. "It's Kimberley, isn't it? If you need me to talk to her—"

"No. It's not that." And if it was, I could handle my own battles, *thank you very much*. No one liked a tattletale. "It's my mama, Dale. She was diagnosed with stage-four pancreatic cancer. I don't know how much time she has, so I need to focus on her care until..." I swallowed the rock that lodged in the base of my throat.

His eyes softened as he sighed. "I'm so sorry, Bekah. I know how hard that must be. My wife was the sole caregiver for her daddy a couple of years ago. It takes a toll."

I nodded. "Thankfully, I'm not doing it on my own. My brother and sister help out, but I live with my parents, so the brunt of it naturally falls to me." Did that sound whiny? "Not that I'm complaining. It's actually a blessing."

"I understand." He blew out a breath. "I'm not going to hold you to the two weeks, though. Unless, of course, you want to stay. Your family is more important than this here job, Bekah." Maybe he was relieved to see me go after all.

"I can't tell you how much I appreciate you giving me a chance, Dale. Truly."

"If you wanna come back later, after..." He rubbed the back of his neck. "Well, later. You just let me know. You always have a place here." The man was a glutton for punishment.

"Thank you."

I retreated to the break room to collect my things and was stopped short by the sight of Kimberley sitting at one of the three small tables around the perimeter. She was engrossed in a magazine and a plate of mac 'n' cheese. If I didn't need my car keys to get home, I would've turned tail and bolted. All the joy I'd held onto since the day before fizzled like a whirlwind romance. *Sticks and stones.*

I was a grown-up, for Pete's sake. Head held high, I crossed the room and Kimberley's line of sight. If she had something snide to say, and she always did, what was it to me? Even so, my fingers shook, making it difficult to open the combination lock.

"Ducking out so soon?" Kimberley asked. "I thought you were on late shift."

"No, ma'am," I said as the lock broke free. "Been here since two." I snatched my purse and dropped the lock into it. As I turned to leave, I was struck by the strangest sensation of peace. *Ask her why she dislikes you.* Where had that come from. As if I didn't know? Obedience was one thing, but I'd have to be plumb crazy to open that barn door.

She forked another bite of mac 'n' cheese. "You think you're too good for this job, don't you?"

Now where would she get a cockamamie idea like that? "Hardly."

I took a few steps toward the door and stopped. She was a strange one. Accusing me of putting on airs when I wasn't the one with salon-perfect brows and eyelash extensions. She probably invested more time and money on her hair and makeup in a month than I had my whole life. *Ask her why she dislikes you.* Maybe whatever her issue was, it didn't really have anything to do with me at all.

There was only one way to find out, and if the Lord wanted me to ask, maybe it was time I stopped avoiding Him. "We've known each other since high school, and you've never liked me. Is it something I did?"

Eyes fixed on her supper, she said, "What makes you think I don't like you?"

I snorted. "Let's say we chalk up the stuff from high school as juvenile pranks and talk about more recent events." I planted myself across from her so we'd be on the same eye level. "You've treated me with complete disdain from the first day I walked into this restaurant. Took pleasure whenever I messed up, and I'll be the first to admit, that was often. Then when Mitch showed up, you maneuvered things for maximum humiliation. Now if this is the way you treat people you like, I'd hate to see what you're liable to do to your enemies."

Shoulders hunched, Kimberley poked at her food with the fork. "Sorry I was such a jerk." Her gaze flickered up to meet mine then dropped again. "Won't happen again." The response was more curious than Kimberley's attitude.

"I don't suppose it matters one way or the other since I won't be working here anymore."

Her head snapped up. "Because of me?"

"No, although you certainly make it easier to leave." I folded my arms. In for a penny... "My mama's real sick, and it's too hard working nights and taking care of her during the day. I know it doesn't look like it, but I need my beauty sleep as much as the next person."

"Yeah, right."

Was that a compliment or a putdown? "What's that supposed to mean?"

She shoved her plate aside. "I'm sorry about your mama. I didn't know. And I am sorry for bein' so ugly." Eyes downcast, she picked at her cuticle. "It's not your fault life's been so kind to you."

The whole world went cattywampus. Unless she'd been living under a rock, she'd have to know about Jonathon's passing, and that Mitch and I were on the outs. How did that equate to life being kind to me? "You sure have a skewed way of seeing things, Kimberley."

She raised perfectly groomed brows at me. "I'll grant you things have gone sideways on you more recently. But when we were growing up, you had everything a body could want."

Was she delusional or what? "I'm at a disadvantage here. I have no idea what you're talking about."

"Only 'cause you don't know any different." She rested her arms on the table. "You know why I'm so good at waitressing?"

I shook my head.

"Been doing it since I was fifteen. Mama ran off when I was just a kid, and Daddy could hardly keep a job drinking all the time like he did."

My mouth dropped and it took a moment to form a coherent sentence. "I had no idea. I thought…" I didn't think, that was the problem. Just like I'd felt judged by my looks, I'd done the same to her.

She swept a hand toward me. "You not only had a mama and daddy that stuck, but you also had your sister and brothers. Then when things took a turn, you come marching in here like this here job was a steppingstone for y'all." She shrugged. "Felt like we were in high school all over again."

How had I not known this before? "Funny, I've spent my whole life feeling like I don't fit in 'cause I was such a tomboy. But you"—I tilted my chin toward her —"seemed so together, always looking like you stepped off the cover of some ladies' magazine."

She shrugged. "If I could pull off natural like you do, Bekah, I'd ditch the beauty products and save myself a lot of money and time." She frowned. "It's my armor."

"Huh." I grinned. "Well, aren't we both a hot mess?"

She smiled back—the first I'd ever seen. "Wish we'd had this talk years ago. We might've been friends." What an intriguing idea.

"Never too late for that, Kimberley. I could always use a friend."

"You and me both." She smiled. "And it's Kim to my friends. You let me know if there's anything I can do for your mama, would you?"

"I might just take you up on that."

As I stepped into the parking lot, a sense of wonder filled my soul. I could have never foreseen that the Lord would use this job as a path toward a most unlikely friendship. If He could accomplish so much with so little, there was no end to His grace.

It was after ten when I parked my car in the driveway. A light shone through the front window. Daddy must've left it on when he went to bed. Just like his morning ritual, his nightly one was steeped in a routine that didn't allow him to be up much past nine.

My mind was still tiptoeing through the conversation I'd had with Kimberley which had me smiling again. Was it possible we could become friends? Wouldn't that be a sweet surprise?

I entered the house through the kitchen and stepped into the family room to cut off the lights when I was startled by movement in the corner. As unusual as it was for Daddy to be up so late, I expected to see him in the recliner. But it was Mama, bundled up with her Bible open in her lap and reading glasses perched on the end of her nose. Her hair was a hurrah's nest after being down as long as she'd been, but her smile was pure joy.

"Wasn't expectin' you home so soon, Sweet Pea."

"Had the early shift, Mama. Wasn't expecting *you* to be outta bed." If her skin didn't have such pallor and her eyes weren't so droopy, I'd have taken it as a good sign. "Couldn't sleep?"

"The Lord was calling to me." She patted the Bible. "Didn't want to wake your daddy, so I thought I'd sit a spell out here."

I leaned over and planted a kiss on her papery-dry forehead. An empty glass sat on the table beside her. "Can I get you something? A glass of sweet tea or some water?"

She wriggled into a better position. "A few minutes of your company would be nice. It seems like we hardly have time to talk these days."

We had the time, but Mama was sleeping most of it away.

I collected a chair from the corner and plopped it down next to her. Her voice had weakened considerably over the last several days, and if she had something to say, I didn't want to miss it. I slipped my hand beneath hers so it was sandwiched between the cool of her palm and the tissue-thin pages of the Bible opened to Psalms 23. I didn't need to see the words to remember the Scripture. *The Lord is my shepherd, I shall not be in want. He makes me lie down in green pastures, he leads me beside quiet waters.*

A chill skittered up my spine. Aside from reading the verses for myself, I'd only ever heard them spoken at funerals. It wasn't pure coincidence Mama had been reading that particular Psalm.

"Tell me about your day, Sweet Pea. How was it?" Mama's eyes were half-closed as if she didn't have the strength to hold them open.

I started to spout off the usual, "Fine" when it came to me that Mama and me might not have many more conversations between us. If I were in her place, I'd want to soak up everything possible while I still breathed air. "Actually, Mama, I quit my job. Dale was kind enough to not hold me to my two weeks' notice, so I won't be going back."

"Is that what you want, or is taking care of me wearin' you out?"

I rubbed Mama's hand with my free one. "Believe me, ma'am, I was not cut out to be a waitress." I chuckled. "Dale was too nice to say so, but I'm sure he was plumb relieved when I told him I was leaving."

"You're too hard on yourself, Sweet Pea. I reckon you can do just about anything you set your mind to." *Just about* being the key phrase. "Won't you miss bein' with your friends?"

"I didn't really have any there, Mama. We were too busy working to socialize." Then a picture of Kim formed in my mind. "Well, there might be one. Do you remember Kimberley St. Clair?"

Mama stared off for a moment as if trying to organize her memories. "Wasn't she that beautiful girl whose mama ran out when she was real young?"

I frowned. "Well, yes, I suppose she's the one. But I just tonight learned about her mama leaving. How did you know?"

"It's a small county, Rebekah. Can't hardly say boo without the entire town knowin' about it, now can you?"

True. But then why hadn't I known? Had I been too wrapped up in my own petty life to give anyone else's a thought? It wasn't like we ran in the same circles, but Kim surely knew enough about me growing up.

"Always did feel bad for that child. Her daddy wasn't worth a lick, neither. Left her to practically raise herself. Your daddy and I talked about taking her in, but the girl was too poor to paint and too proud to whitewash. She'd have none of it. I'm afraid we might have done more harm than good tryin', truth be told."

"I had no idea, Mama." Why hadn't Kim brought it up tonight? Why hadn't I the slightest awareness back then? What else was happening around me that I might have missed?

"No reason to tell you," Mama said. "The things we're called to do in the name of the Lord are best done in quiet." She offered a soft smile. "Now, what was it you were sayin' about Kimberley before we got lost down a wayward path?"

"Hmm?" It took a moment for Mama's question to sink in. "Oh, just that she works at the grill too. We had a nice talk tonight." The story fell flat, but it wasn't like I could bring up the animosity we'd had toward each other. Mama probably didn't have a cantankerous bone in her frail, little body. But she was surely the strongest woman I knew.

I glanced at the words above our joined hands. *Even though I walk through the valley of the shadow of death, I will fear no evil, for you are with me.*

"Oh, Mama," I choked out as my eyes blurred. A vise squeezed my heart so tight it was sure to break. "Why does God have to take you too? Wasn't it enough He took Jonathon?"

She reached toward me with her free hand and wiped a tear from my cheek. "You're gonna learn sooner or later that it does no good to question the sovereignty of God, Sweet Pea. It's something I been meaning to talk to you about."

I sniffled. "What's that?"

"Knowing that when we're called home, there's nothing we can do about it but find it in our hearts to be grateful for the life we've had. God, in His infinite wisdom, knows best. Now I know you feel Jonathon was taken from you too soon, but God's timing is perfect."

"It wasn't perfect for me." I fingered the moisture from my eyes. "I only had Jonathon for five years."

"Oh child," Mama said with a soft smile. "You'll have that sweet boy for eternity. You'll have me and your daddy too." Her gaze caught mine. "Now I got something to say, and I pray you'll accept it with the love it's given."

I straightened my spine and swallowed. "Okay."

"I know more than anyone the burden you've been dealt. But it's not just you who's had to tote it. You wanna blame someone for Jonathon's death, and for some reason you set your sights on Mitch."

My face heated while my mind grappled with the unfairness of the charge.

"That boy is grieving every bit as much as you, and on top of that, he's carrying your blame. A body can only handle so much, Bekah."

"You don't understand."

"Oh, sweet girl, but I do." She squeezed my hand. "When we get dealt what seems an unfair hand, we wanna assign blame. It was God's sovereign plan to take Jonathon home with Him. Nothing you or Mitch could've done to change that."

Words of wisdom I wasn't ready to hear, but oh, if only I had Mama's strength, how different things might have been. "You'd think the older I got the stronger I'd be, but that just isn't so."

Mama's eyes widened. "Now what brought this on?" She patted my cheek.

"I've grappled with my grief over Jonathon for more than a year now, and I feel like my faith is waning. You're facing death and look at you."

"You sell yourself short, Sweet Pea." She squeezed my hand. "My strength comes from my faith, and given time, yours will too. You just have to be a mite patient with yourself and with the Lord, is all."

"I can't hardly stand the idea of you not being here with us." My voice snagged on a wave of emotion and broke.

"Only for a little while, Rebekah. It's hard to consider when all we know of is this here life. But God's word promises so much more than we can even imagine.

Do you remember when Jesus was facing his arrest and spoke to his disciples in the Book of John?”

“‘In my Father's house are many rooms,’” I quoted. “‘And if I go and prepare a place for you, I will come back and take you to be with me.’” The words were easy to memorize, but the promises were a little slow to take root. “I often picture Jonathon in a lush field of grass and flowers, free to run and laugh without any fear.”

“Well, Sweet Pea, you just picture me alongside of him. There will be such joy when I can hold my grandbaby in my arms again. You’re just looking at this all wrong. I’m not dying, child, I’m going to be really living for the first time. Our time here is but a shadow of what’s to come.”

I closed my eyes against the tears that filled them. They leaked out and trickled down my cheek. But when I pictured Jonathon and Mama together in that lush field, a smile was born in my heart. Because one day, I’d be there with them too.

Chapter Fourteen

Mitch

I'd been hard pressed to get Miss Anita's request out of my mind. Prayer was right up there with Gregorian chants as far as I was concerned. Wasn't like I'd never heard it, but the meaning was lost. Even if I believed in a God of the universe, why would He listen to anything I had to say? I figured the best person to answer questions about God would be the one who worked for Him.

Business had picked up over the last week which made community service hours a challenge. I arrived at the church with the sunrise on Saturday determined to clock a good six before getting Caleb to Bekah's for another session. I'd let Brother Paul know I was coming early but didn't expect to find him outside working in the churchyard. Never pictured that being part of his duties. But sure enough, he had a blue tarp spread out and was kneeling on the ground gathering dead twigs and cuttings from the hedges that bordered the walkway.

"Don't you have someone who could do that for you?" I asked once I was within earshot. "Like me, for instance."

He glanced up and chuckled. "This isn't work, son. This is pure joy. Something about digging in the dirt does my soul good."

"To each his own, I suppose." I bent down and snatched up a twig he missed and tossed it onto the tarp. "Surprised to see you out so early."

"Best time of the day as far as I'm concerned." He pushed off the ground with a grunt. "Besides, it's gonna be a hot one today. You takin' Caleb over to Rebekah's this afternoon?"

"Yes, sir. You pegged that one. Once she started working with the boy, she took right to it. Surprised she didn't see through your little plan."

He grunted. "Can't take the credit for it. How's Miss Anita doin'?" He grabbed one corner of the tarp, and I reached down for the other.

"It appears the only thing holding her together is a sweet disposition. The woman is a wonder." I helped Paul drag the tarp around to the side of the church where he'd already begun a burn pile.

"You get a chance to talk to her while you were there last?" He nodded for me to follow him up the back steps.

"Yes, sir. Should have done it months ago." Our footsteps on the tile floor echoed in the emptiness of the church as we walked toward the Sunday school classrooms. "She asked me to do something for her, and I thought maybe you could lead me in the right direction."

"Oh?" Paul glanced at me. "What's that?"

"Just so you know, I'm only askin' as a favor to her." I was backpedaling before I even started. Not the best attitude to go into this with.

Paul grinned. "Wants you to do a little exploring of the Word, does she?"

The man's intuition never ceased to surprise me. "Yes, sir. Don't have a clue where to start. She says to pray, but I don't even know how to do that."

We entered the classroom I'd be painting that day. He sat on one of the low tables while I prepped the supplies. "You and Rebekah never talked about her faith?"

I snapped the drop cloth open and spread it on the floor. "Not really. I mean, she used to bring it up now and again, but I generally tuned her out. It was just a bunch of mumbo jumbo far as I could tell."

He frowned. "Your disinterest didn't bother her?"

Hands on hips, I faced him. "I'm sure it did, but she knew what she was gettin' into when we got married. Said it didn't bother her. Suppose she thought she'd change me eventually. Her mama and daddy tried to tell her different, which might have pushed her the other way. Bekah doesn't like being told what to do."

"Yes, I remember there was a ruckus about it all." How could he not? He almost refused to officiate because of it. "Still, up until Jonathon's death, she attended church every Sunday with her family. Weren't you ever curious?"

I knelt to open a can of paint. "More curious after she stopped."

"Yes," he murmured. "We call that a crisis of faith. Bound to happen to everyone a time or two in their lives." He cleared his throat. "You ever think about the afterlife, Mitch? Wonder what'll happen to you when you die?"

I removed the lid and stood. "Not really." Except the day Jonathon was buried. It was all I could do to keep from climbing down into that hole with his coffin. The idea of him being left alone in that dark box haunted me for days. "I have a hard time believing in a God who would allow all the evil to happen in this world."

Paul nodded. "You're not the only one, son. But that's a struggle a lot of people carry with them to their grave. Of course, by the time they figure that out, it's too late."

I dipped my toes into precarious waters. "You lost your wife and child. You don't see the unfairness of that?"

He was quiet for a heartbeat or two. "All of us are gonna die, Mitch. Some sooner than others. If you think of this life here on earth as the only one there is, you can certainly drown in the evil and so-called unfairness. But what if you knew there was more?"

I crossed my arms. "You mean heaven."

He pointed at me. "Yes, heaven. We'll all live an eternal life, whether we believe in it or not. Truth isn't based on our belief, but the Word of God. Either we'll live it in the presence of God or in eternal damnation. That's a choice we each have to face while here on earth."

I snorted. "A choice? Is it really that simple?"

"Yes." He rubbed his chin. "And no. It's something the Lord has to press upon your heart. Anyone can say they believe in Jesus, but it not only has to be confessed with your mouth, it has to be believed with your heart. That takes a little digging. If you have no desire to know the truth..." He shrugged. "That's your choice. No one can force it on you."

"Sounds complicated." Where were the easy answers I was looking for?

"Start with prayer, just like Miss Anita suggested. Keep it simple. You talk to God like you talk to anyone else. Only you might want to remember He's holy, and a certain amount of reverence would go a long way."

"Talk to him? You mean like you and me are talking right now?"

"Sure." He cleared his throat. "You mind if I pray for you?"

Before Bekah left me, she said she prayed for me all the time. Done in private, so I never actually heard her. Figured that's what Brother Paul intended to do. "Uh, sure."

Closing his eyes, he bowed his head. Not sure what else to do, I followed suit.

"God our Father, we thank You and praise You for Your Son and our Savior, Jesus Christ. We know it's Your will that none should perish but that we would all come to You through belief in Jesus through whose death and resurrection our sins are forgiven. We ask You, Lord, to draw Mitch to You through Your Holy Spirit. Open his heart and mind to understand the love You have for him and the resurrection life he can have when he places his faith in Jesus. We know this is something You desire, so we are confident that You will be faithful to answer this prayer with a resounding yes in Your perfect time. It's in His name we pray."

When Brother Paul stopped speaking, I mumbled an "amen" like I'd heard Bekah do on numerous occasions. Truth was, I didn't understand half of what he said.

"That's nothing like how I talked to anyone I know," I admitted.

"I don't suppose it is. But here's the thing, Mitch. We all talk to God in different ways. You just gotta speak to Him from your heart. You want to know who He is, just ask Him to show you. It's a process that takes time and an open mind. He'll do the rest."

"If you say so."

"You have a Bible?"

"Nope." I reached for a stir stick and dropped it into the creamy paint. I wasn't so sure about this whole business, and if it wasn't for Miss Anita, I'd tell Brother Paul to forget I ever brought it up. Besides, what if there really was something to it? I thought about Jonathon lying in that small casket.

"These days, young people are readin' it from an app on their smart phones. Somehow, it doesn't seem quite right. I have one here you're welcome to. If I was you, I'd start with the gospel of Mark."

I glanced up at Brother Paul and rolled the question I wanted to ask around in my mind a moment. Might be I'd offend him, but the answer could be critical. "You think your wife and daughter are in heaven?"

He nodded. "I know they are. And when my time comes, I'll be reunited with them too."

If heaven was real, I was sure as I could be that's where Jonathon was. Bekah had said something once about seeing him again one day. Somehow, I thought if it were true for her, it'd be true for me too.

Now I wasn't so sure.

Rebekah

Vintage Decor was more a social scene than a shopping experience, especially on Saturday mornings. There was a group of four ladies lounging in the wicker chairs on the front porch with another three sitting on the top two steps. It was no surprise since I'd found the last available parking space in the gravel lot when I arrived for work an hour after opening.

"Good morning, ladies," I greeted while maneuvering around them to reach the door. It was confirmation that my decision to not bow out of work this morning was the right one, although I'd spend every moment away from Mama worrying. She'd had a bad night, but Leah was there. I needed to let go some. My habit of hovering found a new target in Jonathon's absence.

The thought of working with the little boy later this afternoon brought a much-needed smile to my heart. It didn't matter that Mitch would be dropping him off, either. One had nothing whatsoever to do with the other.

"What're you grinnin' about?" Jenna asked with a matching one of her own. She'd turned her attention from the customer she was ringing up at the front desk. Her thick blond hair was piled atop her head giving her the added height necessary to bring her plump body into proportion. She and her cousin Charlotte didn't appear as if they'd come from the same gene pool, aside from hair and eye color. More like Mutt and Jeff.

"Can't a body smile for no reason?" My words got cut off by the sudden bark of laughter coming from the kitchen where three more customers were visible from my vantage point in the foyer. "It's noisier than a hen house in here."

"Yes, ma'am. Charlie's mid-summer sale." She handed the gift bag to the customer. "Y'all come back for those candlesticks, Laura, if you change your mind. They'd be perfect set atop that ol' buffet you bought last year."

"Thanks, Jenna." Laura turned and threw me a smile on her way out.

I glanced around for Darlene. "You all alone here, Jenna?"

"Nope. Darlene went downstairs to see if we had more pieces to set on the shelves in the parlor. We 'bout sold outta everythin' that was there." She rested her arms on the front desk. "How's your mama doin', Bekah?"

"About the same, I'm afraid. Thanks for asking." I swept a hand through my bangs with trembling fingers. One mention of Mama, and a dark cloud threatened my joy. "Why don't I go down and take over for Darlene? Appears she'd be much more useful up here with you. I can find knickknacks as well as the next person."

Jenna shrugged. "Whatever you'd prefer."

Downstairs was just a fancy way of saying the basement, which was where Charlotte kept her stock. There was nothing new in Charlie's store—everything came from estate sales, garage sales, or thrift stores. In fact, she started with her own nana's things left to her when she'd died. Even the furniture was repurposed one way or another. If not refinished, then distressed enough to be chic.

I made my way down the steep steps with caution. They might have been beefed up, and the lighting was much improved over the original single bulb, but it was still a precarious descent. "You down here, Darlene?"

"Over here in the south corner." Her response was muffled by the low ceiling and cramped space. It might be time Charlotte found a better storage facility for her overstock.

I found Darlene bent over an open chest. There were a few objects sitting on the floor beside her. "We need better lighting down here."

"You ain't gonna get an argument from me. I'm gettin' too old for this nonsense." She stood up and stretched back as if to ease a crick in her lower spine. "You come to rescue me?"

"Yes, ma'am. I think Jenna could use your expertise up there with all the customers swarming the place."

Darlene nodded. "Sure thing. You workin' tonight?"

"Nope. Quit my waitressing job the other day so I have more time to spend with Mama."

"You don't say? Might could find you more hours here if you need them."

"I just may take you up on it. Unless I wanna live off the kindness of mama and daddy forever, I need to work." That wasn't completely true. I had money coming to me from Mitch, but pride had kept me from touching it.

"Speakin' of your job at the grill, some girl came by earlier lookin' for you. Said she worked with you there."

"Are you sure?"

"Sure as I can be. Why?"

I frowned. "No one there even knew I worked here except the manager, Dale. He'd have called if he needed to get a hold of me."

Darlene chuckled. "This wasn't no man, I can tell you that."

Strange. Couldn't see Kimberley coming by, but who else could it be?

"How' your mama doin'?"

I picked up a set of silver salt and pepper shakers Darlene had left on the concrete floor and set them aside to take upstairs. "The same. She didn't sleep much last night, because of the pain, but when I came home from work the other day, she was actually sitting up." There was a kernel of hope, buried so deep it'd take a miner to find it, that had me believing it was just possible Mama might beat this thing. If Jesus could raise Lazarus from the dead, surely He could heal one case of pancreatic cancer.

"She's a blessed woman to have y'all for family. Did you work with that little boy? What's his name?"

"Caleb. Yes. Did me good too. Mitch is bringing him by again this afternoon."

Darlene nudged me with an elbow. "I'm gettin' the notion things are less strained between you and Mitch. That true?"

"Why? Because I'm holding a civil tongue?" When she nodded, I shrugged. "Could be Mama's been speaking some truths that are too hard to ignore," I admitted. "Although I don't know what it means, yet."

"You listen to your mama, Bek. She's a wise woman." She collected the other articles from the floor. "Keep an eye out for things bein' mis-stocked, will ya? It's startin' to look like a hoarder's paradise down here."

Even with the basement door closed, I could hear the footsteps overhead and the muted voices of customers as I collected items to be transported up to the shop. It was peaceful in the dank, cool room, and I found my mind slipped easily into prayer. How long had it been since that had happened? Was there finally a healing in my heart taking place now that I least expected it?

The stairs, such as they were, only allowed me to carry a basket with a few items at a time, and once I was finished, more than two hours had passed. With it being the lunch hour, the crowd had slimmed. Fewer customers would allow me freedom to dust and restock the shelves without hindering any voracious shoppers.

"Bekah?" I spun around. Mitch stood just inside the front door.

"What're you doin' here? I thought we were meeting at Mama and Daddy's around four." I peered beyond him to see if he had Caleb, but he appeared to be alone.

"Joe sent me." His hair stood on end like he'd been running his hands through it, and he was fidgety as all get out. "You need to come with me, Bek. It's your mama."

CHAPTER FIFTEEN

Rebekah

In the days since Mama had been diagnosed, I'd come to understand that death wasn't something to be feared—at least not for the one who had a relationship with Jesus Christ. Mama had said her life would just be starting while those of us left behind would wrestle with the loss. I'd had no idea how many people that would be.

The house and yard teamed with dark-clad figures milling about balancing plates of food supplied by numerous church ladies. Food was the universal language for any situation whether celebrating a holiday or memorializing the death of a loved one. There was certainly enough to feed the entire town of Shelbyville from congealed salads to fried chicken. Everyone spoke in muted tones as if they'd disturb those of us who were hanging on by the scantest thread.

With nothing else to do, I propped myself in a quiet corner and tried to melt into the background where I'd become invisible to all but the keenest observer. Mama was now laid to rest beside Jonathon, although I knew neither of them were actually there. I closed my eyes and pictured them sitting together by a stream of water amid tall grasses, colorful blooms, and a kaleidoscope of butterflies. Mama would be able to wrap her arms around her grandbaby once more, and Jonathon would know he was loved. He would never be lonely again. I wished I could say the same for me.

The last few days had been a blur of preparation which gave me little time to give into my desire to crawl into a hole and grieve. Leah and I had scrubbed the house from top to bottom and prepared the extra rooms for Dan, Sarah, and the kids. We asked Daddy to go through Mama's pictures and pick out the ones he wanted for the memorial, but he graciously declined. "I don't need pictures of your mama to remember her by," he'd said. So, Leah and I did it ourselves, which required extra hours of reminiscing over each one with lots of tears and laughter.

Now, I watched my big sister work the room with the same grace and class as Mama would've had things been different. I was no better with a crowd than I was waitressing. Small talk was not a skill set I inherited, and I didn't see the point in it. I was more like Daddy in that way. Wouldn't be surprised if he was squirreled away in his own quiet corner.

"What're you doing hidin' out here?" Joe's deep voice startled a gasp from me. He stood close enough to touch, and yet, I hadn't seen him approach.

"I'm not hiding." *Liar.* "Just watching things from a distance."

He handed me a red Solo cup. "Sweet tea. Drink some. Did you have anything to eat?"

"Not hungry." I took a sip of the tea. I watched earlier as he talked to Mitch, and a litany of questions raced through my mind, but I stuck to a safer topic. "How's Caleb doing?"

"Still hasn't said a word, but he smiles more these days. I think the horseback riding lesson did him good. Left him with a friend of Cassie's today. Given recent events, didn't figure it'd be a good idea if we brought him here." He snatched my cup and took a gulp. "How're you doing?"

I shrugged. "I don't know. It's kind of hard to gripe about her being gone when the alternative would be her suffering. I just don't know why God had to go and take her too." Could I have sounded more like a five-year-old?

Joe slipped an arm around my shoulders and dislodged me from the corner. "Let's go mingle. You need to get outta your own head for a while."

I was too tired to fight him until I saw where he was luring me. Mitch. I spun out of his hold, but he was having none of it. He hooked my arm with his and all but dragged me through the crowd of mourners.

"Bekah, I'd like you to meet my good friend, Mitch." He slung his arm over my shoulders again to keep me from escaping. "Mitch, say 'hi' to Bekah. You two have a lot in common." Then he walked away.

Mitch gave me a crooked smile. "Your brother is a real hoot."

I twisted my mouth. "Yeah. I laugh all the time." He was smarter than I'd given him credit for too.

His smile melted. "I'm sorry about your mama, Bek. There was no one quite like her."

My fingers reached for his tie of their own volition. I smoothed the silky material when what I longed to do was sink into his comforting embrace. It could be I was weakened by despair, but at that moment I missed Mitch more than ever. It would've been easier to stay in my lonely corner and stare at him from afar.

"Mama loved you, Mitch," I said through the knot of emotion that sat at the base of my throat. "That day you brought Caleb by, she couldn't stop singing your praises." My lips twitched. "Who knew you could impress a woman merely by changing her bed?" It wasn't all Mama had praised him for, but I was still working through too many things to give him an opening.

He placed his hands on my upper arms. "Look, Bekah—" His eyes flicked away then narrowed. "Wonder what she's doing here."

I craned my neck to scan the room. There must've been twenty people clustered in groups of twos and threes, but Kimberley stood out in the crowd. For one thing, she was clad in a bright pink dress, like a bird of paradise stuck in a bouquet of dead flowers. For another, she was alone.

"Excuse me, Mitch." I made my way through the crowd offering smiles and accepting condolences as I passed until I was standing in front of her.

"Hey, Bekah." She offered a tentative smile as if unsure of her welcome. "I heard about your mama, obviously." She rolled her eyes. "I hope you don't mind that I stopped by to pay my respects."

"Of course not." We stood together like awkward teens at a school dance. What would Mama do in this situation? "Can I get you something to eat? The church ladies outdid themselves." When in doubt, food.

"No. Thanks anyway." Her eyes roamed the room as if looking for someone in particular. There were enough people to choose from including Brother Paul, Darlene, and Jenna. Various kin and friends of the family were clustered together, as well. "I thought maybe I could just give my condolences to your daddy, but I don't remember what he looks like."

I thought about what Mama had said about her and Daddy trying to help out Kimberley back when we were in high school. Did I dare bring it up? Could be she wouldn't want to be reminded, but she had to know her desire to talk to Daddy would be curious. Then again, things with her were tenuous enough without me stepping in where I wasn't invited.

"I'm not sure where he is, Kim." I turned to look and spotted Dan walking in from the kitchen. "Hey, Dan." I waved him over. "You seen Daddy?"

"He's outside with the kids." Dan glanced at Kim.

"This is Kim. Kim, my younger brother, Dan."

Dan nodded a greeting. "You want I should go get him?"

"No, thanks. I'll take her."

The late afternoon sun had scuttled behind a bank of dark thunderclouds giving a reprieve from the heat. There were as many people outside as in, but I spotted Dan and Joe's kids immediately. They circled Daddy who was sitting in a lawn chair while he appeared to be telling them a story.

"There he is." I pointed him out for Kim. "Would you like me to introduce you?"

Eyes on him, she shook her head. "I got this."

Then I remembered the mysterious woman who'd shown up at the shop the other day and touched Kim's arm to halt her descent down the steps. "Hey, Kim. By any chance, did you stop by the vintage store to see me a few days ago?"

She shrugged. "I was in the area. Dale told me you worked there part time, and I thought to check in on how your mama was doing. Hope you don't mind."

"Not at all." I folded my arms and watched as she made her way across the grass in killer heels as if they were nothing more than a pair of trusty tennis shoes. I wouldn't have made it two steps without breaking an ankle. I glanced down at my own fashionable cowboy boots and scowled. We certainly were an unlikely pair to become friends, but God did work in mysterious ways. Who was I to question His methods?

The creak of the screen door drew my attention as Mitch came out, tracking Kim's trek toward Daddy. He stepped up beside me, and a breeze carried a whiff of shaving cream and soap. "Didn't know you two were so close."

"We're not, exactly," I murmured. "It's kind of a long story, but she knew Mama and Daddy years ago." Kim had reached Daddy, who stood when he saw her. Even from this distance, I could see a smile light his eyes. Apparently, he remembered her as well as Mama had.

"It's funny how God works sometimes," I said, forgetting for the moment who I was talking to. Mitch didn't believe in God, so he wouldn't see the irony in His ways.

Mitch

The Miller clan was a tight-knit group loyal to their own. Hurt one, and the rest would circle the wagons in order to protect. The only kid of a single mom, I was envious. Didn't make it any easier being on the outside, though. I had more than my share of curious stares from a cousin or two, but I wasn't about to disrespect Miss Anita's memory by being anything but cordial. Even when Cousin Stu cornered me out by the maple tree.

"Mitch, right?"

I nodded. He knew my name. From what I'd been told, Stu thought the sun came up just to hear him crow.

"Thought you and Bek split." He crossed his arms as if waiting for the dirt.

"Separated." Two could play at this game. "Where's your wife Misty?" I pretended to glance around for the woman who walked out on him last year after she caught him with another woman. Her best friend, if my memory was correct. A man who lived in glass houses and all that. Nice only went so far.

He scowled. "Dumped me. Can you believe it?"

I made a non-committal sound. The guy was lucky to get her in the first place. Kinda like me and Bekah. Only confirmed my vow to get her back.

Thunder rumbled overhead and the thinning crowd lost a few more to the threat of rain. This was my cue.

"Excuse me, will you, Stu?" I crossed the lawn and went inside through the kitchen. Bekah and Leah were shoulder-to-shoulder working away while Dan's wife, Sarah, and Cassie cleared the table. Even after two hours of grazing, there was enough leftovers to feed a rodeo crowd.

"You need any help?" Three pairs of eyes looked at me like I spoke a foreign language.

"Uh, we're good," Leah said. "There's not enough room in here for another body."

"Then you won't mind if I remove one of them." I caught Bekah's eye. "You gotta minute?"

Bekah frowned, but she snatched a paper towel from the roll hanging beneath the cabinet and followed me out, wiping her hands on the go. Her gray, sleeveless dress hugged her slender curves and showed off toned biceps. Paired with black cowboy boots, it was as dressy as Bekah got. "You fixing to leave?"

"No. I just thought maybe we could talk."

Someone walked past and bumped her. She raised her hands to my chest to keep from knocking into me, and my arms slipped around her shoulders. "It's not the most private spot," she said, stepping away. "Maybe another time?"

I clenched my hand to keep from wrapping it around her arm and dragging her outside. Earlier, she'd run her fingers down my tie, as if it were the most natural thing. Flirting wasn't in Bekah's wheelhouse, so it had to mean something, didn't it? Still, she wouldn't be pushed. If I had any hope of salvaging our marriage, I'd have to come at it from a different angle.

"Just wanted to be sure you're still doing okay." I rubbed my hands down her bare arms and watched as her eyes softened. Trust. That's what I needed to earn from her if we had any hope.

"I'm good." She patted my chest before putting space between us as if softening the rejection. "Since Mama died, we've stayed so busy there hasn't been time to miss her yet."

"Is there anything I can do to help out around here?"

"You might ask Joe and Dan. They're hoping to get all the tables put up before it gets dark. Thought for sure everyone would've gone home by now." Her mouth twisted.

I pointed toward the kitchen with my chin. "They will once the food's put away. I'll see what I can do outside."

The rain had let up, and I saw Joe and Dan hauling folding tables and chairs to Joe's truck. I grabbed a couple of chairs on my pass through the yard and joined them. "Thought y'all could use a hand."

Joe nodded, took the chairs from me, and slipped them in the back of the truck with the stack. "How's it goin' inside?"

"The girls are cleaning up the food. Sounds to me like they're ready for the day to be over."

"Them and me both," Joe said, his attention on something behind me. "Daddy's headin' for the barn. I'm gonna go see if he needs anything." He slapped me on the back and walked off.

Dan closed the tailgate and turned to me. "How's it goin' with Bekah?" His gaze was steady, and I sensed this was more than a casual question.

"I'm takin' it one day at a time. Might be making progress."

He chewed at the inside of his bottom lip—just like Bekah. That wasn't the only similarities between them. While Dan's hair was lighter, he had the same strong chin, straight nose, and blue/green eyes. They could've been twins.

He blew out a breath and folded his arms. "Look, I might be stepping in where I don't belong, but I think you're getting the raw end of this deal."

Was he talking about the blame for Jonathon's death or Bekah leaving me? "I'm not sure what you mean."

"I know you probably think we all stick together"—he shrugged—"and for the most part that's true. I mean, if you'd of done something to hurt Bek, we'd make your life miserable. Even Joe. But her walking out on you 'cause she's broken up over Jonathon? That's not right." It was more words than I'd heard Dan string together before.

"I appreciate it, Dan." I glanced up at the house. "Bekah know how you feel?"

He rubbed his hand along the tailgate. "Nope. We've all been givin' her time, you know? Then Mama gettin' sick..." He cleared his throat. "I think you should know she was talkin' to me about moving to Atlanta. I think that'd be a mistake."

It took a beat to find my voice what with the panic taking hold of me. "When? I mean, when did she talk to y'all about it?" Was I fooling myself thinking things were easing my way some?

"When I was out here last. She hadn't brought it up since, but she gave me the impression she'd make a change once Mama didn't need her anymore." He pushed a hand through his hair. "You might wanna do something sooner than later, Mitch."

"It's not like I can drag her back home, you know." I glanced toward the house as if I could see Bekah through the brick wall. "I thought given time—"

"You don't think more 'an six months is enough time?" Dan shook his head. "You're more patient than me, I'll say that for you."

"Maybe, but you and me both know Bekah's not gonna rush off anytime soon. Not when your dad's left here by himself. And I'm working on something, besides."

"You talkin' about saddling her with that little boy staying with Joe?" He grinned. "Didn't know you were so devious, Mitch."

"Not me," I said with a snort. "That was Brother Paul's doin'. I'm merely using it to my advantage. Now, if you could discourage Bekah from making that move, maybe I'd have a shot here."

But as I walked away, it struck me that I needed more than luck or a decent break to reclaim my marriage. Miss Anita had said Bekah needed a godly husband. If I ever hoped to have the kind of marriage she and John had, or any of Bek's siblings, then I'd need to do more. Be more. And there was only one place I knew to start that journey.

Chapter Sixteen

Rebekah

Preparations for Mama's funeral and the memorial service had kept me in hostess mode for near a week. It wasn't that I didn't miss Mama, but there wasn't time to dwell on it. Maybe that was a good thing. I had immersed myself in grief for far too long, and it hadn't done more than muddle my thinking until I didn't know what was right and what was plain sinful.

Sarah and the kids had flown home the day before, and Dan was leaving the next morning. They had been a buffer for Daddy and me, and I wasn't quite sure how I'd navigate the new normal. If it was a struggle for me, I could only imagine how difficult it was for Daddy. While I had a part time job and plenty of chores with which to occupy myself, he was all but retired.

I was thinking on this while brushing down Siren after a long ride—a first since Mama's passing. Mitch was bringing Caleb for another lesson, which caused a little hitch in my heart. Why was I as nervous as a schoolgirl on her first date? It was Mitch. I couldn't deny the attraction that'd always been there, but it didn't change anything. Every time I looked into his eyes, I saw Jonathon's.

"Have a good ride?"

Dan's voice broke into the silence and drew a yelp from me. "For Pete's sake, Dan." Hand to my heart, I turned on him. "You could warn a girl."

"Whistling my way out here wasn't enough, huh? You must have been deep in thought. Anything worth sharing?"

I swiped the brush down Siren's neck. "Nope. You wanna take a ride? Emperor could use the exercise."

"Sounds good." He petted Siren's muzzle. "Thought maybe we could talk first."

"About?"

"Things."

I rolled my eyes. "Well, that certainly clarifies it. Can you be more specific?"

"You did a great job takin' care of Mama."

"So you've said." I watched as he crossed to the grooming tools hanging on a line of hooks. If he had something to say, why didn't he get to it? "Not that I don't appreciate a compliment now and again."

He nabbed a hoof pick and looked at it like he'd never seen one before. "Now that Mama's gone, what're you gonna do with yourself?" The king of casual.

"Ah. I get it. If you wanna know if I'm still considering moving to Atlanta, why don't you just ask?"

He replaced the pick. "Okay. I'm asking."

I patted Siren's neck before taking hold of her lead rope. "I don't know. I haven't given it a whole lot of thought lately." I led Siren outside to the paddock while Dan trailed behind.

"We've been worried about you, Bek."

I hooked the gate and turned to him. "We? We who?"

"Joe, Leah, and me."

I snatched the sunglasses off my head and jammed them on. "What are you, the spokesperson?"

He snorted. "No need to get ugly. I'm just tryin' to talk to you."

"Well, you're not doin' a very good job of it. If you've got something to say, then say it."

His lips tightened, and a muscle jumped along his jawline. "I told Mitch the other day that you were thinking of moving to Atlanta."

His admission was like a slap in the face, the impact of which had me falling back a step. "What right do you have to talk to him about anything to do with me?"

"He's your husband, Bek. Even if you seem to have forgotten that."

"Yes. He's my husband." I jack hammered a finger onto my chest. "And it's none of your concern what I do or don't do with my marriage."

He met me stare for stare. "I care about you. Isn't that reason enough?"

"I care about you too, Danny, but I don't go around stickin' my nose into your marriage." Heat rose up my cheeks, and it wasn't from the afternoon sun. "If I did, I'd ask why you're letting Sarah call all the shots while you put your own dreams on hold. Or why you're living in Atlanta when we both know you'd much rather be back here with the rest of the family." I folded my arms. "But it's none of my affair, so I'm not asking."

He glared at me. "You done?"

"Just keepin' it real."

"I didn't come out here with a mind to hurt you, Bekah. Yeah, Sarah and I have a few challenges. What marriage doesn't? But we're together and workin' it out. You think pitchin' a hissy fit's gonna be enough for me to slink away with my tail between my legs? Well, it ain't. All of us are worried about how you'll deal with Mama's death since you're still stuck in the muck of Jonathon's. You pushed Mitch away, and now you're trying to push me away." He huffed out a breath and turned to leave.

I pressed my fingers to my mouth and blinked back tears. "Wait." When Dan spun around, I stepped into his arms. "I'm sorry. That was rude and uncalled for. I know you mean well."

He rubbed my back and dropped a kiss on top of my head. "You're forgiven. We all just want what's best for you, Bek."

"I know." I stepped back and swiped at my eyes. "And I know moving to Atlanta is just another version of running away, but I don't know how to get past this."

"Maybe the two of you need marriage counseling," Dan said. "Someone who can help you navigate whatever it is that's keeping you apart."

Mitch had suggested counseling only a month or so after Jonathon had died, and I dismissed it without a thought. "Maybe," I finally conceded. "I don't like the idea of airing our messy lives with a total stranger."

Dan tucked his hands into the front pockets of his jeans. "You like the idea of being divorced better?"

I opened my mouth to answer when I spotted Mitch's truck rattling down the drive. "Speak of the devil," I muttered.

Dan slipped an arm around my shoulders and gave me a quick squeeze. "When you're done working with Caleb, I'm gonna take you and Daddy out for supper. It'll be good to get him out for a couple hours, and you can use the break."

"Thought you were gonna ride Emperor?"

"I will. Just wanna say hi to Mitch first."

He met Mitch halfway to the house then crouched to Caleb's eye level. I couldn't hear what he said, but the little boy's mouth tilted into a smile in response.

I slipped into the paddock and walked Siren out to where I had her saddle set up on a rack, my gaze continually going back to Mitch. My hands were clammy, and my heart raced. Again, with the nervous school-girl reaction. Was it possible to get past my anger and disappointment in him? I'd made all kinds of accusations, but like Mama pointed out, sometimes it's easier to blame the person closest to you than to accept the sovereignty of God.

"What do you think, Siren?" I gazed into the horse's eyes as if she could actually give me an answer. "Am I crazy for thinking Mitch could have saved Jonathon?"

Siren neighed an answer I couldn't interpret, but I had no doubt she thought I was as crazy as everyone else did. But what if I went back to Mitch, and nothing had changed? It wasn't fair that I blamed him for Jonathon's death. In my head, I knew that. And yet those months before I left to live with Mama and Daddy still haunted me. It seemed as if I had lost a little more of my mind every day, and I had taken a piece of Mitch along with it. It wasn't good for either of us.

By the time Siren was ready, Mitch and Caleb were standing side-by-side waiting for me, and Dan was saddling Emperor on the other side of the paddock.

"Hey there." I offered Mitch a smile and ruffled Caleb's hair. "You ready for another lesson?"

Caleb tilted his head back to look at me and nodded.

"Good deal." I turned to Mitch. "If you have something else to do, I can call you when we're about done."

"I thought I'd visit with your Daddy for a bit." Had he said he was going to take a quick flight to the moon and back, it wouldn't have surprised me more. Mitch had never 'visited' with Daddy before. Why in the world would he start now?

"Okay then. I think he's out back in Mama's garden." He turned to leave, and I blurted, "I'm not moving to Atlanta."

Crossing his arms, he faced me again. "Excuse me?"

"Dan told me he told you I was thinking of moving to Atlanta."

He nodded.

"I'm not."

"Good to know." He sauntered away without a second glance.

Was he working at throwing me off my game? First a visit with Daddy. Now, he didn't seem to care one jot that I wasn't running off to Georgia. Maybe it was me he didn't care for. Not that I could blame him. I'd all but charged him with killing our baby, walked out on him despite our marriage vows, and was barely civil. He'd have to be certifiable to love me after all that.

Mitch

There have been experiences in my life that defined who I would be—as a man, a father, and a husband. The moment I saw Rebekah, more than fifteen years before, I knew she would be my wife. I didn't buy into the theory of love at first sight. That's not what it was. Had I been a religious man, I might have chalked it up to God's revelation. Might still could. Only time would tell.

For the past year, I'd let life happen without making any effort, beyond re-acting, to change it. I hadn't known how to fix things for Bekah when Jonathon died, so I backed off. It was too hard dealing with her grief along with my own, and she made it clear where the blame belonged. Right at my own feet, even if I knew different.

I took Miss Anita's advice. Prayer confounded me, but I stumbled through it a time or two. I felt as awkward as a kid performing open heart surgery and about as capable. But it settled my mind some. Miss Anita would have called it peace. Whatever it was, it gave me enough confidence to respond to Bekah without doing backflips over her announcement that she wasn't planning on moving away.

John was in the garden just like Bekah said, crouched over Miss Anita's squash plants. I stopped at the gate, unsure of my approach. The man just lost his wife, and here I was coming to him with my own problems.

He glanced up. "Mitch. What brings you out here?"

"Hey, John. Dropped Caleb off for another lesson with Bekah."

He nodded once. "Good. Then you got yourself some time to kill. Help me get these here vegetables inside, would ya?" He pushed off the ground with a muffled moan and swiped his hands down the legs of his jeans.

"Sure thing." I spotted a couple of baskets stacked near the gate and nabbed them. Sweat trickled down my temples. "Hot time of the day to be harvesting, wouldn't you say?"

"Yep." He reached out for one of the baskets without another word. If John were a monk who'd taken a vow of silence, he'd be easier to talk to.

My mind searched for an opening as I helped fill the baskets with zucchini, tomatoes, and okra. When we were finished, I followed him up the steps and into the kitchen, still unsure about what I'd say. It was easier to face the barrel-end of his shotgun than this silence.

"How are you doing, John?" I didn't ask for the sake of conversation. I really wanted to know. It seemed like the sun wasn't quite so bright since Miss Anita passed. If there really was a heaven, she'd surely be there with Jonathon.

"Fair to middlin'." He slid his basket onto the counter and faced me. "You got something to say, son, or you just takin' pity on an old man?"

I edged my basket next to his then rubbed the side of my nose with a knuckle. "Wanted to ask you for a favor, then realized my timing is probably off. You got enough to deal with as it is."

He pursed his lips. "Don't have near enough to keep my mind occupied. You got need of something, let's talk." He waved a finger toward the family room. "Can I get ya a glass of sweet tea?"

"Sure. That'd go down real good right now."

Once we were situated in the family room, he eased into his recliner. "What's on your mind?"

"Bekah." Elbows on my knees, I clasped my hands.

He nodded real slow. "Been wonderin' when you were gonna get to that. Tried to talk to her a time or two, but the girl's gotta mind of her own."

I chuckled. "That's what Miss Anita said too." The reminder of that conversation wiped the grin from my face. "She said something else, too, though."

"Yeah?" He took a gulp of tea. "What's that?"

"That Bekah needs a strong, godly husband." I peered at him to gauge his reaction. His face was as unmovable as Mount Rushmore.

"My Anita was a wise woman." He dropped his gaze, but not before I caught the sheen of unshed tears. He shifted in his chair, reached back, and pulled a handkerchief from his pocket. A couple swipes of his eyes and nose, and he was composed again. "Seein' as you don't believe in God, how do you intend to be the husband Bekah deserves?"

I cleared my throat. "That's where I could use your help, sir. I've been thinkin' on it some since I spoke to Miss Anita. Only way to know if I can be a godly man is to do a little exploring."

His eyes widened. "A personal relationship with Jesus Christ is a serious undertaking, Mitch."

"Yes, sir. I understand that. That's why I came to you. I figure if anyone's gonna keep me honest, it'd be you."

He frowned. "How so?"

"Well, maybe you'd be willing to mentor me?" I rushed ahead before he could turn me down. "I know you got other things on your plate, and I wouldn't expect to take up too much of your time. I can always ask Brother Paul."

He harrumphed and cleared his throat a couple times. "I don't see why that can't work." He scratched at the stubble on his chin. "You believe in God, Mitch?"

"I don't know. Is it enough that I *want* to believe?"

"It's a start." He eyed me. "Does Bekah know about this?"

"No, sir. And I'd like to keep it that way. At least for the time being."

"Why's that?"

"There's all kinds of things jumbled up along with this. As you probably know, she blames me for Jonathon's death."

"I know she *thinks* she does," John said. "We got a funny way of placin' blame where it don't rightly belong. Birthing and dying are outta our hands." He shook his head. "If I didn't have true faith in the Lord, I'd have a mighty hard time forgivin' Him for taking Anita."

"But that's what I don't get, sir. Bekah's always had faith until Jonathon died. Now..." I shook my head. "She's just as lost as I am. Maybe more so."

"She hasn't lost her faith, son. She's workin' through her anger at God. It's a whole lot easier to push you away than Him."

That didn't sit easy. "Well, I don't want her thinking this whole faith search is just a ploy to get her back. And if I figure out it's not for me, I don't want her to be disappointed."

He nodded. "Probably for the best. Means we won't be able to meet here, you know."

"No, sir."

"How you gonna find time between work and community service?"

My face heated. "You know about the bar fight?"

"This is a small town, son. Besides which, I didn't think those Sunday school classrooms were paintin' themselves." He chuckled. "You got yourself a Bible?"

"Brother Paul hooked me up. Told me to start with Mark."

"Good. Got me a study in mind we could use. Every heard of Max Lucado?" When I shook my head, he went on. "Doesn't matter. You figure out a night a week that'll work, and I'll be there."

"What about Bekah? Won't she wonder what you're doing?"

He waved a dismissive hand. "She don't have to know everything. It'll do her good to wonder." His glance landed on mine. "I've been thinkin' though. You don't ever talk about your own father."

A fist tightened in my gut. "No, sir. He left when I was a kid. Never saw him again."

He nodded. "I remember that. It's just a lot of times, we base our relationship with God on that of our earthly father. When there's a disconnect with one, there's a disconnect with the other. Thought you might want to know that."

"I'll keep it in mind." I finished off my tea and stood. "Thank you, sir. I appreciate it."

"You bet."

I stepped outside with the sense that something pivotal had just occurred. A year ago, if someone told me John Miller was going to mentor me in a Bible study, I'd of accused the person of lunacy. If there was a God in heaven, I had no doubt He could use the deaths of my boy and Miss Anita to turn things on their head. Might be there was a plan afoot after all.

I stopped under the old maple in the middle of the yard and watched as Bekah, Caleb tucked in front of her, walked Siren around the paddock. *Are You real, God? Because, if You are, I'm ready to see what You have for me, Bek, and Caleb. Show me a miracle.*

Chapter Seventeen

Fall 2017

Rebekah

There wasn't a clean spot on the surface of Leah's kitchen counters. Cans of pumpkin puree, plastic bags filled with granny smith apples, and more with pecans were crammed into one corner. Lumps of cheesecloth-covered pie crusts were lined up alongside the sink ready to roll out, and flour dusted every surface including the floor.

Bekah stopped peeling an apple long enough to swipe at her cheek with the back of her hand leaving a swath of flour in its wake. Preparations for the Miller Clan's Thanksgiving dinner was stressful enough without four kids and an overweight cocker spaniel adding to the chaos. It almost made Rebekah grateful she'd never had any babies. Almost.

"When'd you say Gabe's supposed to be home?" Bekah's question ended on an *oomph* when three-year-old Eli ran into her while racing Dillon, the dog, for a wayward tennis ball.

"Sadie!" Leah yelled. "Come get your brother, will ya?"

There was a scuffle of dog and kids, and a scream or two, that put Bekah two steps closer to a nervous breakdown. When it quieted, they were left with a cloud of flour fogging the air.

"I don't know how you do it." Bekah rubbed her temple where a headache was forming. "When did you say Gabe will be home?"

"Not soon enough." Leah spread more flour on the counter and dropped a blob of dough in the middle. "He texted a while ago. Said he needs to get the reports finished, otherwise, he'll have to go back in on Friday."

"Well, I sure hope we can get these pies done before the kids pull off a coup." She popped a piece of apple in her mouth. "You have any dill pickles?"

"Since when do you eat pickles?" She went to work on the dough with a rolling pin.

"I don't know. They taste good lately." Bekah wiped her hands on a paper towel and rummaged through the fridge. "So, do you have any?"

"In there somewhere."

"I gotta stop hanging out here," Bekah mumbled. "I've put on five pounds over the last month."

Leah grabbed her arm.

"Hey." Bekah pulled away and scowled at the white handprint on her red sweatshirt.

"Bek." Leah's stare was intense. "Could you be pregnant?"

"Of course not." She couldn't, could she? "Just because I've gained a few pounds and like pickles? That's quite a leap."

"Maybe, but the only time I've ever craved 'em was when I was pregnant." Leah grinned. "Think about it, Bek. When was the last time you had a period?"

Bekah's pulse leapt, and her mouth went dry. "You know I've never been regular. That's why I haven't been able to get pregnant." That didn't mean it was impossible. "Why, after all these years?" She thought back to that day almost two years ago she and Mitch discussed in vitro. They'd tried for six years before that. Eight years total. *How long did Abraham and Sarah have to wait?*

"Let's go get a pregnancy test." Leah snatched up a dishtowel and wiped her hands. "I'll see if my next-door neighbor can watch the kids for a few minutes."

"Stop." Bekah grabbed Leah's arm. "This is crazy. We got six pies to make still. And it'll take a whole lot longer than a few minutes at the store the day before Thanksgiving." And Bekah was terrified of being disappointed. Of course, she wasn't pregnant. She didn't need to rush out in holiday traffic to prove it.

"We'll go to the pharmacy. No reason a crowd'll be there. If we don't go now, we gotta wait until Friday, Bek. Do you really wanna wait that long?"

Bekah covered a grin with her fingers. It'd been more than three months since her last cycle. Had she gone that long before? "But what if I'm not?"

"Only one way to find out." Leah tugged on Bekah's hand. "If you're not, then you're no worse off. Right?"

Wrong. She'd gotten used to the disappointment. But to build up hope again only to have it dashed? That'd be so much worse.

Leah wasn't taking no for an answer. Within fifteen minutes, she and Bekah were driving to the pharmacy. Bekah's heart hammered in her chest so hard, she feared she'd have an attack before she could pee on the stick. And when they discovered the pharmacy had closed early, tears bit at the back of her eyes.

Bekah sniffled. "Guess we'll have to wait for Friday after all." This is what hope did to a person.

"Not on your life." Leah patted Bekah's hand before zipping out of the parking lot.

The parking lot at Kroger's grocery store looked like the mall on Black Friday. And if they thought the lot was full, the store was a proverbial zoo. Every register had a line of overflowing shopping carts halfway across the store. They worked their way through the maze of people to the pharmacy section where Leah snatched up a test kit, grabbed Bekah's hand, and headed to the registers.

"Why do people wait 'til the last minute?" grumbled Leah.

Bekah bounced from one foot to the other. "You mean like us?"

Leah scowled. "You know what I mean." She tapped the woman ahead of them. "Excuse me, ma'am?"

The elderly lady turned. "Yes?"

"We only have one item." She held up the pregnancy test. "Would you mind letting us go ahead of you?"

The woman's eyes widened, and she smiled. "Certainly." She scooted her cart so Leah and Bekah could pass. "Good luck."

Heat rose to Bekah's cheeks. Did Leah have no shame?

Apparently not, because her sister then eased closer to the man in front of them.

"No, you don't," Bekah hissed, pulling her back. "It's one thing to embarrass me in front of that nice woman, but don't you dare show that man the pregnancy test."

Leah rolled her eyes. "Fine. Be that way."

It was almost an hour later before Leah parked her car into the driveway. "You go on up to my bathroom and take care of this while I release my neighbor."

"Shouldn't I wait until morning?" She'd heard somewhere that it was more accurate that way.

"If you're already gaining weight, I'm sure you're far enough along that it doesn't matter."

Bekah snuck in the front door and eased up the stairs. The television blared from the family room, where she had no doubt four pairs of eyes were glued. Leah and Gabe's bedroom was tucked into the far corner of the house. She slipped into the bathroom, closed the door, and turned on the light to read the directions on the box while her heart hammered in her throat.

Could she really be pregnant? Wouldn't that be the perfect Thanksgiving announcement to make at the family dinner? Her sweaty hands were fumbling to retrieve the test when the door burst open.

"Well?" Leah pinned her with wide eyes.

"For the love of all that's holy." Bekah pushed past her and slammed the door closed again. "I'm just reading the directions."

"Directions?" Leah pretended to pull out her hair. "You pee on the stick. You need directions to tell you that?"

Bekah clamped her jaw and drew in a deep breath. "Do you mind? I don't need y'all standing over me like a crazed prison guard." She waved her hand toward the door. "Git now. I'll come out when I'm done."

"But—"

"Go!" Bekah shooed her away. Alone again, she closed her eyes and willed her heart rate to slow. It wouldn't be the end of the world if she wasn't pregnant. Leah's kids drove her clear out of her mind, so she wasn't even sure she really wanted one of her own. *Yeah, you keep telling yourself that, and maybe you'll actually buy it.*

Bekah did a quick read-through of the directions. She'd been right. It said it'd be best if she waited until first thing in the morning. But now Leah had gone and got her so excited, there was no way she'd be able to hold off until then.

Aside from waiting, she followed the directions to a T as if even one slip up would produce a negative result. Once done, she laid the stick on a piece of tissue paper on the bathroom counter and washed her hands. One to five minutes. She couldn't do this alone. Rushing to the door, she pulled it open and collided with Leah. They were a tangle of body parts for five full seconds.

Leah grabbed her by the shoulders. "So?"

"I don't know yet. Come wait with me." She grabbed her sister's hand, yanked her inside, and closed the door behind them. They moved across the small bathroom connected as if one entity, their eyes glued to the pregnancy stick.

"How long's it been?" Leah whispered.

Bekah shrugged. "I don't know. Maybe a minute." She stared so hard, her eyes watered. At first, she thought she was seeing things when the red cross began to appear. Rubbing her eyes, she bent closer. "Do you see it?"

Leah squealed. "It's a plus sign. My baby sister's gonna have a baby."

The more Bekah wiped her eyes, the more tears filled them. Giddiness bubbled up her throat until she couldn't contain the joy. "Yes!" she screamed. "We're gonna have a baby."

Mitch

As an only child with no kin to speak of, holidays with Bekah's family was a bittersweet affair. Since Mitch's mama had remarried three years before and moved back to Foley, Alabama, he often felt like an outsider when surrounded by the Millers. Like a kid with his nose pressed against the glass, wishing he belonged. How was it he could be in the company of so many people and still feel alone?

Miss Anita had invited Mitch's mama and her husband Eric to come up for Thanksgiving, but she'd declined. Eric had his own family traditions. "You know how it is, Mitch," Mama had said on the phone last night. "Y'all are welcome to come on down and spend the day with us, but I know how close Rebekah is with her own kin."

It wasn't like Bekah's family didn't care for him. Heck, Joe was his best friend. Maybe it was being kid-less. Everyone else had more than their fair share. He'd been working on Bekah to rethink adoption, but she'd dug in her heels. The way she talked, you'd of thought God was going to drop a baby on their doorstep if it was to happen at all. It was a shame. She'd of made a great mama.

He pondered all this on his way home from delivering the last load for the day. Always got a bit melancholy at the beginning of the holiday season, and he was in no hurry to get home. Bekah had been at Leah's all day baking pies. Doubtless, she'd be full of anecdotes about her sister's crazy kids and how he and Bek might've missed a bullet not having any of their own. It was a load of malarky. He saw how her eyes melted every time they lit on a baby. If she thought she could talk her way out of wanting kids, she was one knife short of a set.

At near six, it was already dark when he pulled his flatbed into the drive. Lights shone through the windows—a soft welcoming glow—and he could see Bekah moving about in the kitchen. After a day of baking, she was probably exhausted. Why didn't he think to pick up supper on his way home and save her the trouble of cooking?

He collected the lunch cooler and coat and climbed from the truck. A faint, mouthwatering aroma of Italian seasoning tickled his nose as he moved up the walkway. If he wasn't mistaken, it was Bocelli's pizza—his favorite. Was he married to the perfect woman, or what? She kept his load schedule booked, took care of the house, and even after a full day of holiday baking, plied him with pizza and beer.

"Bek?" He called out as he opened the front door. "Is that Bocelli's I'm smelling?"

She stepped from the kitchen, wiping her hands on a dishtowel, and offered a killer smile. Where was the exhaustion he thought would line her face and weigh her shoulders down? "Hope you're hungry, babe. I got a large."

He tossed his coat over the back of the recliner, set his cooler in the seat, and moved in for a hug. "Starving." He nibbled at her lips then nuzzled her neck. "I could eat something too."

She giggled. "Cute."

"Didn't you go to Leah's today?"

"Uh huh." She walked her fingers through his hair.

"I figured you'd be tuckered out after baking and battling kids all day."

"I got my second wind." She took his hand. "Pizza will be ready in a bit. Come sit down with me for a minute. I need to tell you something."

Normally, a fist to his gut would accompany those words, but how could it be bad when she looked ready to burst with joy? "Okay. Mind if I grab a beer first?"

"Sure."

"You want one?"

She shook her head and slid to the corner of the couch. "I'll just wait here for you."

Mitch stopped in the kitchen entrance and glanced back at Bekah. She was fidgeting like a kid with ants in her pants, clasping and unclasping her hands. She plucked the pillow from the couch and hugged it against her chest then shoved it aside. Maybe it wasn't joy he sensed after all.

"Forget the beer." He dropped onto the couch next to her and reached for her fidgeting hands. "You okay?"

She nodded like the bobblehead he had sitting on his truck dash. "Great." She squeezed his fingers.

"Great. So, what's goin' on?"

She drew in a deep breath and blew it out. "When I was at Leah's today, I got a craving for dill pickles, and—"

"Pickles?" Was this just one of her niece or nephew stories? Maybe he should've gotten that beer.

"Yes. Just listen." She rolled her eyes. "Anyway, I was peeling apples for pies, and I got this hankering. When I told Leah, she made this crazy leap about cravings and pregnancy. Then she insisted we go to the store, and—hold on." She jumped up and disappeared down the hall toward their bedroom.

Mitch scratched his head. What happened to his level-headed wife between leaving this morning and coming home tonight?

Bekah speed-walked back into the family room and thrust something toward him. "Here." It was some sort of plastic stick.

Mitch took it from her. "What's this?"

"Look at the end, babe. What d'you see?" She dropped next to him.

He squinted at the little window. "I don't know. A cross?"

She jabbed her finger at it. "It's a plus sign. Get it?"

Pickle craving. Pregnancy. Plus sign. Did she mean...? "Is this what I think it is?" Mitch's heart rate spiked and captured his breath.

"I'm pregnant, Mitch," She squealed. "We're pregnant!"

"Pregnant?" After all these years? Wasn't he just scoffing at Bekah's assurance that if her God wanted them to have a baby, He'd drop it on their doorstep like some divine stork?

"As soon as we found out, I called Dr. Lenora's office. We got an appointment on Tuesday. I thought maybe I'd schedule you light that day, you know, so you can be with me."

"Pregnant?" It's all Mitch could think to say. Bekah was gonna be a mama, and he was...How could he be any kind of father after the one he had?

"What's wrong, Mitch? You look a little...I don't know...sick." Bekah laid her hand on his cheek. "You're happy about it, right? I mean, I know we kinda thought it wasn't ever gonna happen."

"Of course, I'm happy. Caught me off guard is all." The words came out shaky and unsure. "You're gonna be such an amazing mama, Bek."

"Mitch, look at me." She tugged his hand. "Tell me what's got you looking as if you lost your best friend."

He shook his head as if he could clear the doubts. "I'm thrilled, Bek. A little scared, maybe. I mean, my own daddy wasn't worth spit. Doesn't mean I won't be."

"You're nothing like your daddy, Mitch. You're the most loving, loyal man I know. Bad parenting isn't hereditary, you know."

Mitch hoped not. But he wasn't like Bekah's daddy, either. John Miller had wisdom deep down, which he claimed came from knowing God. Mitch didn't have that. Might never have that. Didn't mean he wouldn't love his kid, though. That was the most important thing. Love.

"We've been waiting so long for this, babe." Bekah snuggled against his chest. "Please tell me you're happy about it."

Mitch held her tight. "If you never give me anything else ever, Bek, I'd still be the happiest man in the world." And if there truly was a God in heaven, he'd be a good daddy, too, despite his upbringing.

Chapter Eighteen

Rebekah

It didn't matter we were heading into August, the hottest month of the year. The sun didn't seem as bright or the air as warm with Mama gone. It just proved what I'd always suspected—her love made my whole world shine. Daddy's, too, I was sure.

Dan had said everyone was worried I'd not be able to handle the loss while still struggling with Jonathon's death. I'd had concerns of my own. And even though I missed Mama something fierce, it didn't weigh on me like I'd expected. Maybe it was because Mama was ready. No doubt she loved us all, but I knew she loved Jesus more. It was right that the Lord didn't drag out her illness until she was wracked with pain. It was a merciful kindness.

Jonathon was just getting to know who Jesus was when he was taken away. Mama would have said his death was the sovereign plan of God, but I couldn't get past the knowledge that Mitch was right there and failed to save him. Was that God's sovereign plan or the failure of one man?

Oh, Lord, why can't I get past this? I know it's wrong. Sinful to blame Mitch. Help me to see things through Your eyes, Jesus. I'd whispered this prayer through-out the night. Every time I woke with a heavy heart, tossing and turning on my childhood bed. There'd been too few peaceful nights over the last fourteen months, and I knew it came from a dark place deep inside.

I dragged myself downstairs the next morning, my eyes weighed down by exhaustion. If I thought I'd be able to sleep, I'd have ignored the alarm. I wasn't looking forward to the day, as Daddy had asked that Leah and I go through Mama's things. Seemed too soon to me, and it wasn't like he needed the closet space. But grief was a private thing, and if this would offer him a modicum of comfort, who was I to argue?

"Mornin' darlin'," Daddy said as I stepped into the kitchen. Once Mama was gone, he'd reverted to his usual routine as if nothing had changed. But I knew it had. Sometimes routine was all we could cling to when our world slid off kilter.

"Mornin'," I mumbled as I made a beeline to the coffee. An intravenous drip of caffeine was what I needed, but as Mama used to say, "beggars can't be choosers."

"You and Leah gonna take care of your mama's things this morning?"

"Yes, sir." I slid onto the chair across from him and dipped my toe in to test the waters. "If that's what you really want."

"I don't need your mama's clothes around me to remember her by, Bek. Besides, I'd rather see you and your sister wearing her things than have them stuffed away in the closet and drawers."

Despite the topic of conversation, a smile tugged at my heart. "I don't think any of Mama's things'll fit either one of us, Daddy." Not in size or style. Although Mama had lost weight over the last couple months, she'd been of good German stock. Leah and I could both fit into one of her blouses.

He frowned. "I suppose not. But she's got herself some real pretty pieces of jewelry the two of you should divvy up. And y'all will need to decide what to do with her weddin' ring."

I pressed a hand to my heart as if it could ease the ache. "That's something you should hold onto. Might wanna offer it to the first grandchild who gets married." Which I'd have no part of, given the circumstances.

He wagged his head. "No, darlin', I'd rather you or Leah take it. You can decide between you."

"Yes, sir." No sense in arguing with him, although I had no intention of laying claim to Mama's ring.

It wasn't a couple hours later I had just finished the outside chores when Leah's SUV came down the drive. I stood on the porch and squinted to see through the glare on the windshield. Was she alone? I surely hoped so. I didn't have the patience or stamina to put on a cheerful front for the kids.

She parked and jumped out. "Hey, there."

"Hey, yourself. You bring any of the kids?"

"I thought we could both use the peace and quiet of a few hours, so no."

I gave her a hug and led the way inside. "You prepared for this? 'Cause I'm certainly not."

"What's Daddy's big hurry, anyway?" Leah slid her purse onto the kitchen table. "I figured he'd of held onto every bit of Mama as long as he could."

"I don't know." I shrugged. "It might be harder on him to have the reminders. Every time I open their closet, I get a definite whiff of Mama's sweet scent. Makes it near impossible not to curl up on the floor and cry." Even as I recounted this, tears fisted in my throat.

Leah rubbed my arm. "You've had more than your share of loss, little sister. Let's get this done, and I'll take you to lunch after. My mother-in-law's got the kids until three, and I intend to take advantage of it."

We headed down the hallway to the bedroom. "Daddy seems to think we might want some of Mama's clothes," I said. "I told him nothing of hers would fit."

"I was thinking we should just fold everything up and take it to Goodwill. I have some boxes and large plastic bags in the back of my car. First thing we should do is separate out what's what."

"Let's start in the closet." I took an armful of clothes and deposited them on the bed. Sure enough, a whiff of Mama's scent rose in the air and snagged at my emotions.

Leah separated a blouse from its hanger. "How're you doin' with everything? I gotta say, you look like a strong wind could knock you over."

"Truth?" I gave her a crooked smile. "I'm lost. And it's not just missin' Mama." I tossed a hanger into the pile. "I feel like I'm sitting out in the middle of the ocean with no anchor. Just drifting through life without a plan."

Her gaze caught mine. "I don't mean to sound critical, Bek, but it's not like that's new. You've been there since Jonathon passed."

"Don't I know it. But somehow, when Mama was around, she had a way of at least pointing me in a direction, even if I didn't move forward." I smoothed the wrinkles from one of Mama's Sunday dresses. "Does that make sense?"

"Not really, no." Leah sat on the mess of clothes on the bed and tugged on my hand, so I'd join her. "You've been in the driver's seat from the get-go, kiddo. If you're not moving forward, you're the only one who can figure out why." That was the closest Leah had come to saying I made my bed, now I had to lie in it.

"I know y'all think I was wrong to leave Mitch like I did."

"No one has a right to judge you, Bek. We haven't had to walk in your shoes, so we can't know what you're goin' through."

"That doesn't mean you don't have an opinion." I sighed. "The thing is, if I could find my way to forgiving Mitch, I'd do it. I know it's wrong, but I don't know how to change it."

"You know what Mama would say."

I couldn't help but smile. "Pray, of course." My eyes caught hers. "I've been doing that, and maybe in time, things will work themselves out. But I don't know if I have time."

"What're you talkin' about?" Leah's voice pitched and her eyes widened. "You're not sick, are you?"

I shook my head. "It's not me, it's Mitch. And no, he isn't sick. It might be he's done waiting on me, is all."

Leah snorted. "Where'd you get such a ridiculous notion?"

"It's not, Leah. Dan told him the day of Mama's funeral that I was thinking of movin' to Atlanta."

"Atlanta? Wherever did he get that idea?"

"From me." I fingered one of Mama's blouses. "I mentioned it a while back. Thought maybe having a fresh start would be a good idea. I didn't expect him to blab it to Mitch, though."

"You're not seriously thinking of moving to Atlanta, are you?"

"Not anymore, no. So, I told Mitch that the last time I saw him, when he dropped Caleb off. He acted like it didn't make a difference one way or the other. Like he'd already moved on."

She nudged my shoulder with hers. "He's just playing it cool, Bek. Don't you get all worked up about it."

"I don't know." I worried my bottom lip. If Leah had seen how blasé he was, she might not be so confident.

"So, ask him."

"What d'you mean? Just flat out ask him if he's done with me?" I let out a nervous laugh. "I don't think so."

"What d'you have to lose? Maybe it'd at least open up some communication between the two of you."

I shook my head. "The last time we had any communication, it ended in a fight." An idea came to mind. "But I bet Joe would know. I could talk to him about it. If anyone might know what Mitch's thinking, it's Joe."

Leah took my hand and tugged. "No, Bekah. If anyone knows what Mitch is thinkin', it's Mitch. Don't go putting Joe in the middle of your marriage. How many times have you told him to stay out of it? Now that it could work in your favor, you're gonna involve him?" She glared at me. "Not fair."

She was right. And really, like she'd said, what was the worst that could happen? I'd been pushing Mitch away for months. If he'd finally gotten the memo, I had no one to blame but myself.

Mitch

For the first time since Bekah had left, I was finally moving in some direction, even if I didn't know where it would lead. Once I told Brother Paul I was studying the book of Mark with John, he decided I should limit my community service hours to Saturdays. Used to be I'd come home from work and veg out on the couch until I couldn't keep my eyes open. But once I'd started with the Max Lucado study, TV didn't hold much appeal.

I sat at the kitchen table and unpeeled the foil from my once-frozen supper. The Bible Paul had given me, the study book from John, and a pen at the ready. We were meeting up the next evening, John and me, and even though half of what I read raised more questions than answers, I was going to give it my best. It beat fretting over Bekah all to heck.

Eyes following the Bible verses, I popped a bite of food into my mouth without tasting it. Mark was telling a story about Jesus healing a man with leprosy. The guy had kneeled in front of Jesus and said, "If you are willing, you can make me clean." So, why was it Jesus was willing to heal some and not others? What did it come down to? I already knew there was no such thing as a "good" person, because sure enough if there was, Miss Anita would have qualified. But Jesus didn't heal her. And he didn't save Jonathon, either.

I was pondering these questions when the doorbell cut into my thoughts. The house was closed up and the air conditioner blasting, so no surprise I hadn't heard anyone come up the drive. A quick glance out the window didn't reveal a car, so maybe a neighbor stopping by. What they'd want with me, I couldn't guess. Had half a mind to ignore it, but it'd be like thumbing my nose at Jesus since I was in the middle of reading Scripture.

I threw open the door and surprise snatched my voice clear from me. Last person I'd have expected was Bekah. Glancing beyond her, I asked, "Where's your car?"

"Parked it on the street. It's too hard to turn around with your big rig in the driveway." She stood on the porch like she didn't have every right to enter. "Probably shouldn't have just shown up like this, but if I called, I'd of lost my nerve."

The possibilities ran through my mind. Was she here to demand that divorce she'd threatened a couple months back? I thought she might be coming around, but Bekah was as unpredictable as a tornado. Just never could tell which direction she was going to blow.

"You're lucky I was even home," I finally managed. "Been doing a lot of hours at the church."

"I didn't think of that." She raised her eyebrows. "You gonna let me in and offer me a glass of tea, or would you rather talk on the porch?"

I swung the door open with a quick glance at the family room. It wasn't a disaster. I'd at least picked up some and even run the vacuum a couple weeks back. "Come on in. Make yourself at home." Lame, since it was her home.

She stepped inside, her gaze sweeping across the room. "Mind if I get myself some tea?"

I pictured the Bible study books sitting on the table. "Let me get it for you. Have a seat."

In the kitchen, I stacked the books and slipped them into the pantry before getting her tea. My supper, now cold, hadn't been all that appealing when it was hot. Now it was just a pathetic commentary on my single status. Was Bekah here to make sure that was permanent?

I joined Bekah in the family room where she was sitting on the couch, hands tucked between her bare knees. Her hair was pulled back in its usual ponytail, exposing her features. Although the late evening sun was slipping behind the sugar maple in the backyard, there was still enough light coming through the window to see her clearly. There were shadows beneath her eyes. A sure sign she wasn't sleeping much. I didn't imagine things had gotten easier since her mama's passing.

Bekah accepted the icy glass from me and took a sip before setting it on the coffee table. "Did you have your supper?"

I hitched my thumb toward the kitchen. "Was in the middle of it when you showed."

"Oh." She wiped her hands on her shorts. "I'm sorry. I don't want to interrupt."

"It'll keep. Easy enough to pop it into the microwave again." I perched on the edge of the recliner and rested my elbows on my knees. Calm, cool, and collected. At least that's how I aimed to appear. Truth of it was, I felt anything but.

"I won't be long." She blew out a breath, her gaze skipping around the room. "It's just, I thought maybe we should talk. You know, about us."

I waited. No sense in jumping in when I wasn't sure how deep the water was.

"The other day..." She cleared her throat and reached for her tea. A couple gulps later, she put it down again. "I know Dan told you I was thinking of moving to Atlanta."

I nodded. Had she changed her mind? Wouldn't be the first time.

"And then, the other day, I told you I wasn't." She flicked her fingers across her bangs. It was a rare occurrence that Bekah was nervous, and it caused my shoulders to tense. "You didn't react."

So caught up trying to figure out what she'd say, her words didn't quite register. "Excuse me?" Had I missed something?

"When I said I wasn't moving. You acted like it didn't mean anything to you one way or the other."

I raked a hand through my hair. "What'd you want me to say, Bek? One moment, you're telling me you want a divorce, that you can't barely stand to look at me. Then I hear you were planning on moving out to Georgia. Now, you say you're not moving, and you expect me to what? To drop down on my knees in gratitude? Beg you to come back?" I clenched my jaw. "Been there, done that. You're all over the place, and I can't keep up."

"I know." She threw her hands up. "Believe me, no one's more frustrated with me than me."

I barked out a laugh. "I wouldn't bet on it."

She dropped her gaze to her lap. "I'm trying to work through things, Mitch. I know I've been unfair to you. Believe me, I do." She tilted her head and dared a look at me. "I guess your reaction threw me off, and I got to thinking maybe you don't care if I work through things. Maybe you've already moved on."

The girl was running hot one minute and cold the next. Impossible. "You're not gonna accuse me of dating again, are you?"

She shrugged. "I couldn't blame you if you did."

If this kept up, I'd be certifiable. "You need to figure out what you want, Bekah. I get you're in a tough spot, what with your mama passing. But you've pushed me away for more than a year, and now you talk like you might could change your mind."

Tears pooled in her eyes. "What I want is to be able to look at you and not see Jonathon lying dead by the pool." She sniffled. "Whenever I see a picture of him, I wonder if he'd have grown to be as handsome as his daddy. Would he of had the same dimples as you? Would his hair be just as thick and curly? I don't want to be reminded of what we lost; I want to be reminded of what we had. And I know I'm making you crazy. I'm making *me* crazy. But I don't know how to fix it."

Her sobs drew me from my chair, and I sat on the couch beside her. She fell into my arms, and I could do nothing but hold her while she cried. My own throat grew thick, and I longed to be able to take her pain away. But I was just a man grappling with a loss of my own. When her tears were spent, she sat up and swiped at her eyes.

"I can't fix this for you, Bekah." I fingered a strand of damp hair off her face. "You wanna go to counseling, I'm in. But until you can come to a place of forgiveness and trust, this isn't gonna work between us. You get that, right?"

She nodded and sniffled while my heart broke just a little more for her. And for me. I could only hope, and pray, that her confusion was a good thing. First step toward a change was realizing we didn't have all the answers. It's what led me to seek out the Bible for myself. Maybe it would lead Bekah to a place of healing.

As I watched from the porch while she walked down the drive, I glanced up to find a lone star twinkling high above us. *If You're there, God, we could sure use Your help.* There was no answer, but for the first time, I trusted there might be one on the horizon.

Chapter Nineteen

Rebekah

When I left Mitch the night before, it was with a blend of despair and embarrassment interwoven with a smidgen of hope. Sobbing in his arms like a lost babe wasn't my finest moment. Still, he'd treated me with tenderness, and it was a reminder of what I'd given up with my bitterness and accusations. If all I needed to move past the tangle of emotions that had me going every which way was prayer and determination, I would be golden. But it wasn't near enough. At least not yet.

I was grateful to have the distraction of work to dilute all the craziness bouncing around in my head. And Darlene must've sensed it was what I needed, because she didn't allow me to slip into the basement, which was my preferred work environment.

"You ain't hiding yourself away in the dungeon like some kinda hermit," Darlene said the moment I walked in the door. "You been doin' this long enough, it's time you worked with the customers."

"I barely know one end of a candlestick from another," I protested.

"Hands on is the best way to learn. Jenna's home with sick kids today, so I could really use your help."

It was a Wednesday afternoon, which was always our slowest time, so she was employing the art of manipulation. Why, I didn't know. But she was the boss, so no point in arguing.

Fortunately, most everyone who walked through the door had a clear vision of what they wanted, so my minuscule expertise wasn't necessary. It left me time to study the displays and identify why one particular gewgaw was paired with another. Was it a color scheme or height or patterns that made the difference? Or maybe those with a keen eye for decor were born to it, like I was born to ride horses. Now if someone needed to pair just the right pad with a saddle, or bridle with reins, then I was their girl.

"Bekah." Darlene stuck her head in the parlor where I'd been examining Charlie's newest decor display. "Someone here to see ya. Y'all wanna take a break, now's a good time."

My heart rate hitched. "Is it Mitch?"

"Not unless he's now a blond bombshell. It's the woman what come lookin' for you a couple weeks back."

Kimberley. The girl could learn to use a cell phone.

When I stepped into the foyer, Kimberley was running her hand across the antique buffet that was showcased for maximum viewing. I hadn't seen but one person walk past it without a double take, and that included me. I'd of been tempted to buy it myself if I'd been back in my own home. Then again, even me, with my limited decor experience, knew this wasn't a piece that would blend with bargain-budget ranch.

"Beautiful, isn't it?" I said, drawing Kimberley's attention.

"Oh, hey, Bekah." She glanced back at it. "Yeah, it would be the start of my downfall. First this piece, then another. Before I know it, I'd be surrounded by furniture that would outshine my apartment. And you know where that would lead."

I smiled. "A new apartment?"

"No. Bankruptcy." She laughed. "Hope you don't mind I stopped by. Wanted to check and see how your daddy was doin'." It was a curious connection she had to Mama and Daddy. Might be worth delving into.

"Would you like something to drink? We could sit out front. It's hot, but the ceiling fans put off enough of a breeze to make it tolerable."

"Sure. Sounds good."

Once settled into a wicker chair, I took a sip of my tea and gazed over the porch railing. Cicadas buzzed while cardinals darted from tree to tree. Charlie had planted Rose of Sharon, delphinium, and red columbine around the perimeter of the porch to attract hummingbirds and butterflies. With the fans spinning overhead, it was like sitting in a private garden in a little piece of heaven. Eden maybe.

"So, your daddy. How's he doin'?" Kim set her glass of tea on the table between our chairs.

I ran my thumb along the condensation of the icy glass. "He's a strong man with a deep faith." I offered a smile. "I don't doubt he's missing Mama something fierce, but you wouldn't know it to look at him."

"I'm sure things are easier on him what with y'all bein' close." Her eyes followed the path of a black and purple butterfly flitting along the pink blooms of the Rose of Sharon. "You're lucky that way." A tinge of wistfulness colored her tone and spurred me toward finding some answers.

"Before Mama passed, she told me she and Daddy knew you were in a bad way back when we were in high school."

Kim stiffened as though I hit a nerve. "Y'all were talkin' about me?"

"I suppose. It wasn't like we were gossiping or anything. The night I quit the restaurant, Mama asked wouldn't I miss my friends there. I told her I didn't really make any, except maybe you."

Kim's head snapped around and her mouth dropped open. "You told your mama we were friends?" The way she looked at me, you'd have thought I handed her a gift. Might be I had.

"Not in so many words, but yeah, sort of. I asked Mama if she knew you, and she did. Said she and Daddy offered you help, but you refused."

Kim dropped her head with a shrug. "I didn't think they'd even remember me. Then when I said hey to your daddy at your house that day, he treated me like I was long lost kin. It was a shock." She glanced over at me. "A good one, though."

"If that's true, then do you mind me asking why you turned them down? I don't mean to pry, but it sounded like things were rough on you. They could of made it some easier."

Her mouth twisted. "You mean 'cause my daddy was a drunk?" She blew out a sigh. "He was a piece of work, all right."

"Then why not take the offer of help? Were you embarrassed or ashamed? Because if that's it, we'd have never made you feel that way. At least not intentionally."

"Oh, Bekah, I know that." She offered a soft smile. "As far as I was concerned, your mama and daddy were like something straight out of a 50s sitcom. I mean, your whole family seemed too good to be true."

I snorted. "Believe me, we had our moments. Still do. There's no such thing as perfection this side of heaven." It was something I'd heard Mama say on numerous occasions.

"I get that, but it's not how it seemed to me."

"But you didn't want their help."

"You gotta understand, Bekah, how messed up my daddy was. Mama up and left him—left the both of us. It was mostly his own fault. He was never an easy person to live with. But it really broke him. That's when the drinking started."

"Must have been awful for you." If it'd been me, I'd have hightailed it out as fast as I could.

"This is a small town. If I'd run off to stay with your family, imagine the shame he'd have felt. First his wife, then his daughter? I just couldn't do that to him. Angry as he'd make me, it just seemed wrong to add to his pain."

Heat stole up my neck and settled in my cheeks as her words took root. Until recently, I thought Kimberley was a stuck-up snob-of-a-girl, and here she was proving to be more charitable than me. I had no inclination if she had a relationship with Jesus, which was something I'd claimed numerous times.

"Bekah? You okay? You look a little flushed." Kimberley stared at me, a frown marring her features.

"I'm fine." I swiped at the perspiration that dampened my bangs. I didn't know her well enough to open up about Mitch and me, but it seemed she had some explanation owed her. "You took me off guard, is all. I don't know that I'd be half as kind or sympathetic as you if I were in your shoes."

"I don't believe that. Your mama and daddy taught you right. I mean, you said your daddy has a strong faith, right?"

I nodded.

"Must've taught you the same." She took a sip of her tea then wiped her damp hands on her shorts. "Me? I don't hold much to religion."

No, but she still acted more Christlike with her daddy than I'd been with Mitch. And, really, there was no comparison. Mitch was a good man, and he'd been a good daddy. I had no reason to fault him as a husband, but it didn't stop me from walking out. Left him to deal with whatever shame came from it without a second thought.

Lord, it's a wonder You don't just strike me down where I sit. I don't want to be this person. Please help me find my way back to You. Help me find my way out of this pit I've climbed into.

"I should let you get back to work." Kimberley's words broke into my prayer. "Thanks for takin' the time to talk to me. Tell your daddy I said hi."

"Maybe you should stop by the house and see him for yourself." It could be the Lord was sending her as my personal Holy Spirit. Never would I have expected guidance to come by way of Kimberley St. Clair. Then again, if God could use a donkey to speak wisdom, He could surely use anyone.

Mitch

It was curious how things had taken a detour since I'd made the decision to delve into the Bible. I wasn't ready to lay it at God's feet, but I sure couldn't discount Him, either. It was a bizarre turn of events that had me studying with Bekah's dad about a God I'd never given much thought to before everything went sideways.

I'd completed the first lesson in the Bible study John chose before we were to meet. It was all about the compassion Jesus had for a man with leprosy. Made me think on Bekah's visit and how broken she seemed over our separation. It came down to one thing—what was Jesus going to do about it? If He didn't see fit to heal Miss Anita or save Jonathon, what made me think He'd be willing to help Bekah?

Never gave much thought to dust and such, but I swiped a rag over the furniture and ran the vacuum anyway. Didn't imagine John was particular, but I wasn't taking any chances. Didn't matter that Bekah and me had married over fifteen years before. John's disappointment over her choice still rankled. I was going to take what points I could.

I'd been up early and had a full day of deliveries but was wide awake as I set the Bible and study books on the kitchen table. Sweet tea at the ready might keep me from getting the yawns before we were done. We'd had some rain, so I'd left the windows cracked all day, preferring fresh air to manufactured. I heard John's truck pull into the drive right at seven. What had he told Bekah about where he was heading? She wasn't one to be nosy, but him leaving at night had to raise a question or two.

I had the door open before John's foot hit the first tread on the front steps. "Hey, John. Welcome."

He stopped on the porch and turned to gaze at the view. "Been a while since I was out here." Long before Bekah had left.

"Hasn't changed any." I led the way into the kitchen and flipped the switch to turn on the light above the table. "Can I get you something to drink?"

"Sweet tea, if you got it." John deposited a Bible and his own study book along with a pen and a pair of glasses. "You get a chance to finish the lesson?"

"Yes, sir." I slid two glasses of tea onto the table and joined him. "Raised more questions though."

"That's not a bad thing. I'd have been surprised otherwise." He took a gulp of tea and set it aside.

"Bekah ask you where you were headed?"

He gave me a lopsided grin. "Not outright. Think she was afraid of butting in where she don't belong. It'll give her something to think on. Now, let's have a gander at the lesson and see what you came up with."

I flipped to the questions and stabbed a finger on the first one. "This one here got me thinking."

John put his glasses on and peered over at my book. "You remember what the leper said to Jesus?"

I nodded. "Yep. Said if Jesus was willing, He could make him clean. Heal him. I get the leper believed in the power of Jesus. But the way he said it got me thinking." I pinned him with a look. "Jesus had to be willing to do it."

John hunched his shoulders. "You thinkin' about Jonathon?"

"And Miss Anita." I tapped the Bible with a finger. "How d'you know what He's willing to do and what He's not?"

John blew out a breath. "That's a good question, son. You know *The Lord's Prayer*?"

"Parts of it," I admitted. "Never paid much attention."

He scratched his chin. "There's a line in there you might remember. 'Thy kingdom come, Thy will be done.' Meaning that the will of God trumps all else. There are some things we can know are God's will. Promises. Says so in the Bible."

"Like what?"

"Well, for one thing, that when He begins a work in someone, He's faithful to complete it. Means that if you decide to pursue a relationship with Jesus, you're sealed for eternal life. He won't turn His back on you. Doesn't mean you won't go through hard things, or maybe even die before you think it's your time. He knows the time and day of your death before you're even born. Even if you don't believe in Him."

That put a whole new spin on things. "That's what Miss Anita meant about God being sovereign."

John nodded. "There are a whole lot of people that believe they control their lives. Truth is, there's no such thing as control. We might fight it, but if God's got a plan, it's not gonna be taken from Him."

"You think it's God's will that Bekah comes to her senses?" I held my breath waiting for some words of wisdom that might ease my fears.

He chuckled. "You're gonna need to be a little more specific, son. If you're askin' me if I think God wants Bekah to come out on the other end of this season healed and whole, then yes. He hates divorce. Sometimes, He allows hard things to get us where He wants us." He held up a finger of one hand while sliding his Bible in front of him with the other. "There's a Scripture verse that speaks of this. 1 Peter 1:7." He flipped the book open near the back and shuffled through some pages. "Here it is. 'These have come so that your faith—of greater worth than gold, which perishes even though refined by fire—may prove genuine and may result in praise, glory and honor when Jesus Christ is revealed.'" He glanced up at me. "The greatest thing we can claim in this life is faith in Jesus Christ. Sometimes it takes a whole lot of hard stuff to reach that point."

It was a struggle to wrap my head around what he was saying. "You're talking about me, aren't you?" I rested my elbows on the table while a heaviness took hold of my heart. "If I'd have believed in God from the get go, maybe He wouldn't have taken Jonathon like He did."

John clapped a hand on my forearm. "You can't look at it like that, son. You need to remember what I said about the sovereignty of God. He knew Jonathon long before you came into the picture."

I raked a hand through my hair. "This is confusing."

"Might be I threw you into the deep end before you learned how to swim. I don't want you takin' on the blame for your son's death. It was God's will, just like it was His will that he took my wife. We aren't in control. Doesn't mean you don't take the proper precautions and make right decisions."

I huffed out a breath. "Maybe you could remind Bekah of that. She grew up goin' to church and learning all this stuff, and she still blames me."

"We've already talked about that, son. You need to remember this is her time of refinement. God's workin' a stronger faith in her through this. Could be He's using it to open your eyes, as well."

I shifted in my seat. "Have to admit, I never gave much thought to all this before. I know you were disappointed that Bekah married me."

He grimaced. "Don't hold that against me. I'm not claiming to have the wisdom of the good Lord, and sometimes that ol' sin nature rears its ugly head. You been a good husband to Bekah, and right now my disappointment is aimed at her hardheadedness." He pinned me with a glare. "But that's between you and me. If we're gonna work together, one thing you need to know is what's said between us here stays between us. And that goes both ways. I'm not gonna blab things you tell me, neither."

I nodded my agreement and hid a grin behind my hand. Never heard John talk so much before. The man was wiser than I'd given him credit for. Just proved that sometimes the smartest people were the ones who were the quietest. Could be there was another lesson in that for me.

We flipped through the rest of the study, and I didn't have the urge to yawn even once. Energy thrummed throughout my body as we discussed point after point. Even if Jesus wasn't real, it surely seemed living like it was written in the Bible couldn't be a bad thing.

Chapter Twenty

Rebekah

I slid the casserole into the oven and pulled salad fixings from the fridge. Routine was the anchor my soul needed when I didn't know which way was up and couldn't have gotten there if I did. I'd have given a year of my life to snuggle into Mama's comforting embrace once more. Being in her company was like setting my sights on the tangible unconditional love of God. Without her, I was dependent on the still small voice of the Lord. With all the clanging going on in my head, it would've been a wonder if I could hear Him even if he bellowed.

Kimberley's visit the previous day kept pushing its way to the forefront of my thoughts. I'd tamp it down, and it'd spring back up like some bizarre whack-a-mole game. There was no doubt in my mind I was in the wrong holding Mitch accountable for Jonathon's death. My heart wasn't catching up, though. Mitch had said I had to find it in me to forgive and trust him if we were to make a go of our marriage. Maybe counseling *was* what I needed, but I wanted to wait on the Lord to guide me before stepping ahead of Him.

I thought about the Scripture in Ezekiel, which is where my prayers led me as I tore lettuce for the salad. *Lord, I pray you will give me a new heart and put in me a new spirit. Please, Father, remove this old heart of stone and give me a heart of flesh. One that will find forgiveness for the things I wrongly hold Mitch accountable for.* I swiped the moisture from my eyes before cutting into a tomato. Had I been slicing an onion, I could have landed the blame of my tears on that.

Daddy came in through the back door with a nod and crossed to wash up at the kitchen sink. "Supper about ready, Bekah?"

"Yes, sir." I scooped up the tomato chunks and added them to the lettuce.

"You doin' okay? Can't help but notice it's been a while since you've taken Siren out."

"Busy is all."

"Busy, huh? Seems to me it's more than that. You gotta lot on your mind?"

I reached for the salad tongs and turned to him. "Working through a few things." Why had I allowed my life to get so complicated? "I sure miss Mama."

"I hear you, darlin'. I miss her too." He leaned against the sink and folded his arms. "But I'm here. I know you and me don't have the same kinda relationship you had with your mama, but I'm willin' to lend an ear."

My throat went tight, and I rubbed his arm. "I know you are, Daddy. You got enough of your own stuff to worry over without listening to me whine about mine."

"Well, I don't think I've ever heard you whining, as you call it. But you gotta know it helps to take our minds off our own troubles by being a comfort to others. We're all of us in this together, little girl. So, you got something on your mind, I'd like to hear it."

If I needed visible evidence of God's love, it was standing right here in front of me. It wasn't everybody who could claim to have a mama and daddy like mine. "I don't suppose it'll come as a shock to you, but it's about Mitch."

Daddy gave me a crooked smile. "You don't say."

I answered with a smile of my own. "Remember I told you Kimberley dropped by the shop?"

He nodded.

"I asked her why she stuck it out at home all those years ago when things got bad. You know what she said?"

He shrugged. "I could hazard a guess, but that's all it'd be."

The timer beeped for the casserole, and I shut off the oven before turning back to Daddy. "Said she couldn't add to her father's shame by walking out on him like her mama did." The wonder of it hadn't lessened. "Can you believe that? From what little she told me, he was a mean drunk who couldn't hold down a job."

Daddy's eyebrows went up. "So, what's this got to do with Mitch?"

Not wanting to see the disappointment in his eyes, I turned my attention to tossing the salad. "I'm ashamed to admit that she was far more forgiving as a kid than I've ever been. Mitch didn't do anything to deserve me walking out like I did. But just admitting it doesn't fix it. Not really. What I know in my head's not matching up with my heart."

Daddy took the salad from me and carried it to the table. "Might be your mama and me didn't do you any favors by takin' you in after you left Mitch."

"How so?"

"We allowed you to run from your feelings rather than face them. If we hadn't given you a place to hide, might be you and Mitch coulda worked things out sooner." Wasn't that just like him to carry the blame that should have landed on my shoulders?

"Oh, Daddy. That's not true. Even if I didn't come here, I would have found somewhere to run. Y'all gave me a safe place to lick my wounds. Only thing is, I don't know where to go from here."

"Well, darlin', where do you want to go?"

Opening the oven, I reared back from the rush of heat. "It's not that simple." I took the casserole out, placed it on the stovetop, and set the potholders aside. "Mitch says I gotta get over this before we can work things out. Who knows how long that'll take?"

He clucked his tongue while shaking his head. "You think you're gonna do this in your own strength?"

"Yeah, 'cause that's been working out so well for me." I gave him an eye roll then retrieved a couple of plates from the cupboard. "I've been waiting on God to change things, but nothing's happened."

He barked out a laugh. "That ain't the way it works, Bekah. Sometimes, you gotta take a step of faith before the Lord intervenes. Besides which, things *have* changed. A few months back, you carried bitterness around like some kinda shield. I couldn't even bring up Mitch's name and you turned sour as a bushel of lemons." He swept a hand toward me. "You hear yourself now? You know what's in your heart isn't right. You wanna make it better. Am I wrong in supposin' you've been praying on it some?"

"No, sir. It seems my mind's consumed with it lately."

"If that ain't change, girl, I don't know what is. We all of us thought you would crumble like an old barn when your mama passed. But you didn't. Instead, you seemed to grow stronger from the loss."

I thought back to where I was a few months ago. He was right. Wasn't it only a short time ago, I couldn't stand the sight of Mitch? Now, there was a longing I hadn't felt since before Jonathon died.

Daddy scooped chicken casserole onto the plates. "Look darlin', I know I promised to give you all the space you need, but it might be time you took that step of faith we was talkin' about."

"In what way?"

He carried the plates to the table while I followed. "You need to move back in with your husband so the two of you can work through all this."

I dropped into the chair. "He made it pretty clear last time we talked that I'd need to get over myself first."

Daddy scooped salad onto his plate and slid it my way. "He really say that, Bekah? 'Cause it don't sound like the Mitch I know."

"The two of you haven't had more than a couple conversations since we've been married." One visit, and Daddy was suddenly an expert on Mitch. "Besides, Mama's been gone only a couple weeks. I can't just up and leave here like that."

"Oh no, you don't." He waggled a finger at me. "You ain't gonna use me as an excuse for stayin' separated from your husband. If you and Mitch had still been together when your mama passed, would you of left him to come take care of me?"

I squirmed under his glare. He was playing hardball, just like when I was a kid. "I suppose not."

"You might think I can't take care of myself, but I can. Just 'cause I miss your mama something fierce don't mean I'm goin' to fall to pieces. She wouldn't want that."

I plopped a serving of salad onto my plate. "But Daddy, I'm not so sure I'm ready to take that step yet. Last thing I want is to fail at this again and hurt Mitch even more."

He placed his hand on mine. "Let me bless the food before it gets cold."

While Daddy prayed over the meal, my mind was so wrapped up in the what ifs, I didn't hear a word. Might be Mitch wasn't all too keen on me coming back. Why didn't he pounce on the chance when I was blubbering like a baby the other night?

"Amen," Daddy finished.

"Amen," I mumbled.

Daddy cut into his casserole with the side of his fork. "You remember the time we went out to Norris Lake, and you were fearful of jumping into the water? You were just a little tyke at the time."

Most would have thought Daddy had switched to a new line of conversation, but I knew better. He was getting ready to make a point. "Was that the one where you bribed me to jump off of the boat dock?"

"That's the one." He pointed his fork at me. "You fought me for the longest time, but I promised if you took the leap, I'd be sure to catch you. Remember?"

"I do. If I remember correctly, I wore you out after I realized how much fun it was."

"But the first plunge, Bekah. That was a leap of faith. The only way you were gonna learn to trust me was to take that step."

"The thing is, how do I know God's gonna catch me like you did?"

He waited for me to look at him before continuing. "'Cause as much as I love you, darlin', it can't begin to touch the love the Lord has for you. He's just waitin' on you to trust Him."

Mitch

Until the day I breathed my last, being around a swimming pool would trigger memories best left alone. Hard to hang out on a summer night with Joe and Cassie without the faint scent of chlorine, the occasional splash of pool water, and squeal of kids to accompany the visit. No sense dampening the fun with my own baggage.

We gathered on the patio and finished up our meal while Jane and Gracie splashed in the shallow end of the built-in pool. Caleb sat on the side with his feet dangling into the water. It was quite a setup they had, which attested to Joe's success. Cassie's too, for that matter. They were a team. Like Bekah and me had once been.

"Y'all get enough to eat?" Cassie started to clear the dishes. "I got some homemade ice cream in the freezer. Peach, strawberry, or chocolate."

"Let me help with those." I hopped up, but Cassie waved me back down.

"I won't hear of it. I'm gonna whip these out, and then we can have dessert. Besides, you did enough bringing me that Annabelle hydrangea. Everywhere I looked, they were sold out."

"It was nothing," I said. "Don't know where my business would be right now if you hadn't jumped in and helped. I owe you a whole lot more than a plant."

"It's nothing." She tapped Joe on the shoulder. "You keep an eye out on the kids, will you?" She gave him a pointed look before hauling a stack of plates inside.

Joe prodded me with his foot. "We can all go inside, Mitch. The kids can find something to do besides swim."

"On a hot August night like this?" I snagged my glass of tea. "Wouldn't think of it. Besides, it looks like Caleb's having a blast." The little boy giggled whenever Jane or Gracie splashed him. Still wasn't saying anything, but he did grin a lot.

"Just wish he'd talk," Joe said. "Been here goin' on a month, and still nothing. Grief's a strange thing."

"Don't I know it." Hadn't I spent the last year or more wallowing in it myself?

"You gonna take Caleb to Bekah's tomorrow? She told me she set some time aside to work with him. They seem to be hitting it off, don't they?"

Last time I saw Bekah, her heart was near broke. But that was an improvement, even if it was harder to stomach than her coldness. "About that, Joe." I sat up and rested my elbows on the table. "It might be best if you take Caleb yourself."

"What?" Joe scowled. "What're you talkin' about? The whole point of this was to get the two of you together."

"Huh." I shot him a glare. "Thought the whole point of this was therapy for Caleb. Maybe help Bekah too. And it appears to be working."

"Okay, yeah." His mouth tightened as he nodded. "But it gives you the chance to talk to her some, too, doesn't it?"

"Sure. It's just that I feel like we might be makin' some progress, and a little space could be a good thing."

"Progress?" Joe's eyebrows shot up. "That's great. Do you think you could be getting back together soon?"

I held up a hand. "Whoa there. We've been separated for close to eight months. It's gonna take more than a few polite conversations to get things back on track. Besides which, Bekah's got some stuff to work out. If we rush into this, things could get worse off than they are now."

Joe snorted. "Rush? That boat's long sailed, my friend." He blew out a breath. "I was sorta hoping things would work out so you might consider adopting Caleb."

I slapped my hands on the table. "Where in the Sam Hill did you get an idea like that? Thought you and Cassie were thinking about it."

"We're only temporary foster care. Brother Paul's getting pressure to put Caleb into the system where he might find adoptive parents."

I shook my head. "Boy, you don't know your sister at all, do you? I tried like crazy to get Bekah to agree to adoption before we had Jonathon. She wouldn't hear of it. Now you decide we're gonna get back together *and* adopt Caleb. Whose brilliant plan was that?"

He squirmed. "As riled as you are, I'm not so sure I should tell you."

I glared at him.

He blew out a sigh. "You already know it was Brother Paul's idea to have Bekah work with Caleb. He thought it'd do the both of them good. The rest we just sorta hoped would fall together."

I groaned.

Joe sat forward. "I know Bekah wasn't open to adoption before. I'm not a complete moron. But look at the boy." He waved a hand toward Caleb who was kicking water at Gracie, grinning ear to ear. "You gotta love him."

"So, what's stopping you and Cassie from adopting him? Appears he fits right in."

He scratched his head. "Y'all don't know this, but Cassie's been planning on going back to school once Gracie's in first grade. She put everything on hold to raise the kids and help me get my business started. If I pushed, I know she'd cave, but it wouldn't be fair to her." He shrugged. "Was hopin' when she did go back, Bekah'd be there to book my loads like Cassie's been doin' for you."

I kept my eyes on the kids. The boy was something else, all right. "Anyone think about how Caleb's gonna feel if he has to go into foster care? I mean, after being with y'all as a part of this family."

Joe slumped back in his chair with a sigh. "Believe me, we've thought about it. Thing is, it's better he was here for a time than being stuck in foster care right after his parents were taken from him. At least there's been some stability."

"I suppose." The thought of that little boy being moved into a group home or even with a foster family made my stomach knot. "How soon is this gonna happen?"

"Don't know for sure." Joe leaned closer. "You think Bekah's getting attached?"

I grimaced. "How could she not? Any of y'all consider how this could backfire?"

"What d'you mean?"

"If Bekah finds out y'all hung your hopes for Caleb onto her shoulders, how do you think she's gonna feel if he ends up in foster care? She's already carrying enough of a burden as it is."

Joe slumped back in his chair. "Hadn't thought of that."

Cassie stepped out onto the patio and yelled. "Y'all ready for some ice cream?"

"Listen, Mitch." Joe clamped a hand on my arm as the kids clamored around the table. "Forget I said anything. I wasn't thinkin' this through. Didn't mean to add to your problems."

Before I could answer, Gracie wrapped her wet arms around my neck, soaking my shirt. "What kinda ice cream are you gonna have, Uncle Mitch?"

I stood and lifted Gracie. "I'm thinking peach. What about you?"

"Chocolate!"

"Let's go see if we can get your mama to give us an extra scoop." I slapped Joe on the back and walked away.

I'd be hard pressed to get even a few bites of ice cream down with the pit that sat in my stomach. If John was right, and God was truly in control, then it might be He was working out something in the background. I surely hoped so. There was only so much weight Bekah's thin shoulders could carry. And now that the thought of adopting Caleb was born in my mind, it wasn't gonna be something I could easily forget.

Chapter Twenty-One

Mitch

Digging into the Bible had shifted my thinking some and opened my eyes to a few truths. I wasn't quite ready to commit, or surrender as John called it, but it didn't escape my notice there was a peace about things I'd not had before.

Take Bekah for instance. A couple months before, if I'd even had a hint she might be softening, I'd have pushed and prodded until I wore her down or made her plumb crazy. But I was willing to wait. Could be the Lord was working on my heart, or maybe I was just getting a little smarter in my older age. Either way, it took the pressure off.

Good thing, too, because there were other areas that had me stewing. Like my truck. Finally was bringing in a steady income when she started failing. Delays when I accelerated, and a distinct acrid scent, told me the tranny was slipping. And if that wasn't bad enough, the new grinding noise when I shifted clinched it. Couldn't work without the truck and couldn't afford to have her repaired. Didn't matter how many times I checked the bank account, the number didn't add up in my favor.

I pulled her into the church parking lot, and she made enough noise to wake the neighborhood. Brother Paul was kneeling alongside the flowerbed and turned to look, hands covering his ears. A tad melodramatic, but he made his point.

"Your truck sounds like a sick cow," he yelled as I climbed down.

"Wish it was. Might be cheaper to pay a vet than a mechanic." I slammed the door closed with more force than necessary. Wasn't the truck's fault she was breaking down.

"You need to get it in today, we can put off your hours. Another week won't make a difference one way or the other."

"Appreciate the offer, but it'll have to wait." For what, I didn't know. A miracle maybe. A rich uncle leaving me a bundle or winning the Mega Millions Lotto, although that would require I play. Never was much for gambling. Figured I made a buck every time I didn't put it down for some pipe dream.

"How long you think it'll last like that?" Paul nabbed the trowel laying in the grass and used it as leverage to push up off the ground.

"It won't, I'm afraid." I could call up Mama and ask if she could float me a loan, but it didn't sit well with me. You'd think a guy could reach near forty without depending on his mama for help.

"What is it, you think?" Paul stared at the truck like it would give him the answer.

"Pretty sure it's the tranny. Been rebuilt twice now, so it's gonna need to be replaced." I blew out a breath. "Nothing I can do about it today."

"No one available to fix it?"

I scratched my head. "A little short on funds, I'm afraid."

"If it's money you need, I could maybe lend you some. How much?"

I shook my head. "Nope. Appreciate it, Brother Paul, but I'm not takin' your money." I waved my hand toward the church. "If you don't mind, I'm gonna get to work. Might as well get something accomplished today."

"Well, hold up, Mitch." He spread his arms wide. "We all could use a leg up now and again. How much you needing?"

"I can't ask you for money."

"You're not asking; I'm offering. How much?"

I tucked my hands into the front pockets of my jeans. "Best guess about six thousand."

Paul's caterpillar brows rose, and his face fell. "Oh. That much, huh?"

"Afraid so. But thanks all the same." I headed inside the church where it was cool, while my brain scrambled for a solution. I could rent a truck, but that'd put me further in the hole. Bank robbery was out, but I wasn't ready to discount the idea of selling an organ. How much were kidneys going for these days, anyway?

I was bending down to open a can of paint when Paul popped his head into the room. "You ever think about prayin' on it some?"

Had to hold back a chuckle. "Can't say I have."

"Couldn't hurt," he said.

The laugh got loose on me, and I glanced up at him. "Well, ain't that a rousing recommendation for prayer." You'd think a man of the cloth could be a little more optimistic.

"Oh, prayer works," he said. "It's just what we want doesn't always line up with God's plan."

"Somehow I don't think God cares much about my truck." *Or me, for that matter.*

"You never know what He'll use to get our attention."

I stood with a grimace. It wasn't as if I was going through something real serious. Like Caleb losing both his mama and daddy or Miss Anita dying from cancer. Or having my little boy die right in front of me and not being able to do a thing about it. But a truck? If God didn't answer any of those prayers, why would He care about something so trivial? I told Brother Paul as much.

"Guess I can understand your thinking, Mitch." Paul rubbed his chin. "But there's a verse in Exodus where God is talking to Moses. He tells him 'I will have mercy on whom I will have mercy, and I will have compassion on whom I will have compassion.' What Moses wanted was far greater than your needs right now, but I believe the Lord desires to show us His greatness. You ask in faith and then see what He does with it. There's another verse in James that says, 'You have not because you ask not.'"

I barked out a laugh. "But a truck? Really? Why would He care one way or the other?"

"Well, son, for one thing, He sees you wrangling with the idea of believing in Him. Might be He'd like to show you some of what He can do. I can't afford six thousand, but He can make it happen. He asks that we bring all our needs to Him. It's not like you're asking for money to spend on something frivolous. This is your livelihood we're talkin' about here."

Still, it seemed a little presumptuous to be hedging my bets on whether I believed or not and asking for a favor. But after Paul left, I set the paint aside and knelt on the floor. Hands clasped, I looked up at the ceiling as if I'd find Him hanging out there with a band of angels or something. "Listen God," I whispered. "I know I'm real new to this whole faith deal. Truth is, I'm not a hundred percent sure I believe it, but might be I'm getting there. The thing is, I'm in a bit of a bind, and if You could see Your way to helping me out, I'd surely appreciate it. And while I got your attention, maybe You could see a way to help out Caleb too. Or, if it's the one or the other, maybe You could help him out instead. That little boy's had more sadness than any kid I know. I'm not sure how You can fix things, but there are a lot of people who believe You hold our lives in Your hands. Bekah, for one, and her daddy John for another. Miss Anita was the kindest person I ever knew, and she said it was because You were in her life. I could sure use that power in mine right about now. What d'you say, God?"

I waited a moment in silence hoping to have some kind of divine revelation. When that didn't happen, I pushed off the floor and got to work. Even if He didn't answer my prayer, I felt better putting it out there.

Rebekah

I woke in the middle of the night, my thoughts swirling with the things of God. I'd never given much thought to how He worked in the background. Knowing the Scriptures and truly believing them were two different things. An omniscient God who saw my entire life before I was even conceived was unfathomable. He knew the wrong choices I'd make and planned accordingly. His Spirit guided me toward the right choices and knew when I'd obey and when I'd rebel. Was marrying Mitch a right choice or rebellion? It didn't matter, because the Lord knew ahead of time what I'd do and would work it out for my good and His glory. At least that's what Mama had always assured me.

I bolted upright with an epiphany. That meant he also knew everything about Jonathon before he was conceived—including the day He'd take him home. The Lord *called* Jonathon home. It wasn't an accident—it was His sovereign will—and He'd been trying to show me ever since. Mama telling me about His sovereignty, Mitch calling me out on my faith, Kimberley sharing her own experiences, and Daddy urging me to take a step of faith. In that moment, the weight of guilt and blame was lifted as if the heavenly hosts swooped down and took them from my heart.

It was only 2:00 am, and I was too wired to go back to sleep. I wanted to call Mitch then and there and beg him to let me come home, but I was afraid I'd come across crazy as a betsy bug. Instead, I searched my bedroom until I found the Bible tucked away on the closet shelf. A step of faith would go a whole lot smoother if I was armed with the Word of God.

Using my phone, I searched for verses on God's sovereignty, flipped to them in the Bible, then read them aloud. One in particular pierced my heart:

All the inhabitants of the earth are accounted as nothing,

But He does according to His will in the host of heaven.

And among the inhabitants of earth;

And no one can ward off His hand

Or say to Him, 'What have You done?'

Isn't that what I'd been doing since Jonathon died, and again when Mama got sick? Accusing God of not fulfilling my agenda. Accusing Mitch of being responsible, when all along, I knew deep down that everything that happened was in the hands of the Lord. We were merely jars of clay to be used as He saw fit. And yet, He loved us enough to call us to Him, to inherit His kingdom alongside Jesus Christ, and give us eternity in His presence. Eternity. This life on earth was just a blink in comparison. Mere seconds.

As soon as it was light enough to see, I slipped out to the barn and saddled Siren. Daddy was just beginning to stir, but I wanted to hold onto this fresh insight like a child coveting a shiny new toy. It was too precious to share until I'd studied it from every angle.

By the time I'd gotten back from my long trail ride and finished attending to the horses, Daddy was gone. He left a note saying he was watching Leah's kids for a few hours. It was just as well. It seemed only right that I saw this through before sharing it with anyone else. Mitch deserved to be first after I'd relegated him to the trash heap over the last year, and I'd be seeing him that afternoon when he brought Caleb for a horseback riding lesson. It couldn't come soon enough.

I dodged probing questions from both Jenna and Darlene at work when they noticed a spring in my step. The hours went by slower than a three-toed sloth as I imagined Mitch's reaction when I told him I was ready to come home. Would he be overjoyed or suspicious? It's not like I hadn't given him reason to be. Hot one minute and cold the next. He didn't share my faith, so would he understand my little epiphany?

Five minutes before my shift ended, I was finishing up with a customer when Mindy Taylor walked in as if the Lord sent her to test my newfound insight. The last time I saw her was the day Jonathon drowned. By the way her smile wavered when she noticed me, I'd say she remembered that momentous event as well. How could she not?

"Hello, Mindy."

"Hey, Bekah. I didn't know you worked here." She accepted the quick hug I offered and stepped back. There was a shadow of sorrow in her eyes and smile. "It's been a long..." The words trailed off as if they could only lead to a dark place neither one of us dared travel.

Better to tread on safer ground. "How are you? How's Keith and the kids?"

"Good." Her head bobbed up and down. "You and Mitch?" She lowered her voice. "I was so sorry to hear y'all are separated." She dropped her head as if ashamed to admit we'd been the subject of small-town gossip. But what else could I have expected?

"We're okay, Mindy. We're working things out."

She lifted her head and beamed at me, hand to her heart. "I'm so pleased to hear that. You think we can get together for a cup of coffee and catch up?"

"I'd like that." And miracle of miracles, it was true. "You have my number. Give me a call when you have time, will you? I'm on my way out, or I'd suggest we get together now."

"No problem, Bek. I'll call sometime next week."

By the time I got home, I had only fifteen minutes to change and prepare Siren before Mitch was scheduled to arrive. Daddy was gone again. No note this time. I sent him a quick text: *Where are u?* A few minutes later, his response came in: *Visiting a friend.* Very curious, though I had no time to think on it. I grabbed a bottle of water and headed outside.

My heart was skipping like flat stones on smooth water when I heard the truck come down the drive. But then it dropped to my cowboy boots when I recognized Joe's truck instead of Mitch's. Caleb's grin when he hopped out of the passenger side was enough to raise it up a couple notches. The little boy had wormed his way into my heart. There was no denying I got more from our time together than he did.

"Hey, Bek," Joe called as he closed the driver's door. "Perfect day for a lesson, isn't it?"

The temperature had dropped by a good ten degrees, and although the cloud cover threatened rain, it hadn't yet appeared. "It is." I rubbed Caleb's back as he threw his arms around me. "You ready to ride, cutie pie?"

He snapped his head up and down once before running off toward Siren. Eyes on Caleb, I waited for Joe to come alongside me. I had to practically bite my tongue in half to hold back the questions bouncing around in my head.

"You're doing wonders with him," Joe said.

I glanced at him. "I'm surprised to see you. If you came to see Daddy, he's not home."

"Nope. Just dropping Caleb off. I have a couple errands to run, then I'll be back for him, if that's okay."

"Sure." I kicked at a rock with the toe of my boot. "Is there a reason Mitch didn't bring him? I mean, he's not sick or anything, is he?" Until I asked, I hadn't even considered it. Here I was once again concerned about only my agenda while Mitch could be down with a summer cold or something worse.

Joe chuckled. "Way to be smooth, Bek." He nudged me with his shoulder. "No, Mitch isn't sick. He's busy is all. Still working off his community service hours." He sighed and crossed his arms. "Besides, he's getting attached to Caleb and thought a little distance might be a good thing."

"What's wrong with getting attached? Kind of hard not to." My own heart melted like butter in the hot sun while I watched Siren dip his head so Caleb could pet his muzzle. "Even Siren's smitten."

"It's just he won't be with us much longer, so it makes it hard."

It took a moment for his words to register. "What're you talking about? I thought you and Cassie were gonna keep him."

He kept his gaze on Caleb. "It's like I told Mitch last night, we're just temporary care givers. He's gonna need to go to a home or a permanent foster family. Best thing for him is a family who can adopt him."

"Why can't you?" Caleb's giggle pulled my attention again. How could Joe and Cassie not want to keep him?

"You know Cassie's been planning to go back to school, Bek. Caleb needs someone who can give him specialized attention. You know, like what you've been doing for him."

Alarm bells went off in my head. "You don't say." Joe was about as subtle as a death metal band at a country western concert. "Do I smell a setup?"

His eyebrows hitched. "Setup? You really think I'd use a little boy who's just been through the nightmare of losing his parents for my own purposes? We took him in because he needed the stability that a group home or the foster system couldn't give him. We never intended it to be permanent."

Was Caleb brought into our lives for a purpose? With my head wrapped up in the sovereignty of God, everything suddenly took on new significance. I couldn't help but see a parallel between this little boy and my own sweet Jonathon. I remembered Mitch's plea for me to consider adoption all those years ago, but I'd refused. Again, I was more interested in my agenda than seeing that the Lord might have other plans.

"I gotta get a couple things done," Joe said as he turned away.

"How long?"

"I don't know. When will you be done with the lesson?"

I shook my head. "Not that. I mean how long before Caleb has to go to a home?"

"Not sure. Brother Paul's getting a little pressure. He kinda went out on a limb here."

What are you doing here, Lord? I sent up the prayer as I crossed the yard toward Caleb. If this was of Him, I had no doubt He'd work it out in his timing. Wasn't that what Mama was trying to tell me while I was whining about her illness and impending death? *Not my will, Lord, but Yours.*

Chapter Twenty-Two

Rebekah

After Joe picked up Caleb, I put a simple dinner together, not sure if Daddy was going to show or not. I hadn't seen him all day and had no idea where he'd gone off to. Whatever he was doing, it was better than him sitting around all day pining for Mama.

Just when I'd decided to eat alone, Daddy came through the kitchen door. "Sorry I'm late. The time got away from me." He slipped past me to wash at the sink. "What's for supper?"

"Leftovers and salad. Hope you don't mind."

"Sounds good." He snatched a dishtowel from the counter and dried his hands.

"Where've you been all day, Daddy? I was starting to get concerned." I put the salad and a dish of mac 'n' cheese on the table.

"No need to worry, darlin'." He sat at the table, waited for me to join him, and blessed the food. When he was done, he picked up the conversation where he'd left off. "Got to thinkin' on what we talked about the other day. You know, how when we get our focus off ourselves and onto others, it's a blessing all the way around. Just thought I'd visit a friend or two who've been havin' a rough go of it. You know, staying busy so I don't waste away." He wiggled his brows at me.

Daddy was a smart one. It was clear where Joe got his not-so-subtle ways. "I get it, Daddy," I said, sliding the salad bowl toward him. "You aren't wallowing in grief, and you're capable of taking care of yourself."

"Well, I'm wallowing a little, and I sure like having my supper fixed, but I don't want you putting your life on hold for me or anyone else." He scooped some casserole onto his plate. "How was your day?"

Such a simple question. "I'll let you know when it's over." I forked a piece of macaroni and glanced at him. "I'm hoping to see Mitch tonight. It's time we had that talk." Just the thought of it had my heart racing like I'd run a record-breaking sprint. It'd be a miracle if I could get three bites down.

"That's good. Past time as far as I'm concerned." He pointed his fork at me. "You better pick up the pace if you wanna get over to see him tonight."

"I'm too nervous to eat," I admitted. "Think I'll just go on over now, if you don't mind."

"Don't mind at all, darlin'. Suppose I best get used to it."

A few minutes later, I gave Daddy a peck on the cheek on my way out the door. Should I call Mitch to be sure he was around or take my chances? Could be he was working late at the church. I put the key in the ignition then punched his number into my cell. No answer. I didn't trust myself to leave a message that would make any sort of sense. I sat in my car for a full minute paralyzed with indecision.

What should I do, Lord? Nothing. Not even an inkling if I should go one way or the other. So, I headed to the house praying for a clear head and the ability to communicate without becoming a blubbering mess like I was the last time I saw him.

Although the days were getting shorter, there was enough light to see Mitch's truck sitting in the driveway, the hood raised. That wasn't a good sign. It had been a peck of trouble since Mitch bought it. I grabbed my purse from the passenger seat and approached the house. The clang of metal on metal and low grumblings met my ears before I reached him.

"Mitch?"

A bang then "Ow. Dadnabit." Mitch stepped from in front of the truck, rubbing his head. "Bek? You should warn a guy."

"I sort of did. I called, but you didn't pick up."

He pulled his hand from his head and peered at it as if checking for blood. "Sorry. Left my phone inside."

"Let me get a look at you." I put one hand against the back of his head and felt around his scalp with the other. His hair was warm and thick on my fingers as I searched for a bump.

"I'm fine, Bek." His voice was strained. "Was more surprised than hurt." He straightened up and took ahold of both my wrists, rubbing the insides with his thumbs.

Could he feel my pulse quicken and hear the unsteadiness of my breath? I stepped back before I made a fool of myself and cleared my throat. "What's going on with the truck?"

He scowled. "Pretty sure the tranny's slipping. You remember how it smelled last time?"

"Uh huh." It was the best I could do while my eyes were feasting on his lips. How long had it been since we'd kissed? Slipping into that train of thought would have me swooning like a Victorian lady whose corset was cinched too tight. *Focus, girl.*

"And the grinding noises it made when shifting gears?"

With a shake of my head to clear it, I turned my attention to the truck. "Didn't you just have it fixed a couple years ago?"

"Rebuilt. Second time, remember?"

Without his truck, Mitch couldn't work. "Can't Jake fix it again?"

"Afraid I need a whole new tranny, but we can't afford it. It'll run a good six grand." Mitch glared at the truck as if it was a disobedient child.

I was so caught up on the normalcy of the comment it took a few seconds to make sense of what else he'd said. We. He'd said *we* couldn't afford it.

"Yes, we can."

He squinted at me. "Come again?"

"That money you've been sending to me every month? I stuck it in my bank account. Haven't touched a dime of it. There's almost $8,000 in there."

His mouth fell open. "What? Why? I sent it so you had something to live on. Is that why you been workin' two jobs?" Was he angry? He sure sounded like it.

Here we were going sideways again when I'd hoped we could move forward. "Do you think we might go inside and talk? I have some things I'd really like to share with you."

He shrugged. "Okay, sure."

Once inside, Mitch hustled me past the family room and into the kitchen like a kid trying to hide his mess. Did he think I cared about the layer of dust on the furniture or laundry scattered on the couch? Even if I did, I was too jittery to henpeck him. Nerves took hold of my voice, and I sent up a quick prayer for much needed spiritual intervention. What I wanted to say was scattered in my mind like flower seeds blown hither and yon. Gathering them all up seemed nearly impossible.

"You okay, Bekah?" Mitch's brows lowered over his piercing eyes as he handed me a glass of tea. He escorted me to the table and sat down on the other side.

"The thing is." My voice sounded like a bull frog, so I took a sip and cleared my throat. "Last time I was here, you said I'd need to get some things straight in my mind if our marriage was gonna work out." Unable to think when our eyes met, I kept mine focused elsewhere.

"I remember."

"I've been doing a lot of praying, Mitch. A lot of praying and thinking and more praying. It was like the things Mama and Daddy said about God's sovereignty had gotten snatched up by the devil and twisted in my mind. It wasn't until I was too sick of my own self that God's truth took hold." I dared a glance. *Please, let there be understanding in his eyes.*

He leaned his elbows on the table. "So, Bekah, what was that truth God laid on your heart?"

The question struck an odd chord. *The truth God laid on your heart.* Had he ever asked such a thing in all the years we'd been married? *God laid on your heart.* It was something Daddy would have said, and the fact it came from Mitch niggled at the back of my mind.

"Bekah?"

I shook my head. "Sorry. What'd you say?"

He ducked as if trying to capture my eyes with his. "I asked you about what you feel God's put on your heart."

Emotion thickened my throat, and I had to swallow. Why had it taken me so long to know the truth? "I realized that Jonathon's life wasn't in your hands. And I know you don't believe the things in the Bible, but I do." I dared to make eye contact. "And the truth of it is, God had the day of our birth and death all laid out long before we were even conceived. He only ever intended for Jonathon to live as long as he did. The same for Mama."

Mitch's stare had me squirming. "But you've always said God is Sovereign, Bekah. I don't get what's different."

"I said it, but I don't think I really believed it. I mean, there are so many things in the Bible that I know in my head, but my heart hasn't quite caught up."

"Like what?" He leaned forward as if to catch every word. He'd never shown an interest in my religion—as he called it. No matter how many times I pointed out that what I had was a relationship, he didn't get it. The truth of it was, I hadn't really gotten it, either. Until the last few days. How'd I go to church my entire life and miss the most important part?

Mitch

When Bekah said I didn't believe in the things in the Bible, I wanted to deny the truth of it. Couldn't, because she was mostly right. There was a stirring inside me to know more. From what John told me last time we met up, that was a start. It was confusing, though. She grew up going to church most every

Sunday. Had a mama and daddy who taught her things about the Bible from the time she was born. After all those years, there'd still been a disconnect when things got rough. What chance did I have? Only time I was in church was the day we married and the day we buried Jonathon. Couldn't count community service hours.

I reached for Bekah's hand. "I really wanna know what you've missed. About the Bible, I mean."

"Okay." She blew out a breath. "One thing is understanding the depth of God's grace." She twined her fingers with mine. "It might seem unbelievable to you, Mitch, but the truth is that everything I have comes from Him. As a gift. Even my faith isn't really mine. There's nothing we can do that has any value without it. That never really sunk in before. And when I think about how wrong I've been." Her voice broke and tears pooled in her ocean-blue eyes and spilled over.

"Hey." I tugged on her fingers. "It's okay."

She shook her head. "It's not, Mitch. It's really not." Sniffling, she snatched a napkin left on the table. "It's like God has shown me how horribly wrong I've been about everything. Blaming you for Jonathon and angry at Him for taking my baby." She swiped the napkin across her eyes and nose. "I only felt God was good when He was giving me good things. As soon as I was tested, I crumbled."

I fingered a strand of hair from her face. "Brother Paul told me that most everyone has a crisis of faith a time or two in their lives."

"Maybe." Her shoulders curved like she was folding into herself. "But the worst thing is that I not only blamed you, but then I abandoned you too. Instead of being the kind of wife Mama would have been, I doubled your grief. I'm ashamed and embarrassed." Tears ran down her cheeks and chin, the now crumpled and damp napkin worthless.

"Let me get you a tissue." I kissed her forehead and slipped out. My gut ached to see her in pain, but somewhere in the mix was hope. If she was working through the anger, then we stood a chance.

When I reappeared, she was standing in front of the built-in hutch, head bent over something. A lot of Miss Anita's things were right where Bekah had left them months ago. Figured she was having a sentimental moment.

"Here you go." As I offered the tissue, she turned.

"What's this?" She held up the Bible study John and me were working through, a crinkle between her eyebrows.

Heat crept up my neck. "Just what it looks like." Should have remembered to put it away. It wasn't like I was embarrassed or nothing. Just wasn't ready to tell anyone about it.

"You've been doing a Bible study?" Her smile and the shine of tears in her eyes were pure radiance. Reminded me of our wedding day.

"So it would seem."

"Since when? Are you doing it with Brother Paul?"

I eased the book from her hand and slid it back where she found it. "What say we tackle one thing at a time." She was so close, I could see the flecks of gold in her eyes and the freckles she hated splattered across the bridge of her nose.

"Why are you acting so cagey about it? I can't believe you kept it to yourself."

That wasn't the only thing I'd kept to myself. Here she was being honest about her failures, and I hung onto a secret of my own. Was there ever justification for a lie?

"Mitch?" She peered up at me. "Are you okay?"

"No. I mean, yes. I'm fine." I pushed a hand through my hair and scooted across the kitchen to put some distance between us. I couldn't think with the scent of her shampoo tickling my nose. And those darned freckles never looked sexier.

"So, why the big secret?"

Her question got caught up in my guilt, and it took me a moment to untangle the two. "No secret, it's just I wanted to dig in some and see where it'd lead before I said anything. Didn't want the pressure of y'all expecting something I couldn't give. I also didn't want you to think I was doing this only to get you back, 'cause that isn't why."

She folded her arms and shrugged. "I understand, Mitch. But you didn't answer my first question. Is Brother Paul the one you're working with?"

John didn't say working together was a secret—just what was said when we were. "No. It's your daddy." I held up a hand. "And don't go naggin' him about it, either. I asked could he keep it to himself for the time being."

"Wouldn't dream of it." Her smile slid into a giggle. "You know how long I've been hoping and praying God would tug on your heart?"

I rested my back end against the counter. "Longer than we've been married, I'm sure. Your daddy said the same thing. He told me understanding how Jesus died for my sins would make a world of difference in our marriage."

She moved beside me so we were hip to hip. "What was it that got you thinking about it? I mean, all these years I've been pestering you about it, and nothing."

I slipped my arm around her shoulders and the heat of her body seeped into mine. She sure smelled like heaven. "It was your mama. Remember that first day you worked with Caleb?"

She nodded.

"Your mama told me you were a lot like she used to be. Stubborn and hardheaded." I smiled when she pulled far enough away to throw me a scowl. "And just like her, you needed a strong, godly husband." Tears were swimming in her eyes again. Couldn't blame her; my own throat was tight. "Maybe if I'd been that for you in the beginning, we'd have come through this a little easier. You'd of trusted me more."

She rested her head on my shoulder. "Oh, Mitch. It wasn't you I didn't trust. Don't you see? It was God. That's what I was trying to explain."

There was a pit of dread that sat square in my gut. The lie sat between us, but what should I do with it? Might be I could talk to John or Brother Paul about it before I confessed something that could hurt her. Hurt the both of us.

"I know we don't have everything figured out yet. Daddy's practically pushing me out the door, but I don't want to rush it. You think we should start thinking toward me coming home?"

I blew out a sigh and closed my eyes. *Thank You, Lord.* "Yes."

"And you'll use that money I have saved up for the truck? I don't wanna be married to a bum, you know." There was a smile in her voice.

Brother Paul was right. Prayer worked. Surely if the good Lord cared about something as trivial as my truck, he'd see fit to intervene for Caleb too. I shifted so I could see her face. "I prayed for it, you know."

She frowned. "Your truck?"

"Yep. For the finances to fix her. Felt kinda silly, but I won't be discounting it so quick the next time." Now if the Lord would see fit to unravel the tangled mess I made. Would it matter to Him that I meant well? Wasn't there a saying about the road to hell being paved with good intentions?

CHAPTER TWENTY-THREE

Summer 2022

Rebekah

Bekah had been a weather junkie all week hoping a little of that Tennessee summer heat would kick in. Why did it have to be so cantankerous? When she was little, once June hit, she could count on it being hot enough to hit the water. Or maybe she just didn't feel the cold then like she did now. But the Lord was smiling on them the day of the Taylors' pool party. It was predicted to be a warm eighty-five with low humidity. Now if she could just convince Jonathon—and Mitch—that he should wear swimmies in the pool, she could relax.

"You gotta be kidding," Mitch said when he caught her slipping them into the beach bag. "Bek, you need to cut loose of the apron strings."

"He's only five, Mitch. Now if he was fifteen, you'd have a case."

"Probably will in another ten years," he mumbled. "I taught him to swim just last month. He's like a little fish." He grabbed the swimmies and started to pull them from the bag, but Bekah smacked his hand.

"It'll be different with a crowd of people. He might get confused or maybe someone'll dunk him. I'm being cautious is all."

"You're bein' overprotective, Bek. You won't let me build him a treehouse—"

"Yet," she cut in. "I said when he's a little older."

"And you practically bolted the training wheels to his bike," Mitch continued. "For someone who claims to put her trust in Jesus, you sure live in fear a lot."

Why couldn't he understand? It only took one second for things to change. After trying for eight years to get pregnant, she treasured Jonathon like a precious gift. Wasn't that how all children should be treated?

"Somehow I can't imagine your mama hanging over the four of y'all when you were growing up," Mitch said. "And I know for a fact, Joe had a wild streak in him."

Bekah didn't want to argue. Mitch might've had some good points, but she did too. "Can we make us a deal?"

Mitch crossed his arms. "Maybe. What d'you have in mind?"

"If you're in the pool with Jonathon, no swimmies. But if he's alone, he wears them."

He nodded real slow. "Sounds reasonable."

"And for the record, Mitch, I don't appreciate you making cracks about my faith. Since you don't buy into it anyway, you have no right judging me." Without waiting for a response, she went to get Jonathon.

There were days Mitch could test the patience of a saint, and God knew, Bekah wasn't one. Certainly, she trusted God, but that didn't mean she should be reckless, did it? Anyone with half a brain didn't drive without a seat belt or walk down an alley in a risky neighborhood. Being practical didn't mean she lacked faith.

Jonathon was tugging a t-shirt over his little chest when she walked into the room. His swimsuit looked to be a mite too big, but it'd fit just about right come August.

"Hey, cutie pie. You about ready to go?"

"Yep." He grabbed his Crocs from the closet and headed for the door.

"Hold up, Jonathon."

He skidded to a stop and turned to her with an eye roll. Probably learned that move from Mitch. "What?"

She sat on his bed and waved him over then put an arm around his thin shoulders when he drew close enough. "Your daddy and I made a deal. You gotta wear your swimmies in the pool unless he's right there with you."

"Aww, Mama. I don't need them. Daddy showed me how to swim." He stuck out his bottom lip and folded his arms. Bekah bit back a laugh. He was the spitting image of his daddy.

She combed her fingers through his hair then hugged him close. "I know you're a wonderful swimmer, sweetie, but there'll be lots of people around, so it's not so easy to keep an eye on you."

"But Mama—"

"You listen to your mama, bud." Mitch leaned against the door jamb. "She's just tryin' to keep you safe. You hear?"

"Yes, sir."

Mitch's support eased the tension in Bekah's shoulders. Even when he didn't agree with her, he always came through. And maybe he was right. Her own mama and daddy never hovered over them, and they survived. Leah's kids all but hung from the light fixtures, and other than the occasional bumps and bruises, they were just fine.

When they arrived at Keith and Mindy Taylor's house, the backyard party was in full swing. The scent of chlorine wafted in the air and mingled with mouthwatering smells coming from the built-in barbecue on the far side of the patio. Kids splashed around in the pool while the adults lined up at a table laden with platters of Boston butt and barbecued chicken, bowls of potato salad, casseroles, mac & cheese, and fruit concoctions. There were so many desserts, they needed a table of their own.

Rebekah wedged the Pyrex dish of congealed salad with whipped cream she'd made between a bowl of pimiento cheese dip and a potato-cheese casserole. No one would be going hungry here today.

"Can I go in the pool?" Jonathon tugged on Bekah's arm, eyes wide and pleading. "Cara and Billy and Reid's already swimming."

"Isn't the weather just so perfect?" Mindy passed by with a platter of fruit and threw Bekah a grin. "Thought it was never gonna warm up."

"It's like you ordered it special, Mindy. Thanks for having us."

"Are you kidding, girl? We don't get y'all over here near enough. Gotta see about getting some more ice." She tapped Jonathon's shoulder. "You gonna get in the pool with the other kids, sweetheart?" She walked off without waiting for an answer.

"Can I, Mama?" Jonathon jumped up and down, the motion dislodging the beach bag from Bekah's shoulder.

"My word, Jonathon. Give me a minute to set my things down." She disentangled him from her arm and glanced around. Where was Mitch, anyway? "Why don't you have yourself something to eat first and then we'll see about going swimming?"

"I wanna go now." His whine was punctuated with a foot stomp.

Bekah bent over to give him a reprimand and nearly toppled over when someone bumped into her. This was not the best place to be negotiating with a five-year-old. She took a deep breath to calm the thread of anxiety that thrummed through her veins. Stick her in the midst of a herd of wild horses, and she was cool as peach ice cream. But all these people? Not so much. She shouldn't have had that second cup of coffee with no food in her system.

"Listen, kiddo, you need to quit your whining. You'll have plenty of time to go swimming after you eat something. We both know once you're in that pool, you won't be coming out again until you're as wrinkled as a prune."

"But I ain't hungry, Mama."

"You *aren't* hungry, sweetie. Don't use ain't."

"What's goin' on here?" Mitch reached from behind Bekah and squeezed Jonathon's shoulder.

Jonathon crossed his arms and jutted out his chin. "Mama won't let me go in the pool."

She raised an eyebrow at him. "That's not exactly what I said now, is it?"

He ducked his head and had enough sense to mumble, "No, ma'am. But I ain't...I mean I'm not hungry."

"Well, I am." Mitch patted his own stomach. "Let's see what we can find ourselves, and then we'll hit the water. What d'you say?" He didn't give Jonathon a chance to argue. He nudged him between his shoulder blades to get him moving toward the end of the food line. "Want me to fix you a plate, Bek?"

Bless Mitch's heart. It didn't matter how crazy he made her some days, he always had her back. She'd need to give him more grace in the future. "I'll get myself something, babe. You just take care of Jonathon." She had to resist the urge to latch onto him so she didn't have to wade into the crowd and make small talk.

She wove through chatting groups of three and four, offering quick smiles and head nods until she reached a quiet corner between the French doors and bricked chimney where she could breathe again. She tucked the bag on the ground behind her, leaving her hands free. If Leah or Joe were here, they'd poke fun at her. The two of them would be fast friends with half the crowd inside a country minute. Why she and Dan got the shy gene was anyone's guess, but it was times like this she envied her older sister and brother. And Mitch. He made an art out of small talk.

Once she had a little breathing room, she was able to appreciate the party from a distance. Most of the people she knew well enough to say hey to, but there were a few she'd never met. Mitch, two full plates in his hands, broke through the crowd and headed her way with Jonathon close behind.

He offered her one. "You said you'd get something to eat, but I know better. You'll hide out here until it's time to go."

Her heart melted a little. "My hero," she said with a giggle. The food must have weighed five pounds. "You don't really think I can eat all this, do you?"

He shrugged. "Don't matter. Eat what you can. Jonathon's gonna share mine." He nabbed a hot dog from his plate and handed it to Jonathon. "You eat this and a little of your mama's congealed salad then I'll take you swimming."

"I can go on my own," Jonathon said before shoving one end of his hot dog into his mouth.

"Nah. I'll take you. Then you can teach Cara and her brothers what you learned last week. Show 'em how you can reach the bottom of the pool. But, if you're on your own, you gotta wear the swimmies like your mama said."

Cheeks bulging with food, Jonathon rolled his eyes. They'd have to work on that disrespectful habit.

Bekah took a couple of bites, but with her stomach in knots, it was all she could manage. It was a perfect day to go riding, and she'd much rather be doing that with her two men than packed into a backyard pool party.

"You're not eating." Mitch pointed his plastic fork at her plate.

"You can't go swimmin' if you don't eat," Jonathon said. "And I'm done." He turned to dart off toward the pool, but Bekah snagged him by the arm.

"You wait for your daddy, you hear?"

Jonathon sighed and danced from foot to foot. "Come *on*, Daddy. Everyone else is already in the water."

Bekah narrowed her eyes at him. "Don't be that way, son. Give him time to eat."

"It's okay," Mitch said, taking Bekah's plate. "I'll go get rid of these and change into my suit." He glanced at Jonathon. "You wait right here until I'm back, you hear?"

"Yes, sir."

Bekah retrieved the bag from behind her and offered it to Mitch. "Your suit's at the bottom." She purposely didn't pack her own so she couldn't be talked into joining them. Sitting on the edge and dangling her feet in the water was enough.

Mitch disappeared inside while Bekah pulled a reluctant Jonathon in for a hug. "I know you think I'm being silly, kiddo, but you gotta give me a break, okay?"

"Okay." He drew the word out.

With a Tupperware container in her hands, Mindy squeezed through the crowd. "Wanna try my famous chocolate chip cookies?" She lifted the lid and held them out. "Homemade." She wriggled her eyebrows. "I don't make 'em too often 'cause Keith'll eat a dozen in one sitting."

"Can I, Mama?" Jonathon said.

Bekah couldn't deny they looked some better than anything she'd ever bought at a store. "What's in them?"

Mindy laughed. "The usual. Sugar, butter, chocolate chips." She shrugged. "I got me a special ingredient that I don't share that makes them extra good."

Bekah opened her mouth to ask what the special ingredient was but snapped it shut. Did she really want Mindy to think she was the helicopter mom Mitch accused her of being? Second-guessing everything he put into his mouth, harping on him to wear swimmies when none of the other kids did?

"Go ahead, kiddo," she told Jonathon.

He had crammed half the cookie into his mouth when Mitch appeared. "Ready, son?"

"You wanna try one of my cookies?" Mindy held out the container.

Mitch smiled. "Maybe later."

While the boys blended into the crowd, Mindy waved another woman over to join them. "Have you met my sister Rachel?"

"No. I didn't even know you had a sister."

Mindy linked her arm into Rachel's. "This is Rachel. Rach, this is Bekah Casey. Bekah and Mitch's little boy Jonathon goes to preschool with Clara."

They'd been chatting for a good ten minutes, and Bekah was beginning to enjoy herself, when a commotion from the pool drew her attention. Her heart kicked into her throat as she pushed through the throng of people to see what was wrong.

"Call 911," a male voice shouted.

When Bekah got through, she saw a drenched Mitch bending over Jonathon giving him mouth-to-mouth. Her little boy was white as a sheet under the shock of dark hair—and still as death.

Mitch

The waiting room was empty aside from Mitch, but he could still hear Bekah's screams while she'd clung to him. Still feel her fists pummeling his chest while everyone at the party stood on the sidelines like a passel of rubberneckers at a fatal car accident. It had taken the ambulance only seven minutes to reach the house, but it was too late.

Jonathon was gone.

Bekah had ripped Mitch to shreds with her words. *How could you let him die? Why didn't you save him? You promised you'd look out for him. You promised.* If he lived to be a hundred, he wouldn't cut loose of the accusations and gut-wrenching pain he saw in her eyes.

And he'd forever remember the heaviness of his lifeless boy lying in his arms.

Even now, sitting in the quiet room, he wanted to defend himself, shift the blame somewhere else. Anywhere else. But Jonathon was gone, and it had to be someone's fault. Either him or Bekah. He couldn't add the guilt of their baby's death to the grief of her loss.

"Mr. Casey?"

Mitch raised his head from his ice-cold hands to see a young woman in pink scrubs—a nurse, no doubt— standing in the doorway. "Yeah."

"Dr. Harper is available now. I can show you to his office."

Mitch needed to use the chair rails for leverage to stand, his body stiff and sore as a ninety-year-old's. His shuffled footsteps trailing the nurse down the long corridor weren't much better. He was dead inside. Dead as Jonathon. The numbness wouldn't last. He couldn't be so lucky.

Mitch kept his eyes on the floor unable to meet anyone's gaze. The staff must've known a little boy drowned today. One sympathetic look, and the scream that'd been building up would cut loose.

The nurse opened a door and stepped aside. "Go on in, Mr. Casey, and have yourself a seat. The doctor will be right with you."

Mitch stepped into the small office and paced from the one window to the door and back, over and over. There weren't more than five steps in each direction, but he was too keyed up to sit. When the door opened again, he was face-to-face with a man near John Miller's age. The hair was a little grayer, and the bags beneath the eyes were evidence that he'd gotten little sleep. Did he carry the burden of his patients' sorrows even after they were gone?

"Mr. Casey. I'm Doc Harper." He offered a veined hand and frowned. "Can't begin to tell you how sorry I am over the loss of your boy."

Mitch couldn't do more than nod as he returned the handshake.

"Have a seat, won't you?" Two chairs faced his desk, and he waited for Mitch to sit in one before he dropped into the other. "What can I do for you?"

It took a few moments for Mitch to swallow down the rock that had lodged in his throat. "I was the one to give Jonathon mouth-to-mouth." He pressed a thumb and finger against his eyes to hold back the flood of tears. "He'd only been under water a few seconds. Didn't make sense that I couldn't revive him."

Doc nodded. "There was a bit more to it, Mr. Casey. My initial findings showed that your boy's airway was blocked."

The doc confirming what Mitch had suspected should have been some comfort, but it only added another layer to the tragedy. It wouldn't bring his son back. "When I was working..." A sob rose up and choked him. It took a few deep breaths to regain a modicum of control. "Sorry." He passed a hand over his mouth and cleared his throat. "I smelled peanuts on...on Jonathon," Mitch finally said.

Doc blew out a breath. "I take it he was allergic?"

"Yes, sir."

"That explains a few things then. Your son's death was pronounced a drowning, because by all indications at the scene, that's what made sense. But I believe anaphylaxis was the true cause. Once we finish with the autopsy, we'll have a more definitive answer."

It had to have been the cookie Bekah let Jonathon have right before he went into the pool. How often had Mitch gotten on her about being overprotective, and the one time she was even the slightest bit lax, Jonathon died? What a cruel God Bekah put her faith in.

"I don't want my wife to know," Mitch said. It would literally kill her. "Is there any reason she has to?"

Doc Harper narrowed his eyes. "It'll be a matter of public record, Mr. Casey. We can't falsify—"

"I'm not sayin' to do that." Mitch clutched the arms of the chair, his fingers digging into the faux leather. "But there's no reason to rub her face in it, is there? I mean, she's practically tied herself in knots to keep him safe, and the idea that one mistake..." He shook his head. "I'd rather she blame me for not watching him close enough in the pool."

The doctor shifted with a frown. "That's up to you, Mr. Casey. The death certificate has to be accurate. Whether she sees it or not..." He shrugged. "The death of your son is a tragedy, but it's no one's fault. It was an accident."

"You know that, and I know that," Mitch said. "But I don't think my wife will see it that way."

Chapter Twenty-Four

Rebekah

It was amazing how a little hope could put a dance in my heart. The sun seemed brighter, the birds chattier, and my steps lighter. Or maybe it was the gloominess that had laid heavy on me for so long was finally lifting enough to allow God's goodness to shine into the dark recesses of my mind. I was almost afraid to let my guard down, which was ridiculous. The nagging sense that something was off with Mitch was nothing more than a lingering case of PTSD. I'd lost both Jonathon and Mama inside of eighteen months. That would make anyone a little batty, wouldn't it?

I pondered these things as I mixed the batter for Daddy's hot cakes. The kitchen window was open, allowing a cool breeze to flutter Mama's starch-white curtains, filling the room with a hint of autumn. It was only mid-August, with heat and humidity predicted to hit the next day and last throughout the week. Didn't matter how hot it got, before we knew it, the holidays would be upon us once again. Mitch and I didn't weather it well the year before. We were barely speaking to each other, and I was packed and moved out by New Year's Day.

But this year would be different. *Please, Lord, let it be so.*

"Hot cakes?" Daddy's voice at my backside had me jumping like a kid caught stealing a candy bar. "What's the occasion?"

I slapped a hand on my chest. "Goodness, Daddy, you scared the life outta me. I didn't hear you come in."

He quirked his eyebrows at me. "Well, darlin', you must've had your head in the clouds, 'cause I made quite a ruckus. Even asked if you'd seen my reading glasses while I was shuffling around in the family room."

My face heated as I hugged the bowl of batter to my chest and gave it another stir or two. "You hungry?"

"Always room for hot cakes." He nudged me with an elbow. "You wanna tell me what's got your mind hijacked?"

I took care to ladle six perfect circles of batter on the electric griddle. "Seems I'll be moving out soon, Daddy. Mitch and I talked last night, and I've finally come to my senses. Took long enough, don't you think?" Even though it's what he said he wanted, I was afraid Daddy would feel as if he was being abandoned, and I held my breath waiting for his response.

"That's good news." He wrapped an arm around my shoulders and gave me a quick squeeze. "Your mama would be right proud of you, Bek." His voice went gruff at the end, and I kept my eyes averted. If I caught him tearing up, I'd be close behind.

"I don't know about that. I'm sure she'd have been prouder if I'd never left Mitch to start with."

"Wasn't a couple months ago, you were ready to hightail it out to Atlanta. I'd say you're making progress."

I scowled and flipped the hot cakes. "Danny's got a big mouth." I figured my baby brother had forgotten all about my desperate urge to flee. "Or was it Mitch who squealed on me?"

He shrugged and moved away with a chuckle. "So, when's the big day?"

"We don't have anything set, but I figured I'd start transferring my things over this weekend." My stomach flipped at the thought of sleeping in the same bed with Mitch after all this time. We'd have to get to know each other all over again.

Daddy buried his head in the pantry. "You know where that blueberry syrup is we got from Florence Lister?"

I rolled my eyes. "On the table, Daddy, along with your reading glasses." Maybe he needed someone to take care of him after all.

"Huh." He stopped by the fridge and collected the plate of butter and a bowl of strawberries. "Are you workin' today?"

"Nope. I'm riding with Caleb this afternoon, and I have a friend coming by for lunch. You remember Mindy Taylor?" I pressed a hand to my belly as if to bolster myself for the pang of grief that would surely come with daring to say her name aloud. But it didn't. Blessed relief.

"She the one that lives out past the old Rutger place?"

"No, Daddy." I started to remind him that it was the Taylors' house where Jonathon drowned, but why bring it up? "Doesn't matter. She came into the shop the other day, and we decided it was high time we got caught up. I didn't figure you'd mind if she came for lunch."

"I don't mind. Won't be here anyway."

It hadn't taken Daddy long to make himself useful after Mama passed. I wanted to ask him about Mitch and the Bible study they were doing together, but I'd promised Mitch I'd keep it to myself for the time being. Just the fact that they were was enough for me anyhow, and I wanted to hold it close like a gift too precious to share.

Once Daddy was done with breakfast, I cleaned up the kitchen and made a passable attempt at straightening out the house. It was a sight better than my own had looked the night before, but I had no one to blame but myself for its disarray. Could hardly expect Mitch to care one way or the other when I'd left him high and dry to fend for himself. I'd get it in order once I moved back in. The thought of it had me giddy as a girl planning her first date.

I tended to the horses and Cheyenne before rummaging in the garden. I came up with a few tomatoes and cucumbers, which I tossed with some spring mix and a light vinaigrette. A little blue cheese and glazed walnuts, and voilà. Lunch.

I'd left the back door open, as well as the window, to get my fill of the outdoors. The leaves of the big maple rustled in the breeze, harmonizing with the thrum of cicadas. Much better than the clunk and whir of the air conditioner. The sound of tires crunching on the gravel alerted me as I was filling glasses with iced tea. Right on time.

I stepped onto the back porch as Mindy was climbing from her car. She reached across the seat and collected her purse and a plate. Seeing that platter topped with cookies was like a flicker of Deja vu. I'd seen a dozen plates of cookies since the day of the pool party. No sense hyperventilating over this one.

"This is a sweet spot." She closed the car door. "Never been out this way before."

"Thanks for being willing to drive out here. I thought it'd be nicer than sitting in a restaurant." Mindy had offered her house, but I didn't think either of us was ready to take that step.

She tented her eyes and peered around the property. "Yes, ma'am, this is a little piece of paradise." Then she waved a hand toward the porch. "One thing you can say about southerners, we don't stand on formality. Don't know many people who actually use their front door." She shook her head and made her way across the patchy grass.

"Isn't that the truth."

"Hope you don't mind, but I brought some cookies. Only thing I can make worth eating." She climbed the steps and joined me on the porch. "Thanks for makin' this happen, Bekah." Her gaze caught mine and she grimaced. "I wasn't aware when I saw you at the shop that your mama had passed. I'm sorry as I can be." She blew out a sigh. "You've had a boatload of loss, girl."

"Seems that way." Because it was that way. But there were plenty of others who suffered more. Like little Caleb. "Guess that's just the ugly part of life." I gave her a quick hug before opening the screen door. "Come on in. Hope you like salad." As she set the plate on the kitchen counter, it was as if the cookies had some kind of power over me. I couldn't shake the image of Jonathon cramming one of them into his mouth as he rushed to the pool. It was the last thing he ever ate.

Mitch

Decisions were a whole lot simpler when I wasn't holding every one of them up against some Scripture verse or another. Seemed the more I learned, the less confident I felt in my own abilities. Always figured being a Christian was more about using God as a crutch to hang all one's hopes on. Now I wasn't so sure.

The upside, though, meant there was someone watching out for me when I faced the hard stuff. Take my truck for instance. I had to believe prayer was the reason Bek showed up with the answer. Didn't figure life would always work out in such a way—God wasn't a genie or nothing—but I couldn't deny it was more than pure coincidence.

It made me want to dig into the Bible more. With my truck now in the shop, I had a couple days free. I could have stressed over the fact there wasn't money coming in, or I could use the opportunity to pick John's brain. There wasn't a man alive I trusted more than him—including Brother Paul.

We agreed to meet at The Coffee Break for lunch. I arrived early, ordered us some food, and nabbed the same corner table where Bekah told me she wanted a divorce. With my Bible, study book, and notes spread out, I waited on John. I could surely use some of his wisdom. So much had changed in the last couple of months, and yet, I felt as if I were right back where I started.

The lie stood between Bekah and me every bit as thick and impenetrable as a brick wall, even if she wasn't aware of it. It made my insides all itchy and edgy.

Steps shuffling up the stairs drew my attention to John as he appeared, his own Bible tucked beneath one arm. There was one couple on the other side of the loft, but other than that, we'd be alone for the time being. He approached the table and took a seat.

"Meetin' in the middle of the day." He slipped the Bible onto the table. "You gone and get yourself retired, did you?"

I snorted. "Hardly. Truck's in the shop getting her tranny replaced. Thought we might as well meet now, then I can pull an all-nighter at the church."

"How many of 'em hours you got left?"

I gazed over John's shoulder and tallied the numbers in my head. "Ten, maybe eleven. Either way, enough to be done with it by tomorrow."

"Good deal."

Justine, one of Evie's girls, topped the stairs with a tray of food in her arms and crossed to our table. "Got you a couple BLT's, some chips, and Cokes." She divvied up the food. "Anything else I can get you?"

I glanced at John. "Took a chance and ordered for you. Hope you don't mind."

"Fine by me." He smiled at Justine. "Think we're good. Thanks." As she left, he scratched his chin and eyed the food. "Bekah made me a stack of hotcakes this morning. Asked her what we were celebrating, and she told me she was moving back in with you this weekend."

"That's the plan." A knot of dread took the life out of my words.

"Thought you'd be kicking up your heels and dancing a jig." John stared at me. "Somethin' wrong?"

I pushed my food aside and folded my elbows onto the table. The secret had been buried so deep inside me, I didn't know if I could cut it loose. Once it was out, there'd be no going back.

"Mitch?" John narrowed his eyes. "You gonna tell me what's going on?"

I cleared my throat. "There's a little matter of a lie between Bek and me."

"A lie?" His eyes hardened. "You cheat on her or something?"

My gaze caught his and held. "No, sir. I've never so much as looked at another woman since the day I met Bekah."

His face softened to the point of a near smile. "Don't suppose it's any of my business if it's between the two of you." He moved the bag of chips from his plate to the table then inspected his sandwich. Pretty sure he was stalling to give me time to confess. The man wouldn't put a bite in his mouth without praying over it.

"The thing is, John, I could use your advice."

He froze. "I'm listening."

This wasn't a random friend I was sharing this with—it was Bekah's dad and Jonathon's grandfather. I needed to tread lightly and feel the situation out along the way. "Is it wrong to lie, even if it's for a good reason?"

He screwed up his mouth. "Son, the thing about lies is that they'll always be found out sooner or later. The longer it sits buried, the more it stinks when it's uncovered." It wasn't the answer I was hoping for. "You wanna dance around this all day or tell me what you're talkin' about?"

I sat up and crossed my arms. "It's about Jonathon. He didn't drown. Not exactly, anyway."

His head snapped back, and he glared at me. "What're you gettin' at?"

"I was with him that day. I mean, right there." I slapped the table. "He wasn't breathing, even though it didn't seem to me he was under long enough to drown. I pulled him out and started CPR, and that's when I smelled peanuts."

"Peanuts?" John's eyes glazed over for a moment before meeting mine. "He was allergic."

"Yes, sir."

"So, you think he had a reaction and that's what killed him?"

I nodded. "I know so. When y'all took Bekah home, I went to the hospital to talk to the doctor. I told him what I just told you, and he said there was evidence of anaphylaxis. They later did a full autopsy and found it's what he died from. I just didn't share it with Bekah."

He slumped against the chair back. "But I don't get it. Why'd you let Bekah believe he drowned? She's been blaming you for it all this time."

"Yes, sir. That she has. But I'd of rather she put the blame on me instead of taking it on herself. Didn't think she was strong enough to carry that load."

John shook his head. "She walked out on you over this, Mitch." He flung a hand my way. "She had you tried and convicted, and you did nothing to defend yourself. Now you're sayin' it wasn't your fault, and you knew it all along?"

I shook my head. "None of that matters now because she's come to a place of acceptance. I don't see the point of stirring it all up again, not when we're setting to get back together."

"I don't know." He rubbed his forehead. "If you believe that, why'd you even bring it up? Could of kept this all to yourself, and no one would be the wiser."

"Except God," I said. "I'm just now finding my way to Him, and I don't wanna mess it up."

John was quiet for a beat. "Well, son, your intentions were good. Jesus taught that we ought to put others before ourselves, and that's what you were doing when you hid the truth from Bekah. Sacrificed yourself and took her abuse. You're a good man." He gave me a faint smile. "Don't let it go to your head none."

I barked a laugh. "No, sir, I won't."

"But there's a few things you didn't consider." He held up a finger. "Let me pray over the food first." He bowed his head, and I did the same. "Father God, we are thankful for every bit of grace You impart on us. I'd like to lift up this here situation between my strong-willed girl and Mitch. You know what's in their hearts, even when they might go about things in the wrong way. We pray You'll bring them back together and bless their marriage. We thank You for this meal and we ask that You use it to nourish our bodies. For it's in Your name we pray."

"Amen."

John nabbed his bag of chips and opened them. "Back to what I was saying." Pointing a chip at me, he continued. "The thing about walking with Jesus is we gotta learn to surrender it all to Him. The good, not so good, and the truly ugly. He don't need us to step in and fix things, you hear?"

"I think so. Tell the truth and leave the rest up to Him."

John popped the chip in his mouth and reached into the bag for another one. "Yep. Now, we both know Bekah was worse than a mother hen when it came to my grandson. You don't know but God had a plan for her in the way things played out. He might've wanted her to go through that trial, and although you steppin' in might've felt like the right thing to do, He already had it under control."

"Yeah, but now that it's done—"

John held up a hand. "But it's not done, is it, son? You got that lie still between the two of you. Maybe Bekah finds out about it on her own, maybe she doesn't. Either way, don't you think it's up to the Lord how all that plays out?"

Definitely not what I wanted to hear. But I asked for wisdom, and I couldn't fault John for laying it out there. The man was a rock.

"Tell me something, John."

His eyebrows hitched. "What's that?"

"Anything ever trip you up?"

He frowned. "Can't get through this life without stumbling a time or two. I'm having myself a hard time digging into God's Word these days without my wife by my side. I don't question the Lord's right to take her, but it's not been easy." His eyes met mine. "You know that better than most, don't you, son?"

A fist lodged in my throat. "Yes, sir."

He smiled and nodded. "Kindest woman I've ever known. Strongest too. Miss her every day, just like I miss that boy of yours." He shrugged. "But I'm not gonna do anyone any good by wallowing in it. Just gotta move forward. And that's what you gotta do with Rebekah."

Chapter Twenty-Five

Rebekah

Mama used to say she always felt the presence of the Lord best while the choir sang during church service. The voices raised in harmony intoning His praises touched a recess of her heart unlike anything else. I imagined it was much like the serenity I experienced while riding Siren on one of the horse trails we'd foraged over the years. God's creation abounded in the birds flitting from tree to tree, cicadas thrumming their own strange rhythm, and the scent of damp earth after a late summer storm. Siren's slow gait eased me into a calm I'd not expected when my thoughts were running in a dozen different directions.

I didn't have the luxury to get lost in a mindless trance, however, because I had Caleb with me. Cassie had dropped him off, and I was to take him back to her and Joe when we were done. I knew Mitch's truck was in the shop, but I'd expected he'd have used the old Valiant he'd kept for emergencies to bring Caleb out. I'd been anxious to see him if only to assure myself that the conversation we'd had the other night wasn't a dream. That he wanted to be together again as much as I did. He hadn't called last night, like I'd expected him to, and I was too unsure to make the next move. But there was nothing I could do about it now. I'd have to put that aside for the moment and focus on Caleb.

It was the first time he'd ridden on his own steed—if Emperor could be called that. At the ripe old age of thirty-two, he had just enough get-up-and-go to keep Caleb grinning at the adventure, but not so much I feared he'd buck or bolt. Still, I kept a slow pace and rode with my body contorted to keep an eye on the two of them. I'd have been better off on a side-saddle—had I owned one.

"How're you doing, Caleb?" I twisted around to see the little boy nodding, grin still pasted onto his face. The riding helmet he wore was Jonathon's, and the decision to use it was like prying money from a miser. "Do you wanna stop for a spell?"

He nodded again.

I pulled back on Siren's reins, dismounted, and ground tied her. "You stay right here, girl." I patted her neck and walked back to where Emperor had stopped then helped Caleb down. "When you find your voice, kiddo, you can just tell me you wanna break."

All I got in response was another smile and a shrug.

"I brought us a little snack." I rustled into Siren's saddle bag and pulled out a packet of Mindy's cookies and two bottles of water. "Let's go cop a squat on that old log over there." I pointed my chin toward a fallen tree that'd been pushed off to the shoulder. It was in the shade of two old maples, the tops of which had created an arch over the trail leaving a kaleidoscope of filtered light dancing on the path.

I plopped next to Caleb and stretched out my legs. "You want some water?" I twisted off the cap of one of the bottles and handed it to him. "We also have some homemade cookies." At least with Caleb, I didn't have to worry about allergies. We'd been assured he had none.

But Jonathon had peanuts. My mind had been so wrapped up in the memory of Jonathon when Mindy presented her cookies the day before, I couldn't bring myself to eat one. I'd planned on dumping them in the garbage the moment she left but realized it would just be proof I was still allowing my grief to overtake common sense. Why waste a perfectly good batch of cookies just because they reminded me of my sweet boy?

Besides, chocolate chip was my favorite, just as they'd been Jonathon's.

"Want one?" I held a cookie out to Caleb.

He scrunched up his nose and arched his brows.

"They're chocolate chip. Don't you like chocolate chip?"

He took it and studied it, first one side and then the other.

I laughed. "It's not a science experiment, kiddo. Just a snack."

He took a bite and chewed, his eyes going wide. Must be pretty good. It was enough to break me down. I took one from the bag, broke a piece off, and popped it into my mouth. It was moist, and sweet, and...I stopped chewing and let the flavors gather on my tongue. It couldn't be. It was merely my over-active imagination playing tricks since I'd just been thinking about Jonathon's allergy. Heart thrumming in my throat, I crumbled what was left of my cookie, removed the chocolate pieces, and put the remainder in my mouth. Mindy had said she used a secret ingredient in her cookies, and I just discovered what it was—peanut butter. No trick.

Closing my eyes, I envisioned that last moment with Jonathon as he'd raced off to meet Mitch by the pool. He'd crammed half a cookie into his mouth. If the peanut butter-laden cookie I just swallowed was the same recipe Mindy used that day at the pool party, then there was a better-than-good chance Jonathon hadn't drowned but had died from an allergic reaction.

I gave him that cookie. Fourteen months of blaming Mitch for Jonathon's death, and it very well could've been my fault all along. How could I ever face him again? *Oh, God, what have I done?* I'd let my guard down just once, and Jonathon had died. I'd killed my child. It wasn't bad enough that I blamed Mitch, but all along, it was my fault.

Caleb's little hand reaching for the bag on my lap brought me out of my own racing thoughts. "Can I have another one?"

I must have been on the verge of losing my mind. I stared into Caleb's clear, brown eyes. "Did you say something?" I held my breath.

He pointed to the bag. "Can I have another cookie?"

The air left my lungs with a whoosh, and I laughed even as tears filled my eyes. "You talked, Caleb!" There were so many emotions vying for my attention, I didn't rightly know where to start. I fumbled into the bag and pulled out the last cookie.

"Thank you." He offered me a brilliant smile then bit into it like nothing miraculous had just occurred.

"Let's get you back to the house." I collected the water bottles and empty plastic bag and jumped up. "My daddy might be home by now, and I'm sure he'd love to hear what you have to say." Someone would need to hear it besides me, or else I really might think I'd lost my mind. But what if that's all Caleb had in him?

"Tell me, Caleb," I said, hefting him onto Emperor's back. "Did you like the cookie?"

He nodded.

I scrambled for something else to ask that would require more than a yes or no answer. "Chocolate chip cookies are my favorite. What's yours?"

He scrunched up his nose like he was giving it some thought. "I like peanut butter the best."

Barking out a laugh, I handed Emperor's reins to him. "Peanut butter, huh? I thought I tasted some in the cookies we just had. Did you?"

"Uh huh. But I like 'em if it's only peanut butter. It's better that way."

I swung up on Siren and nudged her forward. "What else do you like to eat?"

"I don't like broccoli or green beans, but I like French fries and corn."

All the way back to the house, I kept the questions coming. What was Caleb's favorite color? Red. What was his best friend's name? Gunner. What was the best Christmas present he ever got? A dinosaur night light. It kept me from the darkest questions that lingered at the back of my mind: Would Mitch be able to forgive me when I told him it was probably my fault Jonathon died? Would I be able to forgive myself?

As Caleb and I approached the house, I spotted a car in the gravel drive. My heart hitched for the brief moment before I realized it wasn't Mitch's Valiant. In fact, I didn't recognize it at all. A friend of Daddy's must've stopped by—it was about time I had a glimpse into his secret life. He was always off meeting this friend or that. Now, of course, I knew Mitch had been one of his causes. *Thank You, Lord.*

"Let's put the horses out to pasture, Caleb, then we'll go see what my daddy's up to."

"Okay." Such a simple word, but it held a world of hope.

What was going to happen to Caleb? He was finally feeling secure enough to speak, but would that change if Brother Paul had him moved from Joe and Cassie's to another foster home? What if Mitch and I did get back together? Could we adopt him ourselves? It wasn't something we could jump into, and yet, time was running out.

My mind was so fixated on Caleb and his future, I didn't recognize Kimberley leaning against the strange car until I was nearly on her. "Oh, Kim." Hand to my chest, I let out an embarrassed laugh. "I didn't expect you." Obviously. The girl was all the time showing up unannounced.

Her lips twitched. "Didn't come to see you, Bekah. Came to see your daddy." I was still puzzling over her comment when her gaze slid to Caleb who glued himself to my side. "And who do we have here?"

"This is Caleb." I put my arm around his thin shoulders. "Caleb, this is Miss Kimberley. She and I went to school together. We're...friends."

"Hi, Caleb. It's nice to meet you."

I opened my mouth to speak for him then snapped it shut. If he'd talk to a stranger, then I had to believe chances were good he'd not slip back into silence.

"Hi," he said, squinting up at her.

Progress. Kim couldn't know how monumental that small greeting truly was.

She held a book up. "I came by to give this back to your daddy. He said it was your mama's favorite and thought I might wanna read it myself."

I craned my neck to see the title. *Redeeming Love* by Francine Rivers. "He's right. That was Mama's favorite." I hitched my eyebrows at her. "How long have you and my daddy been carrying on?" I grinned to let her know I was only fooling. At least I hoped I was only fooling.

"I came by a few weeks ago to see how he was doing, and we got to talking." She chuckled. "He's got it in his mind I need Jesus in my life."

"He's right about that, too," I said. "There's not a one of us who doesn't."

I only hoped Mitch had enough Jesus in his life to look past my shameful behavior since Jonathon died and forgive me. No one would blame him if he didn't. Least of all, me.

Thoughts were spinning in my mind like a crazed tilt-a-whirl as I pulled my car into Joe and Cassie's drive. Caleb chattered the entire drive, his voice blending with the August breeze that blew through the open windows. Daddy always said God worked in wondrous ways, and He surely was doing so now. With Caleb and maybe Kimberley. Instead of hitching myself to that blessing, I was being tugged in two directions. Joy on the one end and guilt on the other. Mitch had every right to call me on my stuff. Hadn't I all but destroyed our marriage by unfairly blaming him for Jonathon's death?

"We're home." Caleb unbuckled his seat belt and was out the door before I could respond. Despite the brick pressing on my heart, I chuckled. Wouldn't Cassie be surprised when the boy burst into the house demanding a snack?

I followed at a more sedate pace and walked through the front door Caleb had left open. It settled my nerves some to see Cassie kneeling in front of him and swiping at what I assumed were joyful tears.

"You want what?" She asked him with a sniffle and a smile big as Texas.

"Go swimmin' with Jane an' Gracie."

As I approached, she glanced up at me, stood, and rested her hand on his shoulder as if she couldn't bear to break contact. "You did it." Her voice cracked, and she took a deep breath. "I thought it was my mind playing tricks. I made him repeat himself just to be sure."

My throat tightened. "Believe me, I know how you feel, but I can't take credit, Cassie. It was all God." I was starting to sound like Mama. Now if I could just imitate her heart. "We stopped for a break, and he asked for another cookie." A peanut butter-tainted cookie. My stomach knotted.

Cassie bent over Caleb. "The girls are already swimming. Why don't you put on your trunks, and we'll all go outside?"

"Yes, ma'am." He took off down the hall. Squeals, giggles, and the sound of splashing water came from the backyard. Since Jonathon's death, I couldn't be near a swimming pool without fear of being sick. Even now, the thought of those girls in the water with no supervision sent a thrumming through every nerve.

"Are you okay?" Cassie drew closer and rubbed my arm. "You're white as a sheet." Before I could respond, her eyes widened. "They're fine, Bekah. Gracie's got floaters on and Jane's a strong swimmer. I only came in for some lemonade, and then Caleb came rushing through the door—"

"Stop." I ran a hand down my sweat-damp face. "Don't let my crazy turn into your crazy." I blinked back the sudden tears. "Even if it was my place to do so, which it isn't, I've never doubted that you're a great mom." Did I put everyone on edge because of my own neurosis?

Caleb raced into the room and was scrambling to get through the screen door before we could react.

"Hold it," Cassie said. When he turned to her, eyes wide with excitement, she continued. "You need to wait for us before you get into the pool. We'll be out in a minute. Okay? Just let me get y'all some lemonade."

He nodded.

"I wanna hear you say it, Caleb."

I wanted to hear him say it too. The poor child would be pushed to talk until we felt certain it wasn't a fluke.

"'Kay, Miss Cassie. I promise." He slid the screen open and was gone.

Cassie put an arm around my shoulders. "Don't feel like you have to stay, Bek. I

know—"

"Caleb, you're talkin'!" Jane's squeals could be heard all the way into Marshall County. The rest of the kids' chatter was indecipherable, although it was punctuated by high-pitched giggles. It was certainly a day for celebration.

"What d'you want to do, Bek? Go or stay?" Although Cassie was giving me an out, she led me toward the kitchen.

"Actually, I could use a listening ear right now, if you don't mind." Daddy's who I really wanted to talk to, but he hadn't been home.

"You got it." She retrieved a tray from the pantry and moved to the fridge. "You wanna grab those plastic tumblers from the cabinet?" She pointed with her chin, and I obeyed.

A few minutes later, we stepped out into the late afternoon sunshine. Jane, dripping water from her long hair and bathing suit, was tugging swimmies up Caleb's skinny arm while Gracie watched from the steps of the pool.

Gracie hopped up when she spotted us. "Caleb's talkin'," she announced, her eyes almost as wide as her grin.

"Isn't it wonderful?" Cassie slid the full tray onto the patio table. "Y'all want some lemonade?"

Chaos reigned for five minutes, then Cassie and I were left in relative peace to sit and watch the kids. A floral scent mixed with chlorine wafted in the breeze. I closed my eyes and fought against the images of Jonathon's lifeless body lying by that other pool.

"Rumor has it, you and Mitch might be getting back together," Cassie said. The words were gentle, soothing, as if she was approaching a skittish horse. "Is that what you need to talk about?"

"If he'll have me." I tried to laugh it off, but a sob took hold, and it fell flat.

"You're kiddin', right?" She rested her elbows on the table. "He and Joe might have that bromance bond that keeps things confidential, but I'd have to be blind, deaf, and dumb not to know how badly that man wants you back."

Regret sliced my heart in two. If I could go back a year, or even eight months, and change things. God's sovereignty didn't allow that I'd bring Jonathon back to life, but the rest was on me. "I've made such a mess of things, Cassie." I glanced at her face and away again. I couldn't look her in the eye if I hoped to confess my fault in Jonathon's death and the downward spiral of my marriage. How would I ever face Mitch?

"It doesn't matter, Bek." She reached over and covered my hand with one of hers. "Mitch loves you, and I'm sure he's willing to do whatever it takes. I mean, he knows you blame him for what happened to Jonathon, but maybe with counseling, you could see your way to forgiving him."

The confession rattled around in my mind, but it couldn't seem to make it past the lump that grew in my throat as she spoke. "You don't understand," I finally croaked out. My gaze caught on Caleb splashing Gracie in the pool. If it hadn't been for him, would I have ever known the truth of Jonathon's death?

Cassie's voice drew my attention back to her. "Then explain it to me, Bek."

I drew in a deep breath, held it for a moment, and let it out slowly. My heart rate leveled out and the panic subsided. "I stopped blaming Mitch for Jonathon's death a while ago. Before she passed Mama helped me to see how unfair I was being."

Cassie offered a soft smile. "That's good. And Mitch is aware, right?"

I nodded. "But that's not the problem." I sighed. "What he doesn't know," I glanced at her, "and what I just realized, is that it was *my* fault." I pressed a hand to my chest as if to make a point. "And I'm afraid it'll be Mitch's turn to cast blame where it rightly belongs."

Mitch

I couldn't remember when I'd last pulled an all-nighter, discounting the hours I'd spent in a jail cell for drunk and disorderly. Disorderly, anyway. No one would believe I hadn't been drunk. Course, what idiot goes and gets himself in a bar fight when he hadn't even been drinking? At any rate, this one left me with a brain full of cotton and eyes that couldn't quite focus. But at least I'd finished my community service.

After a couple hours of shut eye, I cleaned up the house best I could and headed back to the church to have Brother Paul sign off on my paperwork for court. It'd still been dark when I cleaned up that morning, and I wasn't about to go banging on the pastor's door before he was even outta bed. The long night of mindless work gave me a chance to think on my marriage, the change in Bekah's heart, and John's advice. I knew he was right—any lie between us could cause the potential for a break later down the road. Better to get it cleared up before she moved back in.

It was late afternoon when I pulled my '62 Valiant behind Brother Paul's car. I spotted him crouched over the flowerbed that bordered the parsonage. He had on an old pair of jeans and a ratty t-shirt and looked less like a pastor than I did. Seemed the man spent more time outside than he did in.

He craned his neck as I came around the back of the car and squinted. Could tell the moment he recognized me—eyes widening, he stood. "Will you look at that ol' classic you're driving these days?" He tossed the spade into the dirt and walked toward me. "Boy does that bring back a memory or two. My dad drove a Valiant. What is she, a '63?"

"'62. Passed down from my grandma to my mama and now me. Thought about selling it a time or two, but with my truck in the shop, I'm glad I didn't. Good to have a backup vehicle to get around in."

Paul's eyes caressed the car as he shook his head. "You ever decide to sell, let me know, will you? She'd be a fun project."

I barked out a laugh. "She'd be a project, all right. Needs a whole lot of work to make her dependable, but she's all I got right now."

He looked at me. "You get those hours done last night?"

"Yes, sir." I reached into my back pocket and pulled out the folded form. "Just need you to sign them off, and I'll get this taken over to the clerk's office."

"Come on inside for a spell. We'll have us a glass of sweet tea and catch up."

I followed Paul through the front door into the cool house. Comparing the orderliness of his place against that of mine, I saw where I might could make a few improvements before Bekah came home—if she'd still want to after we tore down the lie between us. Didn't see how she could be upset with me since I was only trying to spare her, but I never could figure out the way her mind worked. Or any woman's, for that matter. Why'd they have to go and make things more complicated than they were?

"You okay?"

I'd been staring at his family room without even realizing it. "Admiring your cleanliness, is all. You have yourself a housekeeper? Can't quite imagine you dusting the shelves."

He chuckled. "A woman comes in once every couple of weeks, but I tend toward the persnickety anyway, so it stays pretty clean. Any progress with Bekah?"

I stepped into the kitchen behind Paul and leaned against the counter while he took a couple glasses from the cupboard. "I believe so, yes. We're talking about it, so that's good."

"I suppose you know she's been attending services with John since Anita passed." He filled the glasses with ice from the dispenser on the front of the fridge. "Looks like the same ol' Rebekah I used to know."

"Yes, sir." I didn't know she was going to church again, but it wasn't a surprise, either.

"And how's Caleb doing?" Innocent question, but I knew better. Once Joe revealed Caleb's situation, I'd been looking at it from every angle. Couldn't take in the boy on my own.

"Not quite sure what you wanna hear, Pastor."

"Guess I was hoping you and Bekah would be open to adopting him. School starts in another couple of weeks, and we're running outta time." He filled the glasses with tea and handed me one.

I sat myself down at the table. "If I'd known from the get-go what y'all were up to, I could of played it straight."

Brother Paul dropped into a chair with a grunt. "Sometimes, you gotta step out in faith and see what the Lord'll do." He took a gulp of tea. "When we first suggested Rebekah work with Caleb, didn't seem you were all that confident your marriage would survive." He raised his glass at me. "Now look at you."

"I get it, sir. But Bekah's never been keen on adoption, and to push her now when we're just finding our way back together might just blow up in our faces."

He leaned his elbows on the table, his blunt fingers wrapped around the glass. "Tell me, Mitch. If it were up to you, would you be open to adopting the boy?"

I drew in a deep breath then blew it out real slow. "The thing is, it's not up to me." I slumped back in the chair. "It's gotta be a joint decision." I hitched an eyebrow. "Truth of it is, it's gotta be Bekah's decision. I could suggest it, but our marriage has to come first. It's a lesson learned the hard way."

"I get it. And I'm proud of how you've grown over the last couple months. We'll just have to trust that God's got his hand on that boy, and He'll find him the right home at the right time."

"Well, you never know." Bekah had become fond of Caleb, but there was more at stake than one little boy's future. I wasn't going to jump in where I should be wading. "Let's just see how God orchestrates things, why don't we?"

Paul's eyebrows shot up, and he grinned real slow. "Well, lookee here. Is that a budding Christian I see sittin' before me?"

I snorted. "Don't act so surprised, Brother Paul. It's near impossible to stonewall the good Lord when He's got you, Bekah, and John on His side." I took a swig of tea and set the glass aside. "No doubt, Miss Anita is up there alongside of Jesus working things on that end as well." A man with half a brain would know the truth when he saw it. Just too bad it took me so long.

Chapter Twenty-Six

Rebekah

There wasn't a minute that passed by I didn't think of Mama or Jonathon. It was a slow road through the mire of grief, but I was seeing such a light on the other side, it made me trust more and more in the Lord and His ways. He certainly didn't need my permission to do whatever it was He purposed, because sure as the sun rose in the east, I'd have made a mess of things had I been in charge. If I'd clung to Jesus when Jonathon died instead of pushing Him aside, I would have never walked out on Mitch and laid all the blame of our baby's death at his feet. *Judge not lest you be judged.* The exhortation in Matthew 7 was a blunt reminder.

For a split second, it entered my mind I could forget I ever tasted peanut butter in Mindy's secret-recipe chocolate chip cookies. Mitch would never know—unless Cassie ratted me out. But it didn't take me five seconds to clear the deceit from my soul. How could I ever face Mitch again if I didn't confess the whole thing? It might take him eighteen months to forgive me, just as it'd taken me that long to forgive him—for something that was never his fault in the first place.

My mind was so fixated on the mess I'd made of things, I'd forgotten about the biscuits I'd put in the oven until the charred scent that poured from it cut into my thoughts.

"Oh, for Pete's sake," I mumbled as I snatched a potholder from the counter before opening the oven door. Smoke poured out, stinging my eyes and nose, and I pulled out the baking sheet and shut off the power.

"Hope you had something else planned to go along with them biscuits," Daddy said, sauntering into the kitchen like he didn't have a care in the world. "They look a might burnt for my liking."

I'd have stuck out my tongue at him if I wasn't trying so hard to be pleasing to the Lord. "I thought they'd spice up the leftovers I'm serving."

He chuckled. "They'll spice 'em up all right."

"Where've you been, anyway? Kimberley came by earlier to drop off a book you lent her." I pointed the potholder toward the table where I'd left Mama's copy of *Redeeming Love.* "Didn't even know the two of you were keeping company." I gave him a cheeky grin. Payback for disparaging my attempt at homemade biscuits.

His eyebrows shot up. "You ain't so old I can't take a switch to your behind, little girl." But his lips twitched with humor. "In your mama's absence, I'm just trying to plant where I can. She was good at spreading a little joy and hope." He turned away from me and flicked the cover of Mama's book. If he felt anything like I did, he needed a moment to refocus his emotions. "Thought maybe you'd be with Mitch tonight. Picked me up some barbecue," he lifted a white sack and put it on the table, "but there's enough for the two of us."

Mitch had called three times, but I let them all go to voicemail. Amazing how one little piece of information can twist a person into a pretzel. If Mama were here, she'd set me straight with some keen words of wisdom. But maybe since Daddy was of a mind to take up where she left off, he'd be able to help me out.

I stared at his back while he fanned through the book. It was a sure bet he was thinking about Mama. A body couldn't walk into this house without seeing her in every crevice and corner. Knowing we'd see her again made the idea of heaven that much sweeter.

I collected a couple of plates and slid them onto the table then went back for drinking glasses. I knew just the thing to distract the both of us from grief-induced musings. "Hey, Daddy?"

"Hmm?" He turned to face me.

A grin worked its way across my face. "Caleb started talking today."

His eyes widened, and he barked out a laugh. "Don't that beat all? I knew you'd bring the boy around, yes sir." He stepped up, wrapped an arm around my shoulders, and gave me a quick hug. "Things are surely lookin' up, aren't they? You and Mitch are workin' through the rough spots, and now this. Your mama would be right proud, darlin'."

The joy deflated like the air from a pricked balloon, and it was all I could do to keep the smile in place. Fiddling with the utensils, I peered up at him. "I have a bit of a problem and could sure use some advice."

He waved a hand at the table. "Have yourself a seat. My office is open for business."

I poured us some tea and sat across from him. He'd had a front row pew to my poor behavior, and now that he was buddies with Mitch, it put things on shaky ground. My stomach was tied in knots along with my tongue.

When I didn't do more than fiddle with my glass, Daddy narrowed his eyes. "What's going on, darlin'?"

My gaze met his for a beat then slid away. "You remember I said a friend was coming by for lunch today? Mindy Taylor?"

He nodded. "Yup."

"I didn't know if you remembered, but it was the pool party at the Taylor house where Jonathon...well, where he drowned." I shook my head. "I mean, died." I scraped my bangs back with a sigh.

Daddy pushed his glass aside and leaned his elbows on the table with a frown. "Okay."

"Before we went that day, me and Mitch kinda had a little tiff. I wanted Jonathon to wear swimmies and Mitch thought I was being overprotective." I took a drink of tea. "You remember how clingy I could be, Daddy, don't you?"

He pursed his lips. "What're swimmies?"

"You know, flotation devices." I wrapped my fingers around my bicep. "They attach to the arm up here and keep a body from goin' under." The more this dragged out, the more my stomach knotted. I waved a dismissive hand. "It doesn't matter, really. The point I'm trying to make is that I tended to hover over Jonathon, so afraid something might happen to him. We can get into a whole theological discussion over God's sovereignty—I mean, Mama reminded me time and again that I didn't really have control over God's plans."

Daddy covered one of my hands with his. "Breathe, darlin'. You're getting all worked up and not making a whole lot of sense."

This wasn't such a good idea after all. I knew what Daddy would say—tell the truth. He'd preached that message from the time I could walk. I drew in a deep breath and then another. "That day at the party, Jonathon was itching to get into the pool. Right before he went in, he asked could he have one of Mindy's chocolate chip cookies. Normally, I would've asked what all was in it, but..." It was on the tip of my tongue to excuse my lapse in judgment, maybe even have the audacity to blame Mitch for making me feel like a helicopter mom. But then we'd be right back where we started.

"But what?" Daddy patted my hand.

I shook my head. "I didn't. Plain and simple, I didn't bother to ask. I let Jonathon take one."

Daddy eased back and dropped his hands into his lap. His eyes didn't meet mine and his mouth was turned down. His thoughts weren't written on his face, like they'd have been on Mitch's, but if I had to guess, he was disappointed in me. How could he not be?

I twisted my fingers together and continued. "When Mindy came by today, she brought some of those cookies." I jumped up and retrieved the covered plate from the pantry and brought it to the table. "Try one, Daddy." It was an odd set of circumstances that the cookies that caused Jonathon's death inspired Caleb to speak again.

He tapped the edge of the plate. "Don't wanna spoil my supper. Just tell me."

"Maybe I'm crazy, but there's peanut butter in them."

With a sigh, he rubbed his forehead. "I don't know why it still amazes me when things come together the way they do," he mumbled.

"Excuse me?"

He lifted his hand from his forehead and waved it at me. "Nothing." Shifting in his seat, he leaned forward. "Let me speed up this here conversation, 'cause the rate you're goin' we'll be here until the Rapture."

"I'm just trying to set up the situation, Daddy. No need to be impatient with me."

"Darlin', you ain't seen impatient—not from me. I take it you're gonna tell me you think Jonathon didn't drown. Maybe, instead, he had an allergic reaction to the peanuts in those cookies"—he jabbed a finger at the cookies in question—"and that's what he actually died from. Am I warm?"

I dropped my gaze. "Yes, sir."

"So, why are you telling me this? Why aren't you discussing the situation with Mitch?"

I squirmed. "I'm gonna tell him. I thought maybe you might know how I can soften the blow."

He barked out a laugh. "What blow would that be, darlin'?" Why was he being so obtuse?

"That I've been blaming him when it's looking like it was my fault all along. When he finds out the truth, I'm afraid he'll be angry with me. And rightfully so."

He thrummed his stubby fingers on the table. "So, you think when it was the other way 'round, you were right to blame him for your boy's death?"

"No, of course not. And I've told him that." Tears bit at the backs of my eyes. "But this is different, Daddy. I walked out on him and was hateful. Maybe it'll be that he can't forgive me in light of all that."

He narrowed his eyes at me. "You've always been a good girl, Bekah. You know how much I love you, and I've been right proud of you from the time you was born. But there are some days you confound me, darlin'. You can't seem to see what's right in front of your face."

What was he talking about? My mouth dropped open, and I stammered.

"The two of you need to stop second-guessing how the other one's gonna handle the trials and such the good Lord allows you to stumble through. It's His way of strengthening your character, and it's about time you got outta His way." He slapped the table with an open hand. "Now, if you don't mind, we'd better eat this barbecue before it's stone cold."

Mitch

Never understood until talking with John what the Bible meant about seeking God's wisdom. Thought maybe if I prayed hard enough for it, the Lord would see fit to make me smarter. Didn't work that way. There was more to it than prayer. Had to read the Bible to know how God thought, understand what it meant to be conformed into the image of Christ, and get myself a manual for living right. Active, not passive. That also meant asking for wise council from people more studied up than I was—which wasn't much.

Once I'd heard what John had to say, I was anxious to talk to Bekah and get it all out in the open. No more second-guessing. I'd called her at least three times and went right to voicemail. The girl was tapping that "ignore" button on me. But why? If she'd changed her mind about us getting back together, she needed to tell me. The thought of it had my stomach flipping like a bunch of crazed guppies, and I wasn't about to let her go without a fight. Whatever giant she had lurking in her mind, I was ready with my metaphorical slingshot, and I wasn't going to wait until she invited me in for the duel.

It was near ten when I pulled my truck into their drive. Thought maybe John would still be up, but there were no lights on as far as I could see. Last time I pulled this stunt, I nearly got myself bit and shot. But I was ready for Cheyenne this time. Had me a piece of leftover hamburger from my dinner tucked into my pocket. That should get me past the first level of home security.

I was just rounding the front porch, heading toward Bekah's room, when Cheyenne's deep growl had me reaching for the bag in my pocket. I crouched down and crooned real low, "Got something for you, girl." Had to go by feel, 'cause it was a moonless night, and I couldn't see a darned thing. In such a vulnerable position, I prayed that if Cheyenne didn't recognize my scent, she'd know beef when she smelled it.

Lights lit up the yard along with the familiar *ch ch* of a rifle being cocked. Cheyenne sat on her haunches, eyes on the burger meat in my hand. I held it out to her then pivoted on the balls of my feet to find John standing on the edge of the porch shaking his head.

He had the gun across his arms like he was carrying a baby. Better than having it pointed in my direction. "You ever heard of calling, son?"

"Tried. Four times. Seems Bekah's ignoring me."

"Huh." He scratched his head. "Might could've come to the door like a normal person."

"Didn't wanna wake you."

He snorted. "Yeah, 'cause this worked out so much better. Might as well get yourself on in here before the skeeters eat you up."

I left Cheyenne to finish the rest of the meat and joined John on the front porch.

"I'll be happy as a pig in mud when the two of you get back together. Might get me some sleep then." His grumbling would've been more effective if his face wasn't lit up with a grin. "I'll wake Rebekah. Serve her right for not calling you back."

"Yes, sir." I followed him inside and waited in the entry while he slipped down the hallway. Couldn't remember the last time I came in by way of the front door. Not even sure why they bothered to have one, except for John to use as a lookout.

Rumbling came from down the hallway before Bekah appeared. She was wearing a pair of gray sweats that hugged her hips and a pink tank that exposed the curve of her belly when she moved her arms. It took a heartbeat or two for my gaze to work itself up to her face. Wariness clouded her eyes and there was a wrinkle between her brows.

She folded her arms against her chest and lifted her shoulders. "You got Daddy a little riled, showing up like this." The heat I was expecting was absent from her tone. This was not the defensive woman of a few months ago.

"We need to talk, Bek. I've been calling you."

"I know," she said on a sigh. "I was gonna get ahold of you in the morning."

"A text to let me know your intention woulda gone a long way."

"You're right. I'm sorry." She offered an apologetic smile. "Why don't you come back to my bedroom, and we can talk."

"Your bedroom?" A picture of John with his shotgun had my voice squeaking. "But your daddy..."

She rolled her eyes and huffed out a soft laugh. "We're married, silly. Daddy's not gonna care if we go in there."

Bekah's room was nothing more than a double bed, nightstand, and dresser. It was as fancy as a cloistered nun's, which meant she'd never really settled in. Should have made the tension in my shoulders ease up, but there was still the matter of the lie that stood between us. And whatever it was that kept her from returning my calls.

She sat on the edge of the bed and patted the space beside her. Despite our marital status, I couldn't help but take a quick glance at the closed door and bend an ear to be sure no one was coming in to defend Bekah's honor.

"I truly was gonna call you in the morning," Bekah said as my body weight put a dip in the mattress. "I know we need to talk, but I suppose I wanted to be prayed up beforehand." That didn't bode well for me.

"You worried about how I'm gonna react to what you have to say?"

She crinkled her nose and shrugged. "Let's just say I haven't set the best example of Christian charity these last several months." She grimaced. "Or maybe ever since we got married."

Sounded like an apology to me. "We've covered that, Bek. You already said you were sorry about how things went down after we lost Jonathon. No need to rehash it."

She reached across the space between us and laid her hand on mine. It was warm and soft, and for a brief moment, it hijacked my brain. Would our marriage always be riddled with baggage from the past?

"The thing is, Mitch, I was wrong."

I shook my head. "Yeah, so you already said." I shifted so I could take both her hands in mine. "You aren't the only one who was wrong, babe. There's something I need to tell you, and I'm afraid it's gonna set us back some."

She slipped her hand from mine and laid it against my chest. "Me first, Mitch. Please. I just have to spit it out or I'm gonna bust."

"Okay. What is it?" Could she feel the thumping of my heart under her hand?

She swallowed hard and stared at me, her eyes welling. "All this time, I've blamed you for letting Jonathon drown, and I don't think that's what killed him." The last few words came out so fast, they tripped over themselves.

It took a beat to process what she said. Was it possible her secret and mine were the same? "Where did you get that idea?"

She dropped her hands into her lap and twisted her fingers together. She stared down at them as if she didn't have the strength to lift her head. "Mindy Taylor stopped by yesterday and brought a plate of her homemade cookies." I didn't need divine revelation to know where this was going. "Same cookies Jonathon had that day he died." She knew.

I rubbed a hand down my face and sighed. "Look, Bek—"

"There was peanut butter in them, Mitch." She glanced up, and her eyes were swimming in misery. "I've blamed you all this time, but it was my fault. I don't think Jonathon drowned."

I shifted close enough to wrap my arm around her shoulders and kissed her temple.

"You aren't furious with me?" Her voice was muffled against my shoulder, but the incredulity was clear. "After everything I've put you through?" She tilted her head to look at me.

I sighed. "I've known all along, Bekah."

She reared back to put distance between us. "I don't understand." She shook her head. "You surely can't mean from the time he died."

Nodding, I linked her fingers in mine. This could be one of those defining moments in our marriage. No more secrets. No more lies. No more blame. "When I tried to give him mouth-to-mouth, I smelled the peanut butter on his breath." Her eyes filled with tears and spilled over. Would there ever be an end to the pain of this loss? "He hadn't been under the water but a few seconds, so I knew something was off when I couldn't revive him. I spoke with the doctor later, and he confirmed it in the autopsy report."

A sob cut loose. "All this time, Mitch." She pulled away from me to fumble on her nightstand for a tissue then blew her nose. "The things I've said to you." Her voice hitched over another sob. "Why didn't you say something? Why did you let me go on blaming you when it was my fault?"

I shook my head. "We're not goin' there, Bek. You wanna be angry with me for not telling you the truth, I can live with that. But didn't you just the other night tell me our boy's death was out of our hands?"

Her chin wobbled. "Yes," she managed. "But if I hadn't gotten distracted, if I'd only—"

"We're not assigning blame." I gathered her into my arms and held on tight. "I did what I did because I love you, baby girl," I murmured. "Maybe it was wrong, but I wanted to protect you from as much pain as possible. The last thing I wanted was you forever blaming yourself for Jonathon's death. We can't change it, but we have to figure out a way to move forward."

"I'm so sorry, Mitch. I've made such a mess of things." Her words ended on a yawn.

I smiled against her hair. "And yet, somehow God's working on us anyway." Gave a man hope.

Chapter Twenty-Seven

Rebekah

A gentle, fragrant breeze caressed my bare arm and coaxed me from sleep to consciousness. With my eyes still closed against the early morning sun, I basked in the cocoon of comfort left over from the delicious dream I'd been having of Mitch. His touch. His kisses. The tickle of his warm breath on my neck and ear. The visions that flitted through my mind could melt a stronger woman into a puddle of syrupy goo.

"Morning, sweet girl." The deep rumble of Mitch's voice had my eyes snapping open. He was propped up on one elbow, his gaze drinking me in like a man deprived of water. His slow smile was contagious as a yawn.

It wasn't a dream after all.

"G'morning." A shiver of pure pleasure ran up my spine as I rested my hand against his bare, muscled chest. "I thought it was a dream."

He nuzzled my neck, stealing the breath from my lungs. "I sure hope not." He shifted his body and bumped his backside against the wall. "This'd be a lot more fun in our own bed. Don't know how you sleep in this thing."

I huffed out a soft laugh. "I didn't hear you complaining last night."

"Won't hear me complainin' now, either." He ran a finger down my arm. "Think I should sneak out before your daddy catches me here?"

"You've got nothing to worry about, babe. He'd be over the moon." I thought about Daddy's reaction last night when I'd confessed my part in Jonathon's death. He hadn't been surprised. "This thing with Jonathon, did—"

He placed a finger over my lips. "Nope. If we're gonna move forward, we got to let the past stay where it belongs."

I curled my fingers around his hand and eased it away from my face. "I don't plan on beating it to death, Mitch. I just wanna know if you talked to Daddy about it."

He eased back a touch, wariness clouding his eyes. "Depends."

I rolled my eyes. "I'll take that as a yes."

He must have figured since I didn't pitch a hissy fit, it was safe enough to snuggle close again. "Are you mad?"

"No." I drew out the word while assessing my feelings. "A little annoyed, maybe. It's an odd notion that you and Daddy are taking sides against me."

"That's not how it came down, Bekah." He fingered a strand of my hair. "I needed someone I could talk to that loves you as much as I do, help me figure out the best way to come clean. Never had a daddy of my own, and for the first time, I feel a strong connection to yours." Well, shut my mouth. If that wasn't enough to make a woman's heart melt, I didn't know what was.

"That's so sweet." I sandwiched his face between my hands and pulled him down for a kiss. Just as our lips met, it hit me that I hadn't told him about Caleb. "Oh, Mitch." I scrambled onto my knees and nearly toppled off the bed.

His eyes widened as he clutched my arm to keep me from falling. "What? What's wrong?"

"I forgot to tell you the exciting news about Caleb."

He slapped a hand to his chest and chuckled. "You took ten years off my life. Do that much more, and you'll put me in an early grave." He sat up. "What's this about Caleb?"

"He talked!" No doubt Daddy heard the squeal that popped out of my mouth like a champagne cork.

"When did this happen?"

"Yesterday. We were riding the trail and stopped for a snack." I grimaced. "Mindy's cookies, of all things, and he asked if he could have another one."

"Never had a doubt." Mitch grinned. "Horse magic, like I told you."

I narrowed my eyes at him. "I don't have horse magic, and if I did, it'd be Siren talking and not Caleb."

"Whatever. That's certainly headline news, though. Means he's starting to feel safe."

"Right? The whole ride back to Joe and Cassie's, I asked him a million questions just to keep him talking. I was afraid we'd walk in the door, and he'd clam up again." I laughed. "You should hear him, Mitch. He's got the sweetest voice." Just like Jonathon's. That had my grin wavering a tad.

"Good timing too. If he's gonna have to go into foster care, it'd be a whole lot easier on him if he's talking." Was that a little manipulation I heard in his tone? If it was, he was good at hiding it.

"Why don't I fix you some breakfast before you go off to work? You got any hauls scheduled this morning?" I scooted off the bed and snatched my robe from the chair sitting in the corner. Why did I feel so modest all of a sudden? I was wearing more than most girls strutting their stuff on the beach.

"No, but I could use a ride to pick up my truck. Jake called last night and said it'd be ready first thing this morning." Mitch climbed out of the bed and pulled on the t-shirt he'd discarded last night then snatched the jeans from the floor and went to work putting them on over boxers as well.

"I can do that." My tongue was thick making it hard to form a coherent sentence. Maybe every married couple needed a little hitch in their relationship to wake them up to what was truly important. I drew in a deep breath and reached for the door handle.

"Wait." Mitch tugged on my arm. "Are you going out like that?"

I glanced down at the robe covering my sweats and tank. "Like what?"

"You know." He flicked a hand toward me. "Dressed like you just got outta bed."

"I did just get out of bed." I shook my head. "Don't worry. I'll change before we leave the house."

"But your daddy—"

"For Pete's sake, Mitch." I rolled my eyes. "If you think me getting fully dressed is gonna fool daddy, then you don't know him very well." I flung open the door and stomped down the hall, stifling a giggle. When did Mitch turn into such a prude?

For all my bravado, I faltered some when I spotted Daddy sitting at the kitchen table with his Bible and coffee. "Hey, Daddy."

He lifted his head, mouth twitching and amusement dancing in his eyes. "Morning, Darlin'." He glanced past me. "Mitch."

Mitch cleared his throat. "Sir."

"Appears you and Bekah worked things out." Looked as if Daddy was going to bust out laughing if I didn't put a stop to this.

"I'm making breakfast, Daddy." I snatched a couple mugs from the cabinet and filled them with coffee. "You want anything?" After adding a splash of half and half to Mitch's, I set it on the table and waved a hand for him to sit.

"I'd rather discuss when y'all are gonna be moving back home." He closed the Bible and folded his hands. "Can't have Mitch here sneakin' in after dark and takin' advantage of my girl." He eyed Mitch's beet-red face and started chuckling.

I slapped his arm. "Leave him be, Daddy. It's scandalous enough for him that I marched out here in my robe and sweats."

Daddy ran a hand over his mouth as if it'd wipe the grin from his face. "I'm sorry, son. You just make it so darn easy sometimes."

Mitch grimaced. "Anything to amuse you, John. I'm here to serve."

"All kiddin' aside, what's the plan with you two?"

I folded my arms and stared at him. "If I didn't know better, I'd think you were anxious to get rid of me."

"Never that, darlin'," he said on a sigh. "Seein' the two of you back together again would bring me pure joy." He thumped the Bible with his index finger. "I bet your mama is lookin' down from heaven praising the good Lord for what

He's done in your lives." As his eyes misted, he blinked and *harrumphed*. "I'd just feel a good sight better if I knew you was taken care of."

A brick laid on my chest as a thought took hold. Might be Mitch was thinking it too, because he stiffened. "Daddy, you're not sick or anything, are you?" He waved a dismissive hand as I knelt beside him. "Don't brush me off like I'm a worry wart. You'd tell me if there was something wrong, wouldn't you?"

He took my hands in his and looked me in the eye. "I wouldn't do that to you, Bekah. As God is my witness, I would never put you through what your mama put us through. I'm gettin' old, sure, and I don't move as well as I used to, but I'm fit as a fiddle." He touched my chin. "If that changes, I promise you'll be the first to know."

I let out a sigh. "I'm sorry. I'm not used to seeing you get emotional is all."

"Course I'm emotional. Every father wants to know his kids are happy and healthy. You and this husband of yours," he nodded toward Mitch, "are comin' off a rough patch. Sure as we're sittin' here, there'll be more. But for now, I pray you'll not take for granted what y'all have. This here life is a blink, Bekah. Seemed like it was just yesterday I was takin' you to kindergarten and now look at you." His eyes filled, and I wrapped my arms around him and held on tight.

It wasn't every girl who was as blessed as me. I didn't ever want to forget it again.

Mitch

Bekah went off to shower and change while I took charge of the breakfast dishes. Squirting soap into the frying pan, I glanced at John as he pushed up from the table and nabbed his empty plate. The man was grinning like an old fool, not that I could blame him.

"Isn't it a wonder how God works things out when you get outta the way?" He slipped his plate into the pan of sudsy water with a chuckle. "Afraid I'd have to hog tie the two of you together until you talked things through."

"Yeah?" I scrubbed his plate. "Your daughter's stubborn as a mule sometimes."

He barked out a laugh and slapped me on the back. "You're just figuring that out, son?" He picked up a dishtowel and took to drying. "Important thing is you didn't give up. I'm proud of you, boy."

My throat went tight, and I had to swallow down the emotion. Thirty-seven years old, and I'd never heard that from a father—or even a father-figure. "Appreciate it, John," I finally managed. "It means a lot to me."

John took the plate from the dish rack. "Shame on me for not sayin' it sooner. It's a plumb miracle you were such a great daddy to that grandson of mine, seein' as you didn't have a role model."

"But I did." I nudged him with an elbow. "You."

He snorted. "I was referring to the fact you weren't raised with a daddy. Or God. If we don't have Him to guide us, it's easy to get lost in our own faulty thinkin'. We haven't touched on Proverbs yet, but that's a book of wisdom rich with advice."

What a strange turn of events. Had John said the same thing to me months ago, I would've disregarded it as the same mumbo jumbo as Bekah's prayers. Now, it was a comfort and gave me hope. It was too bad I wouldn't have any kids of my own to pass it on to. It made me wonder just how far God would go to achieve His end game. I'd barely begun to know who He was, let alone learning to trust in Him.

He took his towel to a fork like he was polishing precious silver. "Bekah told me Caleb's talkin' now." His tone was casual, and his gaze stayed rooted on the fork. John wasn't into small talk, so he was fixing to say something worth hearing.

I put the last plate in the rack and rinsed my hands. "Yeah. No surprise to me, though."

He dropped the utensil in the drawer and looked at me. "Joe tells me the boy's only staying with him and Cassie temporarily. Never was their intention to adopt him."

I nodded. Bekah's dad was about as subtle as a stripper in a church choir. "I know where you're heading with this."

He crossed his arms and jutted out his chin. Bekah didn't inherit all her attitude from her mama. "Now that you and Bekah patched things up, is there any reason you can't adopt the boy?" His aim was true, but he was focusing it on the wrong target.

I swiped my hands on my jeans to dry them. "You know how she feels about adoption."

He rubbed the stubble on his chin. "Shouldn't have to point out y'all aren't the same people you were a year ago, or even a month ago."

"We've been back together all of five minutes, John." It was a gift, and I'd be a fool to step all over Bekah's toes so soon. My gut twisted at the mere idea of it. Or maybe I just ate too much.

John blew out a breath. "Well, son, if it was up to you, would you be interested in taking the boy in?"

"But it isn't up to me." Sounded like Brother Paul all over again. Tension burned across my shoulders, and I rolled them to ease the ache before facing John. "For the first time in over a year, the sparkle's back in Bekah's eyes. I know she'll always grieve the loss of Jonathon—we both will. But it's not consuming her anymore. She laughs and jokes, and—" Some things were best left unsaid. Last night was the first time we'd been intimate since the loss that nearly killed the both of us. "I'm not willing to risk that."

He frowned. "There are no such things as coincidences with God, son. Everything happens in His time. Gotta learn to trust that." He patted me on the arm and walked away, passing Bekah as she came back into the kitchen.

She flashed me a smile. "Ready to go?" The pink of her t-shirt matched the color of her cheeks. She was happy, and I would do whatever it took to keep her that way.

"Yeah."

She rummaged in her purse and came up with a set of keys. "You wanna drive?"

The humid heat and threat of rain received only a passing thought as I pulled the car onto the road. Why did John and Paul have to plant that seed in my brain? It wasn't like I hadn't considered adopting Caleb before, but this wasn't the time. Was it? We'd just gotten past the blame-game and secrets. I might not be walking on eggshells with Bekah, but the footing was still a little dicey.

Bekah patted my leg. "Earth to Mitch."

"Sorry. What were you saying?" I stopped at the turn to Wartrace Pike and glanced at her.

She rolled her eyes and laughed. "I said Daddy seems real anxious for me to move back home."

After making sure it was clear, I turned left toward town. "I don't think he's anxious as much as he's excited. Soon as I get my truck dropped off at the house, we can go back and start packing your things." A thought struck. "Unless you gotta work today."

"I'm not scheduled, but I wanna go in later this afternoon." She tugged at the ragged fringe of her cut-offs. "I was thinking I should give notice. I'm sure Kimberley would love to work there part-time, so I'm going to put in a good word for her. I mean, if it's okay with you."

I took her hand and grinned. "Doesn't matter to me one way or the other if Kimberley works at the shop." If she was quitting, it meant she planned on scheduling my hauls again. Nothing wrong with that.

She huffed. "You know what I mean."

I squeezed her hand. "Yes, babe. I'm thrilled you wanna work with me again."

"I do, but there's something else, Mitch." She blew out a shaky breath. "I've been thinking a lot about Caleb lately." I held my breath for fear I'd miss a word. "You remember before Jonathon was born how you wanted to adopt?"

I let the air out while my heart rate kicked up a couple notches. "Yeah." We pulled up to a red light, and I glanced at her. "What's more, I remember you hating the idea."

"Afraid was more like it." She wrinkled her nose. "The thought of committing to a child and then learning I wasn't capable of loving him like he was my own terrified me."

"So you said back then." The light changed, but rather than follow the line of cars, I pulled into a parking lot. Busy traffic was no place for an important discussion—or for the witnessing of a miracle. *Just started hanging out with You, God, and it's like I'm seeing You all over the place.* I shut off the engine and turned to Bekah. "What's this about?" Everything in me wanted to push, but this had to come from her.

"You remember that story some ten years ago that was all over the news about a woman right here in Shelbyville that adopted a little boy from Russia?" She stared at me like she was waiting for a lightbulb to go off in my brain. "When it turned out motherhood was harder than she thought, she sent him back like she was returning a rejected Amazon order."

Expecting her to bring up Caleb, it took a beat for me to change gears. It was an adoption nightmare if memory served. Practically attached a note to his clothes stamped with "Return to Sender." The whole community was outraged, for good reason. Caused problems with Russia and became a legal battle.

"Yeah. Terry something-or-other."

"Torry," Bekah said. "Torry Hansen."

"Right." The dots were starting to form a picture. "And that's what scared you about adoption."

"What she did was horrible, Mitch." Her chin quivered and she tightened her lips like she was trying not to cry. "But there was a part of me that wondered what I would have done in her place."

I scowled. "Come on, Bekah. We both know you'd never do anything so heartless, even if it turned out the kid was the son of Satan."

Tears swam in her eyes. "No, but I didn't want to take a chance."

I reached out and thumbed moisture from her sweaty face. "That's understandable." Even with the windows rolled down and a breeze blowing through, we were baking in the sun. "Is this what you wanted to talk about? Torry Hansen?"

She shook her head. "Just wanted you to understand where I was coming from then."

Sweat trickled down my back. "Okay." I didn't want to make a move that'd throw her off the track she was slogging through, but dehydration was setting in. "Does this have anything to do with Caleb?"

She wrinkled her nose and smiled. "What d'you think about adopting him, Mitch?"

My lips twitched with a grin, but I forced it back. "You're not worried about him being unlovable?"

"Not at all. I mean, it's gonna be hard on him, because he'll miss his mama and daddy, and I know there'll be challenges, but..." She widened her eyes. "What d'you think? Are you willing? I know we're just finding our way back together, and Joe said he and Cassie can't, but I know if it comes down to it, they'll cave. There's no way they're gonna let him go into foster care."

I let the grin loose, turned the key in the ignition, and cranked up the air conditioner. "You're askin' the wrong person."

Confusion clouded her features. "I am?" Then her mouth parted, and she giggled. "Guess we should ask Caleb, huh?"

"Yeah, but I'm pretty sure he'll be okay with it." I reached over and caressed her cheek. "Not every boy is blessed with someone to love him who's got both horse magic and mama magic."

Chapter Twenty-Eight

Rebekah

For more than a year, Jonathon's bedroom had been closed off like a sacred shrine—holy ground on which nobody was allowed to tread. I knew it was crazy as a Betsy bug, but somewhere deep inside of me, I thought if it remained the way he left it, I wouldn't forget my sweet boy. The truth was, if there wasn't a lick of his belongings left on earth, he'd live in my heart until the day I died. Then I'd be with him again for all eternity.

I stood on the threshold of his room and sighed. There was a clutter of toys and clothes that needed going through and a pile of flattened storage boxes waiting to be filled. Mitch had suggested we keep it all for Caleb, but I couldn't do it. It wasn't because I'd be reminded of Jonathon every time I saw Caleb wearing his t-shirts or playing with his toy cars, like Mitch assumed. It was because the little boy deserved better than hand-me-downs. He needed a fresh start as much as we did, and I'd not make him feel as if he was a replacement—a token child for the one we lost.

Leah put her arm around me as I stood in the doorway. "You don't have to do this, Bekah. I can go through it alone. Better yet, let's leave it for another day. Give you some time to get used to the idea."

"No." I pushed aside the image of Jonathon that last day in his too-big trunks, arguing with me about his swimmies. My throat went tight, and I swallowed a couple times. "Caleb's hardly got enough space to breathe crammed into that tiny room. Besides, it's only got but the one puny window. He'll be much more comfortable here." And I needed to move on.

I crossed to the tall windows and threw them open. A warm breeze blew in along with the voices of Mitch, Joe, and Daddy as they talked over the plans for Caleb's treehouse. It was a pure act of faith that allowed me to trust in God's sovereignty enough to put away my helicopter license. Things were gonna be different this time.

I could practically see Mama smiling down on me from heaven.

Leah's gaze roamed the room. Her organizational wheels must've been spinning. "What do you wanna do, Bekah? Box it all up, or save some for Caleb?"

"We're gonna take the toys to the church. Whatever they can use for the children's Sunday school nursery, they'll keep. What they can't, Brother Paul will make sure gets to Goodwill." I started assembling the first box. "Grab that packing tape off the desk, will you?"

While I held the ends together, Leah secured the flaps. "So, what's the next step in the adoption process?"

I set the box aside. "An independent agency is scheduled to come by on Monday for a home visit, which is one reason I wanna get this done." My belly cramped. What if we didn't pass the inspection? There were so many forms to fill out and hoops to jump through. It'd be a year-long process that could try the patience of Job. Surely, they'd see we'd be better than foster care, though.

"What's with the scowl?" Leah gathered an armful of Jonathon's clothes from the closet. "'Cause y'all have nothing to worry about, you know." She dumped them on the bed and started the process of folding the shirts only a fraction of the size of Mitch's.

Breathe. Where was my faith? "I didn't realize how complicated it would be."

"That's good, don't you think? They wanna be sure he's in capable hands." She pointed a miniature hanger at me. "Imagine how much harder it would be if there'd been family wanting to take him in."

I added a pile of clothes to Leah's. "Motherhood was a whole lot easier when I started with an infant." I sighed. "Although I don't miss the diaper changes and midnight feedings."

Leah held up a light blue shirt. "You sure you wanna give all this stuff away? This is brand new, and it'd fit Caleb."

A movement caught my attention, and I turned to see Caleb standing in the doorway. "Hey, sweetie. Did you finish your snack?"

"Yep." He crossed to the low bookshelf tucked beneath one of the windows and picked up a yellow Tonka Truck. "Is this Jonathon's bedroom?" He slapped at the wheels and watched them spin while my two worlds collided.

I dropped the pants I was folding and crouched in front of him. Mitch accused me of having mama magic, but it was surely on the fritz if I didn't see this coming. That's what I got for wallowing in grief so long. I'd put off introducing my future to my past.

I fingered Caleb's too-long hair from his brow. Time for a haircut. "You remember what we told you about Jonathon?"

He raised his little eyebrows at me. "He died."

I nodded.

"Just like my mama and daddy." He twisted around to put the truck back where he found it while a fist grew in my throat. I knew I'd see my baby again, but what about Caleb? Were his parents lost from him forever? Did they have any faith in Jesus?

Leah sat on the bed clutching a handful of clothes to her chest. "You must miss your mama and daddy a lot, huh, Caleb?"

"Yeah." He plopped onto the floor and reached for a hardcover book lined up in a neat row with others. *Harry the Dirty Dog*—one of Jonathon's favorites. He opened it up on his outstretched legs and flipped through the pages. "They were in a crash." He peered up at me. "That's why I'm gonna live with you and Mr. Mitch, huh?"

I dropped onto my tush next to him and patted his foot. "Yes, sir. We're gonna take real good care of you for them, sweetie."

"But I can still see Gracie and Jane, right? You said."

"Absolutely. Their daddy Joe is my brother." I pointed to Leah. "And Miss Leah's brother too."

"Okay." I'd forgotten how simple the mind of a child was. They took things on faith without question. He lifted the book. "Can we read this?" He batted his long lashes at me and smiled.

I took *Harry the Dirty Dog* from him as my heart melted into a pool of pure love. It took a moment to push the words past the emotion that made breathing a chore. It's all the time it took for my flawed thinking to clear. "Why don't we save that for a little later? I just thought you could do me a favor first."

He scrunched up his nose like he was giving it serious consideration. "Okay. What?"

I pushed off the floor and snagged the box Leah and I had prepared for the first load. "Go through all the books and toys in this room. What you don't wanna keep, put in this box." What did Caleb care if the toys belonged to Jonathon first? His innocent little mind wasn't that complicated, and it was time I took a page from his book. "When we're all done, we'll move the rest of your stuff into here and get your new bedroom set up."

"You mean I get to keep anything I want?" He scrambled off the floor, his hazel-eyed gaze taking everything in like a kid in a candy store. Or a toy store. It was confirmation that it was the right decision.

"Yep."

Leah pulled me aside with a grin. "I don't think anything's going into that box, Bek."

"That's okay. As long as he's happy." I glanced at the clothes we'd been organizing. "You know, you're right about the clothes too. Some of those shirts haven't been worn but a time or two."

He ran a truck along the top of the bookshelf until something caught his attention outside the window. Abandoning the toy, he pressed his nose to the screen. "Can I go outside and help Mr. Mitch build the treehouse?" The child had the attention span of a goldfish.

"I thought you wanted to go through the toys, sweetie." I shared a grin and a shrug with Leah.

He whipped his head around, his mouth dropping open. "Oh, yeah." So many choices, so little time.

I thought about the last Christmas Jonathon was with us, and the excitement over one particular gift. If Caleb wanted to hang out with the big boys, he needed the proper accessories. "I might have just the thing for you." I turned to Leah. "Be back in a flash."

Mitch's garage was a contender for the Housekeeper's Seal of Approval, which was a real head-scratcher. If he was as finicky with the house as he was with his tools, I'd spend a lot less time cleaning. Today, however, it worked in my favor. Jonathon's kid-size tool belt hung right where it belonged, and I collected it along with a hammer. To keep it as authentic as possible, I dug into the gardening box for an old pair of gloves.

Mitch

Stacks of redwood planks, two-by-fours, boxes of 16-penny nails, and tools were spread out over the front portion of our property. Only stipulation to my crew was to leave a good clearance around the old maple tree. Since the day Jonathon was born, I'd had plans to turn it into a boy's dream. Now was my chance. Took a little finagling to get Bekah on board, but that was to be expected. Truth was, we both leaned toward the side of caution these days. Caleb had been through more than was fair, and we were careful to test the waters before jumping in.

"Got you a workbench right here." Joe slapped the sheet of plywood supported by a couple sawhorses. "Let's spread out your plans and see what's what."

John had been picking through the stack of planks and pulled out another one. "There're a few we're gonna need to return, Mitch." He dumped the latest into a growing reject pile. "Spend good money on redwood, you ought to get a decent return."

The smack of the screen door drew my attention, and I turned to see Caleb waddling from the house. Was that Jonathon's tool belt weighing him down? A grin split my face at the sight of a hammer hanging clear to his knees. Bekah must've given it to him, which couldn't have been easy. She was releasing a little more of the pain of losing Jonathon every day. We both were. Wading through the grief was like dancing with shadows.

"Can I help, Mr. Mitch?"

"Absolutely. You got yourself some gloves?" I stifled a laugh as Caleb pulled a pair of Bekah's old gardening gloves from his back pocket and held them up. Now, if I could just find something useful for him to do.

"Hey, Caleb," John called from his position as lumber inspector. "I could sure use your muscle to haul these here boards to the truck. Think you're up for it?" As usual, John was a step ahead of me.

"Sure!"

"Whoa there, cowboy." I knelt in front of him and cinched his belt tighter. "If you're fixin' to help Pop John, it'd be easier if your tools aren't hanging around your ankles." As soon as I cut him loose, he was off to his new job as apprentice inspector.

Joe grabbed a rock from the ground and used it to anchor a corner of the plans to our makeshift workbench. "It's a good thing y'all are doin' for that boy."

I turned my focus on Caleb as he held onto one end of a plank while John carried the full weight. He was chattering like a chipmunk, and Pop John was in his element. "It's a good thing he's doin' for us too." Bekah had taken to mothering again like she hadn't missed a beat. Wasn't sure who talked more—her or the boy.

"Just so you know," Joe scratched his head, "Cassie and me were never gonna let him go into foster care."

I bent over the plans with a grin. "Like that's a big secret." The man couldn't bluff his way through a game of Go Fish.

"Kinda crazy how it all came together, don't you think?" He flicked a leaf off the plywood. "I mean, you and Bekah losing Jonathon like you did, and Caleb losing his parents..."

"Redemption," I whispered. Was just beginning to understand what that meant.

"You expectin' anyone?"

I glanced up to see a car pulling into the drive. "Brother Paul, would be my guess. He called earlier to see if we'd be around. Said he might drop by." As the vehicle parked behind John's truck, I recognized the pastor in the driver's seat. But who were the other two people in the car?

Paul climbed out, opened up the back door, and offered his hand to the woman inside. A man eased from the front passenger side. Couldn't see his face, but he was stiff and slow.

"Gammaw, Pawpaw!" Caleb ran across the yard to the car, the handle of the hammer swinging like a crazed pendulum from his belt, and a rock landed in my gut. His grandparents—Frank and Sylvie Young. Did they change their minds about giving him up for adoption? He'd only been with us for a few days, but the idea of losing him...and what about Bekah? How would she deal with the loss? *Get a grip and quit borrowing trouble.*

Joe and John were offering greetings before I could get my legs moving. Caleb had his arms wrapped around Sylvie's hips. She smoothed his hair from his forehead and said, "It's a blessing to hear your voice again, sweet boy."

Paul slapped my back. "Mitch, have you met Frank and Sylvie Young?"

Frank offered a handshake. "Can't say we have. It's been a while since we've attended services, but I don't remember you bein' there with Rebekah in the past."

"No, sir. I'm a recent convert." Once I got my eyes off myself, I took a good look at them. Some might think their stooped shoulders and the deep lines etched in their faces were signs of age, but grief recognized grief. They'd suffered a blow every bit as significant as ours—and such a short time ago.

"Can't tell you how sorry I am for the loss of your son and daughter-in-law." How fair was it that what caused them pain brought us blessing? "Would y'all like to come inside? I'm sure Bekah would love to see you."

"That'd be nice," Sylvie said, rubbing Caleb's back. "But we don't want to be a bother."

I looked at Joe and hitched my chin toward the house. Message received, he slipped away to get Bekah.

"What're y'all workin' on here?" Frank glanced at the wood-stack. "Looks like quite a project."

I ruffled Caleb's hair. "You wanna tell your grandad what we're building?"

Caleb stepped out of Sylvie's arms and squinted up at Frank. "Mr. Mitch is makin' me a treehouse."

"You don't say. A treehouse, huh? Aren't you a lucky boy?"

"Yes, sir."

"And it appears you found your voice too." He patted Caleb's shoulder. "The pastor here told us you did, but your gammaw wanted to hear it for herself. Where'd you leave it?"

Caleb wrinkled his nose. "Huh?"

Sylvie clucked her tongue. "Pay him no mind, Caleb. Pawpaw thinks he's bein' funny."

I heard shuffling from the porch and turned to see Bekah heading our way with Joe and Leah trailing. If Bekah was concerned about the appearance of Caleb's grandparents, as I'd been, it didn't show. Fact was, she jumped in with a smile and handshakes before I could make introductions.

"I'm so pleased to see you both again," she said. "You've met my sister Leah, haven't you? She's been to church with us a time or two, although she and Gabe regularly attend one in Murfreesboro."

"It's good to see you again, Leah." Sylvie shook her head. "My but y'all have a big family."

Leah grinned. "You haven't seen the half of it. Our brother Dan and his family live in Atlanta. He and Sarah have three kids, and my husband Gabe and I have four."

"We only had the one," Frank said. My gaze connected with Bekah's, and I tilted my head toward the house.

Bekah nodded slightly then spoke into the conversational lull. "Frank and Sylvie, if you have the time, we'd love for you to come in and visit for a bit. You can give us pointers about Caleb."

"If you're sure." Sylvie glanced from Bekah to Frank.

"Absolutely. I have freshly made sweet tea and lemonade." Bekah reached for Sylvie's arm and started walking her to the house.

"While y'all get to know each other," said Brother Paul, "maybe Caleb and Joe can tell me a little more about this treehouse you're building." Everyone else hung back while the four of us went inside.

While Bekah poured drinks, I got Frank and Sylvie settled at the kitchen table. It was nuts to think there was a problem. If I were in their shoes, I'd want to be sure my grandson was going into a good home too. Nothing to worry about.

So, why did it feel like my heart was competing in the Kentucky Derby?

Bekah put a plate of cookies and a few napkins on the table then sat. "They're peanut butter." No one but me would catch the hitch in her voice. "Caleb helped me bake them. Said they're his favorite."

"Don't mind if I do." Frank helped himself. "Bobby was partial to peanut butter too." He laid his hand out on the table, and Sylvie slipped hers into it.

Bekah cleared her throat. "We know how difficult this must be on y'all." She spread a napkin in front of her and fingered out a wrinkle. "There's nothing worse than losing a child. Can't imagine it matters whether they're five or fifty."

"Appreciate it," Frank said. "None of us is perfect, but we might of had an easier time with Bobby if we'd been younger when we had him. Might not have been as old as Abraham and Sarah, but he still was more 'an we could handle. Had a mind of his own, and more energy than we knew what to do with."

Sylvie glanced from Bekah to me. "Bobby had a chance to grow up and make his own choices, whether they were right or wrong. But y'all losing your little one the way you did..." She sighed. "Well, we know you'll be a real blessing to Caleb. It's just—" She clamped her lips tight and shook her head.

Bekah's gaze slid my way. I could see the question in her eyes, and one of us needed to ask it. I reached for her hand under the table. "It's just what, Miss Sylvie? If you have a concern about us adopting Caleb, we should talk about it."

Sylvie's eyes widened. "Oh, no. We're not at all concerned about you and Rebekah adopting Caleb. In fact, we couldn't be happier about it."

Frank nodded. "Not worried a bit. It's just we only had the one boy, and Caleb bein' an only child..." He sighed. "We're just hoping y'all would allow Sylvie and me to spend time with the boy. We're too old to raise him, but it'd mean a lot to us if we could see him now and again."

Tears filled Bekah's eyes, and she pressed a hand to her heart. "That would be a huge blessing to Caleb and to us. With my mama gone and Mitch's mama living so far away, you'd be filling a wide gap." She glanced at me. "Don't you think, Mitch?"

If I lived to be a hundred, I'd never grasp the full extent of God's grace. What was broken and lost, He somehow made whole and saved. "Wouldn't want it any other way."

Epilogue

One Year Later

Rebekah

The day couldn't have been more brilliant, and it surely wasn't dependent on the weather. Had it been pouring rain and windy enough to lay a barn flat, God's grace would still shine through. But it wasn't. Instead, the forecast for that August day was for plenty of sunshine and humidity low enough for locals to wonder about climate change. Perfect weather for a celebration, especially when the person we were honoring requested a pool party.

It was as if we'd come full circle in a way only the good Lord could contrive.

Joe and Cassie's backyard was a bustle of activity, even with all the kids in the water—and there must've been twenty or more. We'd put out a general invitation to friends and family who wanted to commemorate the day Caleb officially became our son, not expecting it to be such a huge turnout. Rather than push away memories of the last pool party I'd attended, I conjured up an image of Jonathon, eyes wide with excitement as he urged Mitch to go swimming. I steeled myself for the ache of grief that always followed such a memory, but it didn't come. Instead, the sound of his giggle filled my spirit along with Mama's gentle words, *Oh child, you'll have that sweet boy for eternity.*

"Bekah?" Mitch's arms snaked around me from behind, and he pulled me back against his chest. "You okay?"

"Yes." The word caught on a sob.

"Thinkin' about Jonathon?" His lips nuzzled my neck, sending a shiver up my spine, while the chatter and laughter around us faded into the background.

"And Mama."

Tightening his hold on me, he whispered in my ear, "I miss them too."

"Okay, you two, get a room." Joe nudged us away from the food table with a smirk. "Some of us have work to do here." He set a platter of meat down and raised a brow at Mitch. "I could use a hand at the barbecue."

Mitch planted a kiss on my lips before following Joe to the grill, and I took a moment to enjoy the sight before me. The kids were playing Marco Polo, and Caleb was it. Eyes closed, he was spinning in circles, neon green swimmies keeping him afloat, yelling, "Marco!"

"Bekah?" I spun around to face Kimberley, whose pink sundress showed off her summer tan to perfection. It was a wonder the girl was still single.

"Hey, Kim." I gave her a hug. "I'm so glad you could make it. Jenna and Darlene are around here somewhere." I scanned the crowd until I spotted them under the patio cover chatting with Frank and Sylvie. "There they are."

"Already talked to them." She touched my arm. "I can't stay, but I wanted to come by and congratulate y'all. I left a little somethin' for Caleb inside."

"But you just got here." Maybe she wasn't single after all. I grinned. "Hot date?"

She laughed. "I wish. Although there is someone who recently joined my church that has possibilities." That's what I was hoping to hear, not that there was anything wrong with being single. The girl worked too hard. It had to be exhausting waitressing at night and putting in a full eight hours at the vintage store most days.

"Well, you better keep me posted." I looked her up and down. "Don't tell me you got all dolled up just to stop by."

"Nope." She widened her eyes with a grin big as Tennessee. "I wanted to be the one to tell you since y'all got me the job at the shop." What in the world could put that sparkle in her eyes if it wasn't a man?

"Charlotte offered me an apprenticeship as an interior designer." It didn't surprise me a bit. Anyone with the sense God gave a goat could see Kimberley was gifted.

I squealed and clapped my hands. "I'm so excited for you, Kim."

"And," she drew out the word, "she's payin' for some online classes. I'll be able to quit the restaurant and work toward a real career. It's like a dream come true." Her eyes misted. "And I owe it all to you, Bekah."

"Don't be silly." I gave her another hug. "All I did was recommend you take my place. You did all the work."

"Maybe, but you opened that door, and I want you to know how much I appreciate our friendship." She hitched her chin toward the pool. "I see Caleb over there. I'm gonna say hey before I take off."

Leah stepped up and threw an arm around my shoulders. "Y'all survived it."

My gaze was focused on Kimberley crouched at the edge of the pool talking to Caleb. "What're you talking about?"

"Everything, little sister." She dropped her arm and shifted so we were face-to-face. "Gabe and me were just talkin' last night about what a rough time of it you and Mitch have had the last couple years. And look at you now—that beautiful little boy is officially yours." Her voice broke on a sob. When did Leah suddenly become the emotional one?

I stifled a grin. "You been craving dill pickles lately?"

"What? No." She scowled. "Very funny."

Kimberley passed with a wave and wink as Caleb came padding across the patio, leaving drops of water in his wake. When he stopped in front of us, I brushed the damp hair from his eyes. The boy's hair grew faster than a thoroughbred.

He grabbed hold of one of my hands. "Hey, Bekah?"

I leaned down. "You hungry, sweetie? Been in that pool so long you're turning into one big prune."

He shook his head, spraying droplets of water like a shaggy dog after a bath. "Can I talk to you and Mitch? I gotta 'portant question." Last time he looked so serious, he asked for a puppy.

"Sure." I glanced toward the grill but only saw Joe and Cassie. "Let's go find him." I gave Leah an apologetic smile and led Caleb through the crowd. So many people. Dan and Sarah at the food table, Brother Paul and Keith Taylor in line behind them. I spotted Frank and Sylvie, Jenna and her husband Cal, Darlene...people everywhere with wet kids darting about. Family and friends.

Our village.

"There he is." Caleb towed me around the backside of the pool where Mitch and Gabe were talking. If he was fixin' to ask for a puppy again, he was wasting a good head of steam. Mitch and me had already decided to take him to Animal Control on their next adoption day.

Mitch must've sensed the urgency of Caleb's quest, because he crouched down at his eye level as we approached. "What's goin' on, bud?"

"I gotta question."

Mitch nodded. "Okay."

Gabe chuckled. "I see this is an important family meeting, and I'm starved." He ruffled Caleb's wet head as he passed.

"Now, bud, what's this burning question you need to ask Bekah and me?"

The child's gaze shot from Mitch to me and back again. "I'm 'dopted now, right?"

"Yes, sweetie." I rubbed his back. "That's what we did this morning in front of the judge."

He sighed. "Sadie said that means you're my parents, right?"

I pressed a hand to my heart as my gaze slid to Mitch's and crouched down so we were all at eye-level. Did we not explain it well enough? What had Sadie said that we didn't?

Mitch put an arm around Caleb. "Yes, Caleb. We're your parents now, just like Leah and Gabe are Sadie's parents."

He scrunched up his nose. "Then does that mean I can call you Mama and Daddy now? Or do I hafta keep sayin' Bekah and Mitch?"

My tear-filled eyes met Mitch's as the pebble-sized wall that still surrounded my heart crumbled into dust. "Caleb, baby." I pressed a kiss to his cheek. "It would give us the greatest joy if you called us Mama and Daddy." *Oh, Lord, You are so good.*

Had I not already believed in the power of Jesus to change lives, that moment alone would have made me a believer.

Also by Jennifer Sienes

Apple Hill Series:

Surrendered

Saving Faith

Illusions

All That Glitters

Providence

Wish Upon a Star

Bedford County Series:

Night Songs

These Simple Gifts

A Sojourner's Solace

Shadow Dancing

Itty Bitty Faith

Tangles and Tinsel

Mayhem and Moonlight

A Canine Christmas

Norfolk Southern Series:

Train-Wrecked Hearts

Did you enjoy *Shadow Dancing*? If so, please leave a review on Amazon, Book-Bub, and/or Goodreads.

About the Author

Jennifer Sienes holds a bachelor's in psychology and a master's in education but discovered life-experience is the best teacher. She loves Jesus, romance and writing—and puts it all together in inspirational contemporary fiction. Her daughter's TBI and brother's suicide inspired two of her three novels. Although fiction writing is her real love, she's had several non-fiction pieces published in anthologies including four in *Chicken Soup for the Soul*. She has two grown children and one very spoiled Maltese. California born and raised, she now lives in Middle Tennessee with her real-life hero and husband.

Visit her at www.JenniferSienes.com

www.ingramcontent.com/pod-product-compliance
Lightning Source LLC
Chambersburg PA
CBHW032238310726
48973CB00008B/2201